Praise for
A Negro and an Ofay

"Fans of Walter Mosley and George Pelecanos are going to devour Danny Gardner's brilliant new book. *A Negro and an Ofay* breathes exciting new life into noir fiction."
—Jonathan Maberry, *New York Times* bestselling author

"Elliot Caprice is a terrific character with his own Midwestern territory and Danny Gardner tells his stories with style and cunning."
—Peter Blauner, *New York Times* bestselling author
and co-Executive Producer of CBS's *Blue Bloods*

"Danny Gardner's masterful debut engenders echoes of the greats. I had the impression I had somehow stumbled across a previously undiscovered work of Chester Himes, or Jim Thompson, or Walter Mosley—or all three magically rolled into one."
—David Corbett, prize-winning
author of *The Mercy of the Night*

"Immersive, poignant and utterly enthralling. Written from the middle of America's great racial divide, it's satirical, cool and irrevocably honest; imbued with an inherent nobility that rivals any modern day hero."
—Tom Avitabile, bestselling author
of *Give Us This Day*

"*A Negro and an Ofay* is a smart, crisp, historically accurate, and unapologetically racial narrative that signals the arrival of a strong, necessary voice in crime fiction. This is the best debut you'll read in a long time."
—Gabino Iglesias, author of *Zero Saints*

"Elliot Caprice is a complex mix of muscle and brain, of toughness and heart, of doing wrong and only sometimes getting it right. *A Negro and an Ofay* reads like a long lost Raymond Chandler, one that he wrote from the south side of Chicago."
—Lori Rader-Day, Mary Higgins Clark Award-winning author of *Little Pretty Things* and *The Black Hour*

"Hard-boiled don't get much harder than this. Danny Gardner hits all the right notes, but with enough swagger and voice to make it completely his own. Elliot Caprice is a fantastic character, stuck between two worlds—black and white, good and bad—and I really hope to see more of him."
—Rob W. Hart, author of *South Village*

"One of the best tools Gardner has in his toolbox…is his sense of humanity."
—Scott Waldyn, *Literary Orphans Journal*

"…it manages to be smart, historical, and about identity/racial issues while retaining all the entertainment value that pulpy thrillers bring to the table. This is a book with a carefully crafted plot that touches on a lot of issues that were as relevant six decades ago as they are now."
—Out of the Gutter Review

"This is a stunning debut! A powerful combination of brilliant storytelling and a breathtaking grasp of dialog subtext that strongly reminds of Mamet. Gardner is destined to become a big name in this writing game."
—Les Edgerton, author of *The Genuine, Imitation, Plastic Kidnapping*

"Elliot Caprice is a trouble magnet and that makes for a great character."
—Simon Wood, author of *The One That Got Away*

"Plenty of hardboiled patter and a dense plot with a great sense of place and wonderful dialogue."
—Eric Beetner, author of *Rumrunners*

"Gardner speaks truth through fiction. *A Negro and an Ofay* forces us to look into the brutal mirror of our past in the hope we might understand our future. With his sharp as a whip crack writing, Gardner may just change the world"
—Paul Bishop, author of *Lie Catchers*

"There's a naturalness and ease about this book despite a complex and dense plot. It flows effortlessly, and the dialogue has a wonderful cadence to it. I feel like if Gardner told me a tale on the spot, it'd be surprising, dramatic, and entertaining. To me, that's a born storyteller, and it comes through loud and clear in this electrifying debut."
—Sarah M. Chen, author of *Cleaning Up Finn*

"It finds a way to address issues of race and class without getting sidetracked, and, in fact, builds these issues seamlessly into the plot instead. What results is a totally unique detective in Elliot Caprice, who struggles with issues that feel both familiar and totally alien to the genre, not to mention the reader."
—Michael Pool, *Crime Syndicate Magazine*

"This young author is not only the heir apparent to Chester Himes and Walter Mosley, but the subtle social commentary laced almost invisibly within the beautifully crafted saga of an African American police detective fighting the ramifications of a frame that derailed his career, along with routine racism in 1950s Chicago, shows the promise of a contemporary James Baldwin or Ralph Ellison."
—Will Viharo, Digital Media Ghost

A NEGRO
AND AN OFAY

DANNY GARDNER

A NEGRO AND AN OFAY

THE TALES OF ELLIOT CAPRICE

DOWN&OUT BOOKS

Down & Out Books
3959 Van Dyke Rd, Ste. 265
Lutz, FL 33558
www.DownAndOutBooks.com

Cover design by JT Lindroos

ISBN: 1-943402-67-1
ISBN-13: 978-1-943402-67-0

To Chicago, my love.
May your south and west sides rise again.

CHAPTER 1

As he came to, with blurred vision, he detected light. It didn't shine so much as claw at the brick walls, like the slender fingers of angry ghosts. An endless flight of concrete stairs coiled away from him. He was headed downward, though not by his own volition. He remembered drinking in a roadhouse joint. "Black Night" was playing on the juke. He understood how Charles Brown hated to be alone. A shot of corn. A friendly chippie. More corn. An offered dance. By the time Brown's brother was in Korea, he heard hard words behind him. "Get your hands off my woman, red nigger." The absolute wrong thing to say to him when he had been drinking. "Fuck you" this and that. A shove. The juke stopped. A fist for that fat, greasy, chicken-eatin' mouth. He heard something behind him.

Then black.

His head hurt. He heard ringing. Assumed blood in his ears. A moment later, it sounded like jangling. He figured chains or keys. His hands were bound. His wrists were cold. He thought he was cuffed.

Hoped he was cuffed.

He had accommodated himself to incessant disorientation while in Europe, where he would climb out of his tank and find himself immersed in bullets and bombs and shouts and screams. In the din of war, he learned to disregard the senses that failed him and focus on his singular survival. That's how Elliot Caprice returned from the Battle of the Bulge with all his limbs. And most of his wits.

He shifted his feet.

1

"Take it easy, boy."

Boy.

"Shit, I'm in the bing."

"Shut your hole," the fat jailer holding his feet said. He hadn't seen the skinny jailer holding him by his arms until he rolled over after they dropped him on his face.

"If you can talk, you can walk," Skinny said.

"Easy to see which one of y'all picks up the donuts in the mornin'," said Elliot.

"You are in the custody of the St. Louis County Sheriff. You'll be detained until you can appear before a judge. Got it, smart guy?" Fatty said, just before he kicked Elliot in the ribs.

Elliot rose to his feet. Skinny pushed him down the stairs.

"Why am I here when I vaguely remember bein' dry-gulched in Belleville?"

"You had a police issue thirty-two on your person," Skinny said. He produced a key ring. "Get comfortable. Make friends."

He shuddered as the cell door slammed behind him. It sounded eerily similar to the lid of his M18 Hellcat. The blast of body heat combined with the cold limestone felt just like ol' Lucille's air-cooled engine exhaust. He was rudely reminded of the involuntary smells men create when their glands respond to despair; sweat and filth, rushed through the air on panicked breaths. Elliot immediately turned back toward his jailers.

"Look here, constable. How's about my phone call?"

"No calls on Sunday. Gotta wait until morning. Could be in front of the judge by then," said Skinny.

"That'd be too bad for you, halfie. Beatty is a hangin' judge," said Fatty.

"I'm colored. They're all hangin' judges."

"Ya know, Nathan White," said Fatty, as he looked at the docket. "You keep that attitude, you may not get in front of the bench. You're in the Meat Locker, pally."

The infamous Meat Locker was the massive desegregated holding cell underneath the St. Louis County Courthouse. As broad as it was long, it was nearly standing room only. Only a few pendant lights hung overhead so inmates depended upon street light that passed through the barred, narrow windows above. Elliot wondered if anyone walking by knew what was down there, in the depths, stowed underneath St. Louis's poor excuse for a palace of jurisprudence.

Elliot was amazed at how, although drunk and disoriented, he managed to give his alias. Nathan was his middle name, the first name of the uncle who adopted him as a baby—Nathan "Buster" Caprice. White was for the most mysterious half of his racial heritage. He resolved to use only one name, unlike the litany of aliases of the con men he encountered during his time on the Chicago Police Department. A liar is only as good as his memory. Elliot's life depended upon his deceptions.

He shambled through the bodies of poor unfortunates forced to integrate until he found a cot on the other side of the cell. The galvanized bucket chamber pots had overflowed. He'd missed the only meal of the day. He was booked on a Sunday. No small blessing. It gave him time to figure on his situation. The gun needed an answer. He was once a Chicago beat cop. His record would be examined. After that, the guards drop a dime. Elliot somehow hangs himself in the shower. The screws split the bribe. Fatty takes the bigger cut.

He laid on his back with nothing else to do but serenade himself with curses. One for drinking too much. Another for his weakness for the blues. A third for the corresponding weakness for big-legged women. Above all, he cursed himself for not playing the game well enough at Bradley Polytechnic. When life had him by the short hairs, he often fantasized about being a good student who graduated on the Dean's list. Then he could have traded on his near-whiteness to land a job in the front office of some industrial farm in Illinois. Could've had a nametag. Maybe a desk. Dated some chippie from the secretarial pool. Perhaps that would have kept him from enlisting in Patton's Third Army. He would have never followed every other discharged colored to the big city. He wouldn't have taken the police academy test while drunk, just to show how much smarter he was.

He wouldn't have ruined his life.

"Hey, yella. That's my cot."

Elliot opened his eyes. A mountain of a man had taken a seat on a cot across from him. He was dark as midnight and stood well over six feet, as tall as he was broad. He had the scarred hands of a fighter. The lines in his face outlined a massive skull underneath.

"Yeah, white boy. Get it up," came a much slighter voice.

"You a cannibal, big man?"

"What's that smart shit you say there?"

"How else you got a voice comin' out ya ass, if'n you didn't eat a fella?"

A smallish man, no more than five feet tall, stepped from behind Mountain. If he felt better, Elliot would've laughed.

"Watch it, light-skin," the big man's tiny flunky said.

"Seems like y'all got yaselves a couple of cots already. Push on."

Elliot closed his eyes again, until he felt the jump of Mountain's kick at the cot's legs.

"Ain't nobody tell ya? They all my cots."

"You want a cot, you gotta ask us," said Flunky.

"Ovah there, jawin' with the jailers, soundin' like you Jimmy Cagney. You-dirty-rattin' wit' them ofays," Mountain said. He assumed a fighting posture. "You ain't white yet, high yella, but you keep tryin'. Now, up it."

"What yo' name is, corn pone?"

"This here is Frank Fuquay. Folks around our parts call him Big Black," said Flunky.

"What parts would those be?"

"Yazoo County, Miss-sip!"

"Yeah, Lawd!" Big Black said.

"Is that so? My daddy was from around that way," Elliot said.

"Yo daddy, huh? No doubt sum' cracker that took the long way home one night."

That was the last slur of his mixed race Elliot intended to hear. Big Black's buddy was a short-stack, but it was still two against one. Uneven odds were nothing new to him, so he resolved to play it cool.

"Tell you the truth, he was 'bout as inky as you."

"What you say?"

"Yeah, boy. It took a whole lot o' snowflake to dilute that much buck. You a tall drink of Darkest Africa, Big Black. Whycome you got no white in you at all? Yo granny wasn't pretty enough for the slave foreman?"

"I know you ain't gonna take that, Frank!"

"Shol' ain't!"

Big Black's swiftness would have startled Elliot, had he not set him up for it. From his lower position, he delivered a fierce heel kick to Frank Fuquay's left knee, just above the patella. Most folks don't know healthy joints have enough give in both directions to protect them from injury. Big Black found out the hard way. The glazed concrete floor, slick from the tears of the miserable, let him down. Frank fell forward. Elliot swerved out the way. Big Black hit the floor. Before his monstrous opponent could recover, Elliot knelt, grabbed him by the throat and placed his entire two hundred pounds behind the knee he slammed into Big Black's chest. It made a loud sound. The sort a paddle makes when one beats the dust off a rug. The air rushed out of the bruiser's lungs. Flunky stayed put, shouting commands.

"Kick his ass, Frank!"

"Shut up, Tony."

"Yeah. Shut up, Tony," Elliot said, as he looked around at the other inmates. All were too miserable to get involved.

"Let me see if I can tell it. Sixty-six runs right up through

Yazoo. You two jackasses steal some shoes and make the trek on up to the big city. Ain't that many pigs to stick up this way, so you opted to break the law. That's how you in heah. That 'bout right?"

"Fuck you," the big man said. Tony finally fell silent.

"See here, Big Black," Elliot said. He squeezed his fingers tighter around the bully's neck. "Instead of wastin' ya time pickin' on folks—Lord knows who you tryin' to impress—y'all need to get your stories straight. In a minute, them ofays gonna slide some confession papers in front of you. As I doubt you know how to read, there's a good chance your black ass gon be puttin' his X on somethin' someone else did, on top of your own mess."

"You fo' real?"

"Happens all the time. They'll string you up and have ya mama pay the shippin' on your body. She'd have to take up a collection for your big ass. Better stop makin' hay and start makin' friends, Big Black. Somebody gonna have to write to yo' mama about how her big, dumb baby boy wound up hangin'. Or you could write it yourself. If'n you know how to write. Okay there, Big Black?"

Frank attempted a struggle. Elliot put more weight behind his knee.

"Okay, Frank Fuquay. All the way from Yazoo County, Miss-sip?"

Elliot glared into the Big Black Mountain's eyes.

"Gotcha, boss."

"What?! Teach this yella nigger a lesson, Frank!"

"Shut up, Tony," Big Black said.

Elliot let his hand go slack. He lowered his voice to a whisper.

"We's all afraid up in here," Elliot said. He allowed Frank Fuquay up off the disgusting floor. "And get rid of the little guy. He's trouble."

"Fuck you, high yella!"

Elliot took to his cot. He was content to rest after getting himself through a scrape without anyone coming up dead.

For once.

CHAPTER 2

Even in the din of the jail, he was tired enough to sleep away the headache were it not for the memory of Izzy Rabinowitz's voice, as clear as if he were in the cell with him.

"The straight path ain't for you, kid. You're neither fish nor fowl. You're meant to play the margins."

Truth told, the longest he stuck with anything was when he collected for Izzy's outfit, which was from the time he was twelve until he went off to college at twenty. Since he took his first steps, he was resentful. An abandoned baby, bequeathed all of his parents' piss and vinegar. A city boy trapped in farm country. Father meets Mother in Chicago, makes her pregnant. Dies in the race riots. Mother finds Father's brother to abandon her bastard. Doc Shapiro, there at bastard's breech birth, takes him under his wing to keep him out of trouble. Shapiro's cousin, Izzy Rabinowitz, the loan maker, shows up at the back door of Doc's small office. Out in the car was a thumb-breaker suffering six stab wounds to the torso. Bastard cleans up the blood without a flinch. Asks a lot of questions about what happened. Finally, bastard finds purpose. No more overnight stays in the Southville County jail for mischief and mayhem. No more beatings with the mule strap in Uncle Buster's barn. Belonging. Acceptance. Praise. He was good—great—at doing dirty work for the most powerful Jew in the Midwest. That he never had the stomach for it was his little secret.

Yet Bradley Polytechnic Institute was his choice. He applied. Passed the entrance exam. Made the grade for an entire year. At an advisor's suggestion, he allowed himself to join the forensics

8

team. He even made a friend: John Creamer of the Lincoln Park, Chicago Creamers. It was a funhouse mirror pairing, as John was far too much of everything that Elliot lacked altogether—money, charm, good social standing. At least they shared some whiteness. They studied together. Ran together. Allowed each other into their respective worlds. Their friendship almost made Elliot forget how much he hated college.

In the south, it was Jim Crow. In the north, an understanding. Upward past the Mississippi, outside of farm country, it was hard to find anything as explicit as a hung sign or body. A Negro needed to know his place. Though Elliot knew, he really didn't give a shit.

The night of Elliot's first speech competition he won his debate. John pulled him away to celebrate. That meant they'd both be white that night. The two found a union hall speakeasy in Champaign where they could drink and dance with white girls from the University of Illinois. At the height of the party, they found themselves surrounded by angry white boys.

"Lookin' colored tonight, I guess," Elliot said, with a cackle.

Creamer was plucky when drunk, so he took off his tie and put up his dukes. Elliot pulled a snubbed-nose .32 from his ankle, concealed just how Izzy taught him. Saved them both a lot of trouble. Once the mob dispersed, Elliot ordered another bourbon from the bar. John Creamer pleaded to dangle, but Elliot paid him no mind. The snowflakes were dazzled by their show of joie de vivre.

Officers of the Urbana Police Department arrived.

"Give me the gun," Creamer said.

Something in the way Creamer took it upon himself bothered Elliot. The insistence. The eagerness.

"They won't search me. Give it to me, now."

The pistol was out of Elliot's hands for three seconds before John Law was upon him. He was dragged out to the squad car.

Behind the police station, he tasted paving gravel.

"The colored part of me tries to follow the rules," Elliot said. "Only the white boy in me figures they don't apply to him."

He was sober by the third boot heel to the ribs. Silent by the fourth blow of the nightstick. Creamer finally arrived when he was unconscious.

They were halfway back to Bradley when Elliot told John Creamer to take him back to Southville. Once the car pulled in front of the Caprice family farm, they exchanged handshakes. John returned Elliot's gun. The moment was somber, yet hollow. Whatever commonality the two shared was trumped by the reminder from the college town dicks. The most they'd ever be able to do was stick up for one another. Moreover, Elliot knew stashing the gun for his colored friend made John Creamer feel good.

That made Elliot feel as if he owed the wrong white boy a favor.

It was late, five hours until morning. Elliot didn't have his key. There was no waking Uncle Buster once he was asleep, so Elliot let himself into the barn, the place where he once took his beatings. The discomfort of hay on hardpan was buffered by the return of his most dependable friend.

Resentment. It never left him. Not for a second.

The only clue that morning had come in that windowless cube of misery was the sound of wood on iron. Fat and Skinny had returned.

"When do we get grub?!" one voice said.

"I wanna talk to a lawyer!" went another.

This triggered a cacophony of pleas, all of which would be ignored. Elliot saw his jailers had been joined by a third man dressed in a suit. This was what cops referred to as a barrel check—once suspects in a crime are identified, the investigating detectives first search the lock-ups for faces matching descriptions. Depending upon the detective, near matches worked as well as exact.

"Shaddup, you mooks!" No one complied, so Fatty attacked the bars once more.

"Shut up! Or Christ on tha cross, I'll turn the boiler on!"

"This is Detective Sergeant Molak from the Chicago Police Department," Skinny said. "He's looking for two suspects wanted for narcotics trafficking."

Tom. Molak. The Polak.

Elliot remembered him from the Chicago Police Academy. Spoke fluent Polish. Politically connected uncle in the Hegewisch community. Too weak to pass the fitness test. The sort everyone figured would quit. Or wind up superintendent. He was slight of build, had hunched shoulders, smallish eyes, and a Sephardic nose that he stuck everywhere it had no business. No way he was in St. Louis for the department. Not by himself. Elliot hoped he wouldn't be spotted. His number might be up.

"I'm looking for two men—one colored, one white—both known narcotics traffickers. They were last seen Thursday evening in the Clifton Heights neighborhood," Molak said. "Anyone sharing information leading to their arrest will be looked upon favorably."

"We have a bunch of new shines as of Friday," Fatty said.

"That'd be a good start, Andy."

"My name isn't—"

"The Negroes, yeah, pally?"

Fear crossed the minds of even the recidivists. Frank Fuquay, only just prior so cocksure, now sweated bullets.

"Say, Big Black," Elliot said, in a hushed tone. "You one of the fellas they lookin' for?"

"Naw. We got picked up fo' burglary."

In the strained light, Elliot could see youthful ignorance behind his eyes. His current predicament afforded him no opportunity to shepherd a young fool, but he couldn't just let the kid twist.

"We stole sum stuff from an ol' lady after she paid us to haul rubbish out her cellar."

"Every colored, line up along the bars here! Don't make me tell you twice!"

The colored inmates lined up face front along the bars, enough for two rows. Elliot sidled next to Frank.

"Listen here. You so big, you'd have been pegged before he came down here. It's gonna be alright," Elliot said.

"Yeah?"

"Line up, look straight ahead at the wall. Answer every question in an even tone of voice."

"What that mean?"

"Just. Like. This," Elliot said. "Yes. No. Name. Age. Whereabouts you were when. You wait until they ask. If they don't ask, you don't say. They'll pass you by. Got it?"

Frank Fuquay nodded.

"How you know this stuff?"

"Let's go."

Frank Fuquay followed Elliot to the bars, where they took spots at the very end, Frank second to last. Elliot last. His ploy was to use the dichotomy to throw off identification. To the lazy of mind—Elliot remembered Molak as particularly lazy—all faces blur into black. Hues diffuse. Even the mélange is lost. Had he considered it, Elliot could have relaxed, as he completely let himself go. His clean cut, tip-top exterior on the force was now overgrown. Mass of ungreased curly hair. Dark farmer's tan. Drunken red eyes. Shit, he could barely recognize himself.

Unfortunately, Molak was uncharacteristically aggressive, demanding names, hometowns, whereabouts. The rat kept coming. Elliot's ribcage felt like the floorboards in a Poe tale. Molak stopped, gave a slender, dark-skinned man the once over before he questioned him. Elliot was two places from being exposed. Frank Fuquay emulated Elliot's body posture. Next, Molak gave Frank the up and down.

"Name."

"Frank Fuquay, suh."

"What's he in for?"

"Burglary," Skinny said. "You're not lookin' for a guy this big, are ya?"

"Maybe," Molak said. "Relax. You ain't makin' detective tonight, Andy. Where you from, country?"

"Mis-sippi," Frank said, using the tone Elliot suggested.

"What're ya doin' up here in Saint Louis?"

"Nuttin' much, lately."

The other detainees snickered.

"Shaddup!" shouted Fat. Molak looked up at Frank once more before he flipped the page on the clipboard.

"Show me the whites."

"Alright, file out," Skinny said. "Every white man up here, right now!"

Frank hung close to Elliot as they returned to the crowd of blacker faces.

"How was that, boss?"

Elliot took back his cot. Frank Fuquay claimed the cot across from him. Elliot watched the bars, hoping for an opening as Molak checked for a white man of the description.

"How you know so much?" asked Frank.

"I've been through this before."

"You don't seem like a crook."

"That's 'cuz I'm not."

Elliot noticed Molak's disappointment.

"That scrape we had earlier? You coulda mussed me up good," Frank said. "I couldn't peg you fo' a bad guy after that."

"Don't be so sure."

The white detainees filed out, openly complaining about the accommodations. The difference in temperament was striking. The stratums of society functioned in white folks' favor, even during incarceration. Any colored fella with the sense God gave him knew to count his blessings. The indifferent jaws of the machine could care less which colored man's blood lubricated its gears.

Elliot left Frank Fuquay behind as he hustled for the bars.

"See here, constable!"

"Yeah?"

"How's about that phone call now, boss?" Elliot faked deference of the white man's nigger.

"Later," Skinny said.

"Promise to make it quick."

Skinny paused to watch Fatty and Molak walk up the stairs.

"Gimme your hands."

Elliot threaded his hands through. Once cuffed, Skinny opened the cell door. Elliot walked out. Skinny grabbed him by his collar.

"Try anything, I split your head."

"Head's already split, boss. I'll be no trouble a'tall."

As Skinny kept watch near the stairs, Elliot picked up the receiver of the payphone. His request for a collect call made him shudder. To evade hell, he'd return to perdition in the land of string bean farming where organized crime was regularly done in the light of day.

"Southville County Sheriff," went the deep baritone.

"George?"

The other line made no sound. Only breathing.

"Georgie...it's me...Elliot...you there..."

"I'm here," George said, his voice trailing off.

"Listen, Georgie. I can't give it all to you on this call, but I'm in a tight spot. I'm locked up in St. Louis."

"St. Louis?"

"In the Meat Locker."

"Good Lord."

"I didn't have any ID on me. I'm in the docket as Nathan White."

More silence from George.

"No one here has seen or heard from you in ages. Now you just call out of the blue—"

"You gotta help me out, Georgie Boy."

George had to be the straightest man ever born of Southville, but no one could make him sin like Elliot Caprice.

"What do you need me to do?"

"Get me moved up on the docket. I'll take my chances with the judge."

"Elliot, I'm the Southville County Sheriff. You're in St. Louis."

"You're the sheriff now?"

"Long story. Which you would know, if—"

"Look, fat boy. I'm sorry I whited on you," Elliot said. "On everybody, but I'm gonna have to make it up to y'all later. Right now, I'm in the mother of all jams?"

"All these crazy stories on the wire," George said. "Some folk said you were dead."

"Well, Sheriff, I stay in here any longer, they weren't lyin'."

Elliot never exaggerated his predicaments. His life was so wild, he lacked the necessary creativity for embellishment.

"I'll figure out something," George said. "Stay dormy 'til I get there."

"Hey, Georgie."

"Yeah?"

"Maybe bring a lawyer?"

"You're a trouble magnet, you know that?"

"Ain't neva been any different, Georgie."

Elliot replaced the receiver on the payphone carriage. The bars opened. He reclaimed his cot, where his new best friend Frank Fuquay still waited.

"How'd it go, boss?"

"How'd what go?"

"Ya phone call? I figure you got an angle."

"I'm all out of angles, big man. That's how I'm here."

He prayed for the throbbing in his head to cease. He also

prayed for his new shadow to leave him be. Both prayers went unanswered.

"I on't know whether to ask you how you got yose'f in heah or how you gon get out."

"The same, both ways," Elliot said.

"I don't get it."

"Big Frank, you best to keep it that way."

CHAPTER 3

Sheriff George M. Stingley, Jr. hung up the phone slowly, as if he knew as soon as the receiver hit the carriage he'd be involved in his dear friend's dirt. Before Elliot's call, the holiest man in Southville was in the county jail gathering the personal effects left behind by, quite possibly, the unholiest: the late Sheriff Willis Dowd. Seventy-two hours earlier, when Dowd suffered a heart attack in a Sugartown sin den, Special Deputy George was called in to keep everything quiet. The county bosses remembered his late father, the Right Reverend George M. Sr. of Greater Grace Pentecostal, in particular, his willingness to go along to get along. It was expected that George Jr. would be a chip off the old block, thus, by fate or circumstance, he was appointed the first Negro county sheriff in the Midwest. As it happened in Southville County, it served as no occasion to update the history books.

George catalogued his options, which were few, as he possessed little faculty for corruption. He may have inherited his father's heavyset frame and rich baritone, but morally he took after his mother. In her house, it was personal discipline. Strive for that greater grace. First act saved so, by God's mercy, you may be saved. In George Sr.'s church, it was redemption, forgiveness, tithe, washed in the blood, tithe, calendar of events, women's auxiliary announcements, tithe and see you at Bible Study, where you may tithe again. As the son of a preacher, George was raised to be politically savvy, enough so he knew his backroom promotion put a target on his back. Handling things himself would be politically suicidal. Better to field support from Elliot's adopted community, the Southville Jews, of which Izzy Rabinowitz was their most influential constituent.

Deputy Ned Reilly hauled in Pete Simms, who was ripe for the drunk tank. George was so troubled he almost didn't notice them enter.

"You alright, George?"

"Yeah."

"You sure? You have that look on your face," Ned said, twirling his finger in front of his nose.

"Elliot Caprice just called."

"He's still alive?" Ned struggled to keep Pete on his feet.

"He's in the Meat Locker," George said. "Make sure you process Pete."

Ned finally got Pete on the bunk in the cell. The booze-hound was snoring so soundly he didn't bother to close him up inside.

"Pete's just off the wagon again. He's been no actual trouble."

"Drunk and disorderly. When he sobers up, his wife can bail him out."

"That's a bit harsh, doncha think?"

George looked across his glasses into Ned's eyes. His jowls squeezed against his shirt collar. Behind George's back, Ned referred to it as his preacher's stare.

"Ned, I'm the new Negro sheriff, fresh on the heels of the white sheriff that died between the legs of a prostitute. Let him dry out. Treat him real nice. Bake him a cake, but make sure some file somewhere shows he was booked. I should be back tomorrow."

Ned Reilly was the son of poor farmers left wrecked by the Dust Bowl. They fled to the fields of Southville when Ned was too young to remember. His was the sort of white man whose beginnings hadn't afforded him the status of race. Black or white was never an issue. Ned kept score on haves and have-nots. He chided fat cats. Big shots irked his ire. Taking orders from his old friend George was easy, so long as no one tried to make a fool out of him.

It was Elliot Caprice's favorite pastime.

"You headed to St. Louis to bail your buddy out?"

"Are you giving me grief about it?"

"Not at all, Sheriff. What you want me to say should anyone important come callin'?"

"Say I'm out paying a professional courtesy."

"Fair enough."

George had the door halfway closed behind him when he stuck his head back in.

"Ned."

"Yeah, George?"

"We'll give Pete a break this one time. I'm guest preaching for my mother on Sunday. I expect him to be at church."

"I'm sure ol' Pete will be there, George."

Most around Southville liked to say that were it not for the power to arrest folks, George wouldn't have anyone in church at all.

The Sheriff sat in his personal car outside Doc Shapiro's storefront office for at least fifteen minutes before he ventured inside to appeal to one of the heavies of a community he had been raised to distrust. George hadn't developed the affinity for Jewish folk the way Elliot had. He was raised in a Pentecostal church steeped in a tradition of blame naming. Jews took more than enough blame for imagined crimes. Yet George Stingley was no bigot. His appreciation for the Old Testament more than New afforded the two men at least some commonality, other than love for Elliot.

On a good day, one could observe patients of all stripes in Doc's waiting room. The aged, slender, Lithuanian Jew was Southville's only physician. Sure, folks could go up to Rockford or even Peoria, but then they might have to pay.

19

A bell chimed as George opened the door. Doc Shapiro was examining a screaming child in his exam room. Two other children waiting were mortified at what may happen to them. Their mothers admonished their fears, demanding they not become an embarrassment. When the exam room door finally opened, a feisty Irish boy no more than six years old flew out shouting a litany of tear-soaked curses. He hobbled into the arms of his mother on his bandaged left foot as he rubbed his right buttock. Doc Shapiro followed, flannel shirt, rolled sleeves—no lab coat—looking every bit a humble Teamster than a doctor of medicine. He was tall and gaunt. He had big, scarred hands, and a head full of white hair. No one knew where the scars came from. Elliot Caprice may have given him the snow up on the hill. Even at his age, Doc was still the kind of handsome that made him look as if he was in charge. He noticed George standing near the door but did not acknowledge.

"Just a little tetanus shot was all I gave him," the doctor said, his smooth tenor softening the harsh edges of his Eastern European accent.

"He gonna be alright?" asked the boy's mother.

"Change his dressing daily."

The woman spoke to Doc in a lowered voice.

"I'm afraid I can't pay you just yet. See, his daddy is off in Chicago findin' work on account of us losin' this year's crop. I promise as soon as he comes back…"

The good doctor interjected out of mercy. He was always privy to Southville's gossip. So many grandmothers sit in his waiting room. He knew her husband left in a drunken huff weeks prior. The crop wasn't lost. The money for seed disappeared down his gullet. Doc never intended for her to pay. Most likely, no one in his office that day would either. It was a wonder how ol' Shapiro made a nickel at all.

As Doc showed them out, he turned his attention to George.

"Sheriff Stingley."

"Doctor Shapiro, I was hoping we might have a word."

"As you can see, my waiting room is quite full."

"It's about Elliot Caprice."

Doc Shapiro ushered George into his examination room and closed the shades.

"Go on, Reverend."

George's father took away his robes years ago, yet folks still thought of him as clergy.

"He's in jail in St. Louis."

For a moment, George wondered why he felt the way he did when he delivered bad news to parents.

"What are the charges?"

"Most likely, being colored while minding his own business. He's in under an alias."

"Are you able to help, George?"

"Not much, I'm afraid. I've been sheriff less than a week. He needs a lawyer."

"He needs his friends, my boy."

In the space of a short conversation, he went from "Reverend" to "George" to "my boy." George sat in the chair near Doc Shapiro's desk.

"We kept in touch until he moved to Chicago." George shook his head.

"Ah. Chicago."

"Rumor has it he was on the cops, but fell into some dirt. I hadn't heard from him for two years. Today, out of the blue..."

"He needs you."

"It's Elliot Caprice we're talking about. He needs an angle."

George's hint wasn't subtle. Doc cut his eyes upward in surrender.

"I'll have to make a call."

"To Rabinowitz?"

"This bothers you?"

"I won't be connected to any friend or associate."

"Rest assured, Sheriff. Your lawyer is neither friend nor associate of Isadora Rabinowitz."

Doc dialed a number. George wanted to bolt from the room.

"Ya. It's Shapiro. Is my cousin in?"

They made conversation in Lithuanian Yiddish. Doc scribbled notes on his apothecary pad. George wondered whether that was one of his methods for concealing secrets. When he hung up, he handed George the note.

"Here is your attorney, Reverend. There will be nothing to pay. You will fetch him from his office in Springfield. His name is Michael Robin. He is a good man, like yourself."

If George wasn't so dignified, he would have rolled his eyes.

"I have one request," said Doc.

"Of course."

"Please bring him here."

"He won't come."

"Mention it concerns his uncle. He will come."

George thanked the good doctor, then left as fast as his burly frame could manage.

CHAPTER 4

George could have driven 80 to the 155 but chose U.S. Route 66, the long straight line of asphalt that cut right through Illinois's flat farmland. A big colored man driving an official vehicle better travel as straight a path as humanly possible. The figurative was closed off the moment he accepted Elliot's collect call. The literal connected the southern United States right on through to Chicago. He'd be far safer traveling the Mother Road.

Rows of corn stalks glistened in the hundred-degree sun. Cascading arches of illuminated water provided a glorious backdrop, against which wretched lives harvested the grain of kings in the unrelenting sun. Occasionally George glimpsed the dusky faced field-hands completely unable to tell which were Negro. They were lashed together in the bonds of lesser work. Each dolorous soul colored in deep hues of despair.

By noon, he arrived at a nondescript office building that served officers of the Sangamon County circuit court, which was barely a block away. He found Michael Robin and Associates listed on the directory, but as Wills and Probate. George found this odd but not disheartening, at least not until he opened the door to room 202. It was the tiniest two-person office ever rented. Every small window was open, plus a large standing fan in the corner was going. A colored girl in secretary's attire franticly rummaged through boxes of records that dominated the floor space.

"Excuse me," George said. He went unnoticed. "Miss!"

Startled, she leapt to her feet. The file she held in one armpit went free, its contents fell on the floor. George knelt to pick them up.

"I didn't mean to frighten you."

"Next time, knock."

"I did. Called out, too."

George handed her the folder.

"My name is George Stingley, Southville County Sheriff."

"Shapiro's man, yes. Elaine Critchlow, paralegal."

"I don't think I've ever met a Negro female in the legal profession."

"Negro female, hmm?"

"Yes," George said, legitimately pleased. "I think that's wonderful."

"You know, Harriet said the same thing."

"Harriet?"

"Tubman. We used to discuss my future when she brought me north on the Underground Railroad. Attorney Robin will be just a moment."

George took off his hat, needing something to do with his hands to ease his embarrassment. Mike Robin entered the room. He was younger than George expected, but gray at the temples. He had a stern look about him. Strong chin. Piercing gaze, with what George's mother referred to as accusing eyes. His dress was modest: dark suit, white shirt, tie, Florsheim shoes, wire-frame glasses. George wondered if having a colored woman in his employ complicated his reputation.

"Reverend Stingley."

They shook hands. George appreciated Mike's grip, which was strong. The grip was the tell. He experienced a lot of weak handshakes once he traded his vestments for a badge.

"I do a lot more policing than preaching these days."

"Yes, of course." Mike turned to Elaine. "We'll be up in St. Louis for the rest of the day, maybe into the night."

"It's too hot. Once I file these affidavits, I'm going home."

Elaine flipped her file shut. "Great meeting you, Sheriff. Good luck in St. Louis."

She opened the door, but turned back around.

"Oh," Elaine said. "Perhaps this is a country thing, but when you refer to a lady as a female, it makes you sound like a breeder. Bye now."

She shut the door. George looked over to Mike Robin.

"The court clerks love her," Mike said. George loosened his tie.

They arrived at the St. Louis County Courthouse in time to see Elliot brought past in a group headed to court for hearings. George approached a St. Louis County deputy. Instead of professional courtesy, he was given the third degree, including an inspection of his badge to verify its authenticity. Mike Robin stepped in.

"You have my client in custody. He's entitled to conference with his counsel."

As a Midwestern Jewish attorney was more believable than a Negro County Sheriff, Elliot was unshackled. They found an office no larger than a cubby to talk. Once behind a closed door, Mike sat across from George. Elliot perched himself next to his friend, so he could get a good look at the stranger.

"Who's this?" Elliot asked.

"Mike Robin. He's a lawyer."

"I'm an attorney, actually. There's a difference."

"Robin, huh? Like the bird." George's insides tensed. Elliot had the shit starter sound in his voice.

"Something like that."

Elliot looked Mike up and down. He then leaned into George's ear.

"You brought me some cop-a-plea tryin' to pass—"

"Now hold on a moment, Caprice," Mike said. A clerk knocked at the door.

"Five minutes!"

"Are you crazy?" George said.

Elliot rose from his seat. George pushed him back down.

"Hey, preacher man!"

"Do you want to stay locked up in here?"

"How you know he's a decent lawyer?"

"Attorney," Mike said.

"This is Doc Shapiro's man, Elliot."

Elliot stood up straight. He looked more afraid than when he was in the cell.

"Doc knows I was arrested?"

"I asked him for help—"

"You told Doc I was in jail?"

"I had to do something," George said.

"Not somethin' like that!" Elliot ran his fingers through his hair. "Christ on the fuckin' cross."

"That's not what's important now."

"The name Robin isn't to hide my Jewishness, Caprice."

Mike took off his glasses. It was all in the eyes.

"I'll be damned," Elliot said. "All grown up, huh?"

"Been out of law school four years."

Elliot had never seen Mikey Rabinowitz, as he wasn't allowed inside Izzy's home. He had claimed it was a business rule. Elliot knew it was because he was colored.

He turned to George, speechless.

"Shapiro didn't say a word." George raised his hand as if he was testifying. In court, not church. There was a second knock at the door.

"Wrap it up!"

"Sheriff," Mike said. "Would you help us out, please?"

George stepped outside to appeal to the deputy who thought he was a fraud. He shut the door, leaving the two who had never met, but knew each other well, alone.

"We don't have much time," Mike said, replacing his glasses. "We need to discuss the—"

"I thought you were fat."

"What?"

"Izzy used to say you were fat. Liked your sweets too much."

Mike shook his head.

"I lost a lot of weight in college."

"Where was that, exactly?"

"Caprice, we don't have time—"

"C'man."

"Illinois."

"Good school," Elliot said. "I went to Bradley for a hot second."

"I know. My father would rub it in my face."

"I don't doubt it."

Elliot fell silent.

"You know," Mike said. "I tried to get into Bradley. Illinois was my second choice."

"How'd you get into Illinois, but not Bradley?"

"Jew quotas." Mike shrugged.

"Ain't that always the way."

George returned.

"Any longer, they'll drag you in front of the judge."

"What's the plan, Mikey?"

"I made some calls," Mike said. "Turns out you're still a cop."

"Impossible."

"Verified with the Superintendent's office." Mike consulted his notes. "Assigned Detective Elliot N. Caprice, badge 47-9509-B, Wentworth district. Current status: suspended."

"Suspended from my neck, maybe."

"That would explain the gun they found on you," George said.

"Nobody needs to know that."

"Why not?"

"I got my reasons, alright?" Elliot ran his fingers through his hair again. "What else?"

"What do you mean, what else?" George said. "The gun is their case against you."

"Sheriff, what are you investigating these days?"

"What do you mean?"

"Southville is the crime capital of Illinois farm country," Mike said. "There must be something."

George thought a moment.

"Before Sheriff Dowd died, he was looking for some rum-runners who brought unsealed Kentucky bourbon into the county."

"That's how you became Sheriff?" Elliot laughed. "God really likes you, Georgie."

"Don't blaspheme."

"Hey, better you than that fuckwit Dowd."

"When you speak of the dead, say something good," George said.

"Dowd is dead. Good."

"It could work," Mike said.

"What could?"

"Nathan White is a material witness to a felony committed in Southville County, Illinois. You called his attorney to get him to comply voluntarily and found out he was in here." Elliot and George looked at Mike, then to each other.

"Takes after his daddy."

"No need to insult a guy," Mike said. "You have jurisdiction. He was a criminal in Southville before St. Louis."

"Wouldn't be lying about that."

"Give it a rest, fat boy," Elliot said.

"I don't have a writ from anyone in authority," George said. "Besides, that's a federal crime—"

"Nathan White is a colored degenerate they pulled off the floor of a juke joint. No offense."

"Nathan says 'none taken.'" Elliot leaned back in the chair.

"There's still the gun."

"It's over a hundred degrees outside," Mike said, laughing. "Gun or no gun, if you can help them cut down their caseload, you could get Julius and Ethel Rosenberg out of here."

"Do you understand my position?"

"Psst." Elliot put his hand up to his mouth. "George is a colored sheriff."

"Don't make fun, Elliot."

"Oh, believe me, I'm not. I'm sweatin' bullets over here."

"I can't stand up in a court of law and pretend cops from another county finding an unregistered firearm on a suspect is just some little thing. Even if I am the Sheriff of Perdition."

"George has a point, Mikey," Elliot said. Mike finally rolled his eyes at the sound of his kiddie name.

"The gun isn't connected to any crimes, is it?"

"None I can remember."

"Wouldn't be the first time the cops planted a gun on someone." Mike shrugged. "That will be my argument, if I have to argue."

Mike Robin was game. George Stingley was wary. Elliot Caprice was desperate. George nervously rubbed his chin.

"Georgie," Elliot said. "If I don't dangle, I'm white. In the worst way."

Another knock on the door. George's jowls pressed into his collar.

"Sheriff?" Mike stood up.

"Shit," George said.

Hard-luck prisoners jammed the courtroom. As some fool long ago chose the west side of the building to put the windows, the heat from the afternoon sun made everyone impatient, law or accused. The police's disregard for due process was plain. It sickened Mike Robin to see rows of colored faces suffering the wounds of police brutality. So many black eyes. Swollen jaws through which pleas were mumbled.

After hours of barking legalese in layman's terms to the throngs appearing pro se, the judge was exhausted. The public defender must have gone fishing. When Nathan White's case was called, Mike approached the bench with Elliot. The judge was so happy to finally see one other steward of the court he was lose for the play.

Just then, George and Elliot learned the difference between a lawyer and an attorney. Lawyers make trouble for their clients. Attorneys make trouble for everyone else. Mike Robin cited statutes. Alluded to filing motions that would tie up the process. Threatened to file injunctions. Demanded segregated accommodations to protect his client. Before long, the gavel-banger was glad Elliot was someone else's problem, just as little Mikey Rabinowitz who used to be fat said would happen. Nathan White was swiftly remanded into the custody of the nigger sheriff with the badge that could have come out of a gumball machine. The only snag in the scam was Elliot's fingerprints. Once processed, they were forever linked to his alias. Now Elliot Caprice would be on the hook for Nathan White's crimes, thus poor ol' Nate had to die, yet Elliot didn't mourn him. He had kept him alive far longer than expected. He deserved to rest.

The return trip to Springfield was silent. The experience left each man reflecting upon his part.

George knowingly attested to the legitimacy of a false identity. Were it ever to get out, it would be another reason for his opponents to push him out of public office. Only the Lord he prayed to knew how much the job dampened his spirit. He spent his life playing respectability politics, yet it earned him no respite from the community's bigotry. Just another reason to tip-toe instead of live full-throated, which is what he truly deserved.

It would be no time before Mike heard from his father about getting himself involved with Elliot. They would fight. He would hear about how he was supposed to bring the entire *mishpachah* into respectability. How he could have hired another Jew, rather than a colored girl. How Izzy paid his way through law school to work for his father, not be some *schlepper* in Springfield, taking pennies from farmers. In his bones, Mike could feel the battle coming.

Elliot was broke, down, and busted. When he reached out to George for help, he dragged all his Southville folks into it. Doc Shapiro. Izzy's favorite kid. He put George's success—corrupt as it was—on the line, just for getting drunk in the wrong joint while on the lam. Damn them big-legged women. Sure, he was thankful to be out of jail, but where would he go? Not back to Southville. That'd be a worse tangle than if he remained in the Meat Locker.

"You really put it on 'em in there, Mike," Elliot said, breaking the silence. "I've seen nickel-slick, but that was dime-smooth."

"You deal in probate, right? Wills and such?" George said.

"Keeps the lights on as I log time on race cases."

"A lot of money in race cases?" Elliot asked.

"I have my reasons," said Mike. "So what will you do, Caprice?"

"What do you mean?"

"Sounds like you're done with being a cop. What's next?"

"Mindin' my lonely." Elliot smirked as he watched the road.

"Is he always like this?"

"Don't ask."

"Right here, midway up the block," Mike said.

George parked in front of Mike's apartment building. It was

inelegant, meant only for working folks, not well-off ambidexters. He had cut himself off from his family. Izzy would drop dead if he knew his son lived in some WPA joint.

The trio got out of the car. Elliot approached Mike.

"See here, Mikey," Elliot said. "I know it wasn't easy for you to do that favor."

"When the good doctor calls, you don't say no."

"Ain't that the truth."

"Thanks for everything," George said.

"Good luck in the job, Sheriff. That's a hard town to serve."

They shook hands before Mike put his arm behind Elliot's shoulder. He led him to the side. George stood by the car.

"Not to pry, but if you don't have plans in the interim, I could use a crafty fella at the office. I'm up to my neck in estate administration but my process servers keep quitting on me. You may knock on the door of the occasional weirdo, but you shouldn't have to get your hands dirty. It's easy work."

"I'm going to put dinner away, Michael!"

The three looked skyward to see Elaine standing in the window appearing most unlike a paralegal. Tousled hair. Modest nightgown, but a nightgown nonetheless.

"I'm coming already," Mike said.

"Miss Elaine," George said. He tipped his hat while looking at his feet.

"Sheriff. How's the breeding coming along?"

"Obviously, I should go," Mike said. "Consider my offer."

"Thanks again, Mikey." Elliot waved goodbye, which was a lot.

Once Mike Robin was gone, George opened the door of the cruiser.

"Don't that beat all?" George said.

"Fella said he had his reasons."

Off the two went into the night one white man short of a safer ride on the Illinois highway system.

* * *

They rode in silence, no radio, no conversation. They had been friends since forever, so George could feel Elliot's ticks. Elliot could feel George feeling them. Southville was the last place he wanted to be. Best to stop it before it started.

"Look here, Georgie," he said. "Get me on to the station up in Lincoln."

"We're going back to Southville."

"You're goin' back to Southville. I'm goin' to Kansas City."

"Elliot, you just got out of jail."

"Don't worry, fat boy. I got folks who served with me over that way. They'll put up with me for a while."

"Doc Shapiro made a request, which we both know was an order. You need to see him."

"He probably just wants to catch up. I'll call him myself once I'm in KC."

"He said it's about your uncle."

"What about my uncle?"

"He wouldn't say."

"Fuckin' Doc. He and Rabinowitz, the Sanhedrin of Southville. What do you know about it?"

"Can't say I've run into him, really."

"Good job, Georgie." Elliot grew agitated. "Southville County's holiest can't do a ride-by to make certain the goddamned Caprice family farm hasn't burned down? Her eminence Mother Stingley didn't have a pie you could take him?"

George abruptly pulled over to the shoulder, slammed on the brakes and shoved the gearshift into place. He could hold his composure better than most, but mention his mother in less than pleasant terms and George would come right up out himself.

"I should have hung up on your arrogant ass—"

"Language, Georgie."

"You may be surprised to know that while you've been gone,

life moved forward. Elliot Caprice isn't the most important person—"

"Whoa."

"I'm have responsibilities to an entire county. I don't have time to step and fetch for your precious Jews—"

"Hey, watch it now, George."

"Go to hell, Elliot!"

"Man, you gonna burn through all your allotted curse words for the month."

Elliot joked because he was nervous. No one wanted to face George Stingley when he was done playin'.

"Alright, Reverend." Elliot raised his hands in surrender. "Alright. I'm not tryin' to be an asshole. I'm just under the gun is all."

"I stuck my neck out for you, again."

George punched the steering wheel with his big, black fist. The cruiser went silent. They didn't look at each other. A few cars passed by, their headlights cast light through the dark moment between friends.

"I didn't say thank you," Elliot said.

"What else could I have done?"

"You could've hung up."

Another car passed. This time, it slowed down to look inside their vehicle.

"It's getting dark. We better get on."

George started the cruiser.

"You're welcome." George said. "I'm just glad you're alright."

They pulled back onto the highway.

"My uncle, huh?"

"Tell him it concerns his uncle. That's all he said."

"Damn."

The year Elliot spent on the run, he hadn't thought once that Uncle Buster could have needed him. Even before, the extent of their contact was brief letters containing money Elliot knew the proud man would never spend. Occasionally he'd call making small talk, but nothing more. He never let on about what he was doing. It was safer that way. When everything fell apart, he chose to run rather than track his misery back to Southville. It was the right thing to do. Still, in all, he wasn't there for his uncle. Buster Caprice was more man than most, yet he was only a man. In the time he was away, Elliot forgot that he would eventually grow old.

"You think it's something serious or Shapiro just playing games?"

"Doc doesn't play games."

"Where am I taking you, Elliot?"

Everything within Elliot told him to say the train station in Lincoln.

"I guess we're goin' home."

CHAPTER 5

It was a chilly Chicago night, but the final package Elliot carried made it hot as summer. He tapped at his chest to feel the thick manila envelope through his black leather jacket. He worried his nervous sweat would ruin the contents inside. The risk was enough for him to reconsider the entire score. He should have pulled up stakes the minute he was left out in the cold, but his guilt about his past as the youngest, blackest member of the Roseland Boys wasn't going to resolve itself. Besides, he was a Caprice. That meant he always finished what he started, personal risk be damned.

The northbound Red Line train pulled into Addison station. Only a few late riders— likely third-shifters headed home from the stockyards—were on the car with him. He pulled down his black eight-panel cap to obscure his face. For good measure, he fingered his service revolver in his right pocket. Just before the doors closed, he hopped off. A quick check of his surroundings yielded no additional worry. He traveled late enough where it would be easy to spot a tail. If things had to get messy, no witnesses.

He felt the heft of the gun in his pocket as he trotted down the stairs to the street below. The southbound train passed overhead as he checked all directions before he jogged west, cut-ting through a neighbor's walk to the alley behind Bill Drury's place.

The garage door was closed, which left him standing in the alley, out in the open. Like an asshole. Whatever Bill was doing, he wasn't covering Elliot's ass, per usual.

He stood off to the side near some city ashcans, just outside a pool of greenish amber streetlight. Drury had until twenty to show before he'd dangle.

"Thousand one...thousand two..."

He saw light through the side-door window pane. Elliot banged on the door. Up it went. Drury stood on the other side, chewing on a stubbed cigar, making that same annoying Cheshire cat grin.

"You're late," Elliot said.

"I was having dinner."

Elliot pushed past him.

"Please. Come in."

"Goddamn it, Bill," Elliot said. "I don't mind tellin' you I'm tired—"

"Why don't' you come up?"

"What?"

"My daughter made pot roast."

Elliot stared through Drury, blinking at the utter mundanity of the offer. The notion of retiring to the man's eat-in kitchen to enjoy dinner was absurdly enticing. Maybe, after they look at the contraband for which he risked his life, they'd discuss the Bears' chances at the championship. Debate White Sox versus Cubs.

"Man, I should've been gone."

"She makes a damn good pot roast. I made her leave it on the stove, in case you wanted some."

Drury smiled. Not like a jerk, but an honest-to-goodness, happy to see you smile. Elliot and Bill had become something close to good friends. They related to each other's absurd level of rage at society gone wrong. They both loved being a cop, but despised what had become of the Chicago Police Department. They mutually exploited each other—Bill wanted fame and fortune, Elliot wanted payback—but they respected each other, in a twisted sort of way. Sure, Drury would throw him under the bus if he had to, but Elliot expected that of white folks. Besides, Drury was a North sider, which was far different than

South Side ofays, who figured they shouldn't have to look at colored folk once they came home from working with them all day. He was good Chicago. By comparison, Elliot was barely allowed to stand in Izzy's back yard. Drury was once brass, and here he offered up his daughter's pot roast to a half-colored mule. Elliot almost felt bad at what he was to say next.

"We can't do this again, Lieutenant."

"You serious?"

"One day, I'm gonna wind up steppin' on my own dick. This shit is too hot."

"Don't worry, kiddo. I've kept you out of it."

"Oh, I bet you have."

"Hey, have I ever screwed you before?"

"After Kefauver, there ain't much screwin' left."

Elliot pulled the envelope from his jacket. Drury took it.

"This is heavy," Drury said.

"Don't I know it."

The latest delivery was about an inch thick. This haul was the real deal.

"You did good, Caprice. Goddamn, pally. This is a score."

"The last score."

"I'll assume there's nothing in here about—"

"You know our deal, Bill."

"Rabinowitz would be the cherry on top," Drury said. "You don't owe him anything."

"I know I don't." Elliot looked over his shoulder. "If we're going to stand here, can we at least close the garage door?"

"Let's have a drink. To celebrate. C'man."

"I'll have one in your honor. Once I'm back on the South Side."

Elliot offered Bill a final handshake. Drury hesitated.

"Caprice, you've got the mind of an arch criminal." Drury took his hand. "With the heart of a cop."

"So, I'm fucked either way."

Drury laughed, looked as if he wanted to say something else, but the sound of thunder broke through the garage. His jaw exploded. His chest went next, which left a mosaic of blood and flesh on Elliot's face. On instinct, Elliot yanked his service revolver from his pocket. His left shoulder caught fire.

"Elliot," George said. "Elliot, wake up."

Elliot opened his eyes. Straight ahead, through the rolling dusk, were the poorly sequenced street lights.

"Are you alright? You were thrashing about pretty good there."

Elliot said nothing.

"I figured I'd let you sleep," George said. "How's your head?"

"Still attached. Guess we're here."

"Yep."

She sat as he remembered her: a patchwork of farmland. A few industrial employers. Neighborhoods for all the different classes, sectioned off by race. It supported two congressmen but only one hospital. The fire department was modern. The only law was George. The main drag was paved as were the affluent blocks. The rest were still dirt roads lit by gaslight. Nearly equidistant between St. Louis and Chicago, and situated along the Illinois River, Southville was the midpoint between Missouri bondage and Chicago freedom. It bore the appearance of small town U.S.A., which was good for mobsters like Frank Nitti, who used it as a place to stash loot. In time, the town was flush, so much that folks got used to finding an occasional body in the corn stalks.

George hung a right at Aberdeen Avenue.

"New lights, huh?"

"Yeah. Roseland Boys got the city fathers to put them in last year."

"Why you would ever want to be sheriff is beyond me."

"My father wanted me to want it."

"They do that, don't they," Elliot said. "Be thankful you had the one, Georgie Boy. I got three fathers. Ain't nan one happy with me."

George stopped the car outside Doc Shapiro's. The light was on in his exam room.

"Case in point."

"It's good to have you around again," George said. "Will you stay?"

Elliot grunted.

"Well, just let me know whatever you do. If it's safe to say, I mean."

"Thanks, Georgie. You did me right."

"Let me know if you want to meet up at Duffy's later."

"Duffy's? When did you start drinkin'?"

"When I started fishing bodies out of the river for a living."

The sheriff pulled off. Elliot walked up to the door. It was locked, so he walked around the corner to the alley. The special entrance was cracked open. Doc saw them pull up—he saw everything. He wondered when the last time one of the Izzy's crew was brought in for triage.

Doc was doing busy work: replacing consumables, sorting records—everything he himself used to do. This meant he was ill at ease. Rummaging through his things was a sign he was rummaging through his mind.

"What's that ya say there, Doc?"

He didn't turn around, which made Elliot feel even worse.

"*Zay mir moykhl tatenui.*"

Doc walked over to Elliot. He took his ward's face in his old doctor's hands, which smelled like antiseptic and tobacco, his only vice.

"Ever the doctor."

Elliot winced. Doc noticed the swollen area on the rear right side.

"What did they do to you?"

"Nothin' I probably didn't have comin' to me."

Doc sat him down in the examination table. He looked in Elliot's eyes. "Follow my finger." He moved it up, down, then across. Elliot blinked wildly.

"You're concussed. You're also in the bottle."

Elliot rubbed his forehead.

"It's been a hard night. Month. Year."

Doc walked to his medicine cabinet.

"George mentioned something about my uncle?"

"He's no longer on the farm. Last I heard, the bank put it into receivership."

"The farm's been foreclosed?"

"*Meynt azoy.*"

Doc returned with aspirin. He handed them to Elliot, who swallowed them without water. Doc grabbed his stethoscope and listened to Elliot's pulses.

"I took a shot upside the head."

"*Shtum.*"

"I'm fine."

"Take off your shirt," Doc said.

It was easy to see why Elliot hesitated. He had fresh scratches from the wallops along with so many old scars. Those from the war that bore keloids Doc recognized. Newer ones, circular in composition, he did not. One was on the back of Elliot's left deltoid. Its match was at the front of the same shoulder, irregularly shaped."

"What *katsev* treated you?"

"Doc—"

"Why didn't you go to a hospital?"

"What sent my uncle to a bank for a loan?" Elliot said, changing the subject. Doc exhaled.

"A big canning company from out west came to town offering contracts to plot owners. Buster held out."

"Unk's no sellout."

"His work-hands were being hired away, so he took out a loan for the planting season. After that, he fell ill."

"His heart?"

Doc nodded.

"Losing the farm has only made it worse."

Doc used a stethoscope to listen to Elliot's pulses.

"If the farm is seized, where is he?"

"The SRO across from Sugartown."

"Ugh. Betty's joint."

"Room twenty-one. I offered up my place."

"Nah. He wouldn't." Elliot rubbed his temples. Doc put away his instruments.

"At least you are here," Doc said.

"Don't know what I'm gonna do about it. I have some war pension checks comin' to me, but that don't sound like it's gonna be enough." Elliot put back on his shirt.

"Go talk to him."

"Maybe tomorrow"

Doc waved Elliot off.

"It's late. He's probably asleep."

"*Shoyn yetst.*"

"Fine. Right after you're done chewin' my ass."

Doc slapped him on the thigh, hard.

"By the way, nice touch sending in Mikey Rabinowitz."

"Isadora didn't appreciate it."

"How'd he know?"

"How wouldn't he? Michael refuses to help his father, even now that he needs him."

"Hard to believe he needs anyone."

"There's a new player in the loan racket. He's running out of allies. He's trying to legitimize, and fast."

"He's not broke, is he?"

Doc took a seat atop his desk.

"No. His finances are still intact, but his influence has waned. This new character trades on fear. Everyone wants to stay out of the fray."

"At least his green is still long. I may be asking him for a loan."

"I can give you my answer now if you like."

Elliot's stomach dropped when he heard the voice. Izzy Rabinowitz stepped in from the rear alcove. He didn't favor Doc Shapiro in appearance much at all. He was the same height as Mikey, but had much harder facial features that he concealed underneath a gray fedora that perfectly matched his powder gray fresco suit. He wore white spats atop his deep gray Florsheim Imperials. The spats matched his hat band. The shoes matched his mood. Izzy never bothered announcing himself. If he called upon you in person, it wasn't for pleasure.

"Isadora."

"Ira." Izzy took off his hat. "Figured you'd be here, kid. I see you're in one piece."

"Mikey is really good at what he does," Elliot said.

"That's one opinion," Izzy said. "The cops, kid? Figure I taught you better than that."

"You taught me a lot. Learned a lot more through observation."

"You sound like your preacher friend, our new sheriff. Can you believe it?"

"You didn't make that happen?"

"This shit-show of a government is all goy. Well, minus one."

"A Southville con took place without you?"

"There's that mouth." Izzy sat in a chair. "Glad I was able to help your defense."

"I don't remember you bein' there."

"Your half-colored brain go soft, kid? You know how it works, as does Mikey."

"Don't hassle him about it. If he wasn't there, I'd—"

"Aah, give it a rest," Izzy said. "Fuckin' Clarence Darrow. I don't mind tellin' ya I don't like your attitude."

"I just didn't expect to run into you when I'm in dire straits."

"Everything's gotta be on this kids terms. Ira, he hasn't changed a bit. So what, kid. You need work?"

"Sheeeit—"

"How you figurin' on makin' good on those expert legal services that saved your *tochas*?"

Elliot hopped up from the exam table. He had enough height on Izzy to seem threatening. He wasn't crazy—Elliot kept his hands soft—but Izzy went too far.

"You don't get to claim that for yourself."

"Watch your mouth, kid."

"I called George. He asked Doc to help. Doc called Mikey, not you, which I'm sure pissed you off 'cuz all roads have to lead through Izzy Rabinowitz."

Izzy stood. Using the hand speed of a much younger man, he grabbed Elliot by his collar.

"Isadora," Doc said, aghast at Izzy's aggression. Elliot did nothing. Their eyes locked. This was a battle of wills.

"You wanted to try it straight. I told you it wouldn't work out. You could've come back to me, but you ran off to the war."

"There was a draft."

"You know they were passin' over coloreds."

"Not this colored!"

"Half-colored. The stupid half."

Doc jumped between them before Elliot could do something he'd regret.

"Not in my place," He said, to Elliot. He turned to Izzy and said nothing. Only stared. *A breyteh deyeh hoben.* Once Doc spoke, no one else dared say shit. Not even his younger cousin Isadora, the Midwestern rainmaker. Izzy let go of Elliot's collar. He retook his seat.

"You know what hurts the most, kid? I stopped bein' good enough for you, but you join the most crooked bunch of bastards in all creation. Chicago PD makes my organization look like the Little Brothers of the Poor."

Elliot looked away. Doc was relieved the argument ended.

"So what can I do for you? As if I haven't done too much already."

"Ask him, *boychik*," Doc said. Elliot exhaled. All he could muster was a statement.

"I have to get the farm out of hock."

"The farm," Izzy said, sarcastically.

"I can't have my uncle in that fuckin' flophouse."

"Hey, he went to a bank. He took his chances."

"He didn't know what he was doing." Elliot felt guilty hearing himself say it.

"Believe it or not, I like Buster. Everyone does," Izzy said. "But I'm sure that bank note ain't small potatoes. If you don't pay, I'd have to sell it anyway. This is a bad pony for everybody. Let it go."

"Isadora—"

"Don't Isadora me, Ira. I got a guy movin' in on me. Sets up in Rockford, callin' himself The Turk, of all things. How's a Jew supposed to take that?"

"As a threat," Elliot said.

"These are tense times, kid."

"Don't be cruel, cousin."

"You give him the money," Izzy said. "And once it's down the drain, you'd have to start chargin' all the poor unfortunates."

"Give half. I'll cover the rest for him."

"Doc, stop."

"Come back to work for me, and—"

"I ain't gonna do that," Elliot said. Izzy almost looked hurt.

"Ask me for anything else."

Izzy looked away. Elliot took a moment to ponder his consolation prize.

"I could use a car."

"You remember where the yard is. Go see Amos. Pick one out."

Izzy stood.

"I'll pay you for it after I get my war pension."

"Relax, kid. I'm flush with cars. Every *schlepper* wants to use one to cover their vig, like I'm fuckin' General Motors."

Izzy took Elliot by the chin. There was a hint of affection, but only just.

"You've never looked so bad, kid. Get your shit together." Izzy turned his back. The conversation was over.

"Cousin," Izzy said, as he walked toward the door. "Let yourself out of this office once in a while."

"Cousin," Doc said. "Best to Rebecca."

Elliot stared at the floor.

"I meant what I said—"

"No, Doc."

"The money doesn't matter to me, *boychik*."

"That's 'cuz you ain't got it. You the onliest Jew that doesn't care about his *mazuma*."

"There are a few of us."

"Yeah. You and Abraham Heschel. Maybe I can get the other half from him." Elliot stood up. "Nah, Doc. I have to deal with this by my lonely."

Doc went to his desk for his strongbox. He took out a sawbuck."

"Nothin' doin', Doc. C'man."

"*Shtum. Folg mikh.*"

Doc pressed the ten-spot in Elliot's hand. Elliot looked down to the floor in shame.

"Isadora is right. You look like shit. See your uncle."

Elliot nodded, rose to his feet and left.

He could have cut through Sugartown to shorten the walk to Miss Betty's SRO, but he didn't trust himself to avoid stopping for a drink. One would lead to several. That would lead to trouble. Uncle Buster would see him worse for wear, but not drunk to boot. He ventured over to Pettingill Road, the east-west drag named after one of Southville's founders. From there, he'd keep to the unlit stretch of back road along Route 30. Questions dominated his mind. Was he somehow so important to Izzy that things would take a turn in his absence? Was Uncle Buster dying without the farm or was it always killing him?

The war changed everything. Most of his compatriots in the 761ˢᵗ knew little of Jews. For the average Negro, the existence of concentration camps was an abstraction. Just another example of how ofays do each other when there were no niggers around. Once Patton took colored regiments deep within German territory, they witnessed atrocities that eclipsed the tortures of Jim Crow. For Elliot, it was personal. This one could have been Doc. That one could have been Izzy or his wife or one of his sons. The alienation of Negroes and Jews into third-class citizens was a grim commonality. To Elliot's mind, something similar befalling Negroes was more than possible—it was likely. All it took was another economic depression. Maybe some masterful propaganda. Then the next concentration camps to be liberated would hold colored bodies. This was his motivation for joining the Chicago Police Department. That, and being cheeky. He desired to legitimize himself. Perhaps help legitimize colored folk overall. Sure, the stable paycheck was nice. Serving as an example of the social legitimacy of post-war Negroes was more important.

At least, that's what he told himself.

The dirt stretch ran out. He jogged through a clearing in the remains of a defunct string bean farm. In the distance was the four-story tall, fifty-yard long monstrosity that was Miss Betty's SRO. It began as temporary housing for migrant workers. The first two floors were built from the ground up by displaced area farmers, courtesy of FDR's Work Protection Administration. By the close of the WPA in 1943, it had become a shanty for drifters. It was of no more use to the government, so it was deeded back to the county for the sum of one dollar. Somehow, Betty Bridges, one of Sugartown's prevailing women of the night, managed to gain legal possession of the shanty. Perhaps it was through blackmail or something equally nefarious, but it certainly wasn't her charms. Once the vagrants were driven out by her raucous personality plus a well-compensated Sheriff Dowd, she used the money she squirreled away through the years to recondition the place. Miss Betty's Single Room Only was born.

The last time Elliot saw it, it had a newly built third floor of brick. Now a fourth floor sat atop the third, constructed of reclaimed wood. He snickered when he saw an electric sign outside. Of course, the "Miss Betty's" part remained lit, but on alternating circuits blinked "single rooms only" and "no guests."

He walked inside. A few sleeping indigents were seated in the lobby around a television that only offered static. Elliot wondered if the old bag charged tenants to watch by the minute. Her brother Percy, as clueless as ever, was asleep in the booth underneath a racing sheet. Elliot ducked around an old payphone booth. When the coast was clear, he darted up the stairs. As he approached room twenty-one, he took a deep breath before knocking softly. Behind the door he heard snoring louder than a dying bear moaning. He opened the door to find Nathan "Buster" Caprice dead to the world. He shut the door as quiet as he could, but his next step touched a creaky floor board. Buster sat up straight. He reached for a hickory axe handle he kept near his bed.

"Unk. It's me."

"Wha?"

"It's me, old man. Wake up."

Elliot took a step back while Uncle Buster fumbled for the

light switch over the bed. He didn't want to see the business-end of that hickory. Buster's eyes adjusted to the light.

"How long you been standin' there?"

"Just now. I ain't been back but a minute."

He was black as night. His coarse gray hair made him look regal. His deep-set, piercing eyes had dark pupils which were framed by yellowing whites. Specks of red brought on from decades in the sun looked like constellations.

His shoulders were broad. His neck was thick. He looked more boxer than farmer. He put the hickory down. Elliot noticed that his large, calloused hands trembled.

"How long have you been sick?"

"Shapiro tol'?"

"I was just at his office. I come up from Springfield," Elliot said.

"That old Jew stay tellin' tales, don't he? Damn Walter Winchell—"

"What are you doin' in this shit-hole? Doc said he has a room for you, at least until you get on your feet."

"He do enough for me already."

Buster sat up on the edge of the bed. He reached for a bag of Drum tobacco and his rolling papers on the end table. Elliot watched as his uncle's old black hands make a perfect smoke, shakes or not.

"Want one?"

Buster lit one for him before he rolled one for himself. Elliot sat down next to Buster on the bed. He filled himself not only with smoke, but the memories of long, sleepless nights on the front. Of stakeouts, where coffee and cigarettes kept him alert.

"Why didn't you tell me about the farm? I could've helped."

"I figure you wuzn't comin' back. Why bother you wid'it?"

Buster took a long drag. He sucked in a bit more air, which caused the smoke to dance on his palette. He looked like one of the sculptures Elliot saw in Italy—the Mouth of Truth.

"Well, I'm here now. How much do we owe?"

"Thirty-one hunned," Buster said, releasing the smoke.

"Christ, Unk?! Were you buyin' slaves?"

"Roosevelt's old program ran out. These big food companies come through buyin' up crops, seasons in advance. Other farms got money to pay health insurance 'n such. Just wanted to keep our field hands, is all."

Buster took another drag.

"Soon as I got sick, they all up and quit anyhow. Ain't dat always the way."

The smoke escaped his nostrils as he spoke, like an old black dragon.

"How long we got until we lose it?"

"Fella at the bank—"

"Loan officer."

"Who else?"

"Shit, you could be takin' your financial advice from the janitor for all I know."

"Can I tell it?"

"Tell it."

"The loan officer said our back acreage is locked, sum'n or other."

"Landlocked."

"That's it. Said they have ta get some approval for an ease-ment, they called it. Can't sell it until that comes through, 'cuz the bank wanna divide it up." Buster took another drag.

"So there's time."

Elliot used his fingers to pull out the ember at the end of his cigarette.

"How thangs in the big city? You still on da cops?"

"Man, I can't show my face back there."

"Ya caught up in some dirt?"

"Yeah."

"It's good you back in Southville. Dirt the natural order o' thangs 'round heah. You look tired."

"Tired ain't the word."

"There's enough bed fo' two. We'll sort Betty out tomorrow." Buster patted the mattress. He rolled on his side to make room for his nephew. Elliot laid the opposite direction. It bothered him how much safer he now felt. It was a testament to just how bad he'd fucked up his life.

"I should've never left."

"Sure you should've. You restless, like yo' daddy wuz. Better you take that fight out in the world than keep it locked up in yo'sef."

"Did he stay in a fix all the time?"

"Jefferson caused trouble. Most of ya trouble ain't yo trouble a'tall. It's everyone else's. Like that preacher's boy. The fat one."

"Georgie."

"Either it was him or one of dem kids from Roseland. As soon as they got picked on, you out deah fightin'. Pull a gun wit' dat rich boy down at college. You go to tha war. You join tha cops." Buster yawned.

"I just can't abide bullies is all," Elliot said.

"Ya stay out of the sun long enough, you look white. Most folks would trade on that, but naw."

"Some things just ain't right, Unk."

"Some thangs ain't s'pose ta be right."

Elliot turned onto his side. The powerful simplicity of Buster's words eased him of his guilt, at least enough to fall asleep. Were it not for the snoring, he would have enjoyed the first real night of rest he'd had in a year.

CHAPTER 6

Elliot opened his eyes to twilight that peeked out from the tears in the vinyl pull shade over the window. Sparrows and blackbirds argued over territory. Crows provided commentary. Uncle Buster was still asleep, the violent snoring reduced to a low grumble. Elliot walked out into the hall. It was too early to encounter anyone else, so he had no need to sneak. He felt free.

The facilities on Uncle Buster's floor weren't the worst place Elliot had used in his year laying low. He needed a toothbrush, a razor hadn't touched his face in days, but at least he could free himself of his funk. After hosing off, he went back to the room. He took some scrap paper and a pencil from the end table.

Unk,
Gone out to take care of some business.
Be back around dinner.
—e

Those two simple sentences scrawled on scrap paper may as well have been a detailed manifesto. It was a personal declaration he wasn't going anywhere until matters were resolved. He snuck down the stairs to find Miss Betty's lobby empty. Percy was in the booth, still parked behind his racing sheets. Elliot tapped on the counter.

"What's that'cha say there, Percy?"

The racing sheets came down.

"Elliot Caprice. I'll be damned."

"Look here, I'm back in town takin' care o' thangs. I'm stayin' up in my uncle's room."

"I don't think Betty's gonna like that too much."

"Betty still take cash on the barrelhead?"

"You know that, cousin."

"Betty can mind her goddamned bidness. Don't go skimpin' on his accommodations neither. He old, but he ain't stupid. Ya get me?"

"Sure, boss."

Elliot swiped two dimes from the counter top.

"We square?"

"Sho', Elliot. I ain't neva minded you nun. It's just my sister. You know how she can be."

"Yeah, I know. That's why this ain't no permanent arrangement. I'll give this back to you later."

Elliot walked over to the pay phone.

"Hello. This is Elliot Caprice. Is Attorney Robin in?"

The lunch counter at the S.S. Kresge on Pettengill had prices affordable enough to make the segregated accommodations bearable. Had he gone anywhere else more comfortable, the undesired attention as the prodigal son returned would have slowed him down. The seating sections were blanket corporate policy, administered by absentee management. Graffiti scrawled above the "colored patrons only" sign read "Colored folk wouldn't eat here!" Good ol' Southville.

He took his coffee as he had on the job: black and strong. He used it to chase down two hard-boiled eggs plus toast. It took him all of ten minutes to eat without pleasure. A cop's breakfast. Just enough to keep him on his toes. He laid down a dollar, the tip equal to the bill. Once fed, his brain bathed in caffeine, Elliot was prepared to get himself a haircut and a shave, some duds to show up to his meeting looking professional, and to claim the wheels Izzy gifted him from the yard. It was the colored man's post-prison trifecta.

Elliot wanted to make it to Boots' Barber Shop before it opened, but soon learned Boots had already been busy an hour, his waiting chairs filled with the asses of neighbors Elliot would rather not enjoin in conversation. Boots had been cutting Elliot's hair from the time he was a boy, when Uncle Buster realized he couldn't trim the child's wild miscegenated locks without messing it all up to hell. He knew Elliot well enough to see that he wasn't there to socialize, so Boots took him next. A few customers gave dirty looks, but no one spoke up. Elliot Caprice had enough of a reputation that no one wanted to test him, especially not fresh out the joint. A master raconteur, Boots did all the talking. He filled Elliot in on Southville current events as he gave him a classic taper, keeping it higher on the top so he could part it naturally. After a straight razor shave, Elliot felt, if not like a new man, at least a clean one. He tried to pay but Boots would have none of it.

"Welcome back, baby boy."

"Thanks, Boots."

"See you in two weeks?"

"Sure."

A neighborhood barber is a Negro's priest.

For one so frequently subjected to Izzy's brutal collection techniques, Spats Culpepper couldn't have been happier to see Elliot at the door of his tailor shop. Elliot wondered if he still had a thing for the ponies. When his wife Nanette—a slender older creole whose fast hands and keen eye made her a whiz at alterations—saw Elliot, he knew. She blurted out canned excuses why her husband didn't have Izzy's money. It took five minutes for Spats to get her to relax, which was good because she was liable to reach for the pistol she kept in the thread drawer. For years, Spats had been Izzy's go-to for suits. On a few occasions, Elliot managed to dissuade his boss from having something on Spats broken if, for no other reason, he still had tailoring to finish. Those favors Spats never forgot. He granted

Elliot easy credit terms out of gratitude. Elliot chose a two-piece, on the lighter side of charcoal gray, cut from open-weave wool to keep him cool. He chose a powder blue shirt and grey tie, a pair of Florsheim Imperials a half-size big, but good enough, and a straw Panama hat that perfectly matched. Nanette performed the alterations at record speed just to get Elliot out of their boutique. She loved ol' Spats to a fault but would have no parts of any of Izzy's crew, past or present, friends or not. Elliot didn't blame her for disliking him. When he thought back to those days, he didn't much like himself.

As Elliot walked to the Roseland Boys' auto lot, he saw himself reflected in the large shop windows along the main drag. He felt better now that he had cleaned up. He had a purpose again. One far closer to his heart. He almost felt relieved until he remembered how he spent the intervening years tending white folks' business while he allowed his own to wither on the vine. He had only himself—and perhaps a world that lavished upon colored men the means to destroy their own lives—to blame. His time in the war gave him such high hopes. The camaraderie of patriotism was infectious. Once he returned to racial segregation's tyranny of despair, it made him feel stupid for believing it could be any different. He wasn't the first colored man back from overseas to find himself locked out of post-war opportunity. He may have been the angriest. Now he was fresh out of jail after being on the skids. It was bad enough he was broke. Now he owed three people favors. He may have been clean, but it was no triumph.

Amos was hard at work chopping a Cadillac for parts when Elliot walked into the shop. Pity the poor bastard for which his '50 Coupe de Ville made good on his marker. He stood six feet tall, was broad-shouldered, had a thick neck, strong arms, and hands made for hurting men. Amos was well into his fifties, as indicated by a graying mustache underneath a receding hairline that fell back well past his temples. He almost looked fatherly until you ventured close enough to notice the scars.

"What's that'cha say there, Dangerous Doyle?" Elliot said. Amos dropped his wrench and wiped his hands on his smock. He approached Elliot dukes up.

"Na what'ya gawna do if I chrow da straight right?"

Amos threw a slow yet menacing fist. Elliot dipped at the knees. He rose on the other side and feigned a double right hook: one to the body, one to the temple. He kept his guard hand planted on his right cheek.

"Deahs da stahf, babe."

Everyone Amos liked was "babe."

"Gawt youah trailin' hand up."

"Fundamentals."

"Nobody minds deah fahkin fandamantas."

Elliot snickered when he realized he missed Amos' mush mouth.

When work was slow, Amos taught Elliot fighting techniques. Elliot learned the brutal art of incapacitation: eye gouging, temple smashing, fish-hooking, limb-breaking. Uncle Sam may have taught Elliot how to kill men, but Amos taught him how to save his own life, taking the next man's life in the process.

"Izzy let you know I was comin'?"

"Shah. I gawdah go bayhk ta dis chawp. You fin' a cah an' I'll get da keys."

Elliot walked the rows of parked collateral. The yard sat on an acre behind Sugartown wherein some of the finest automobiles stretched end to end. Elliot was interested only in those stored underneath tied-down tarpaulins. He knew those were Izzy's keepers. The rest may have looked nice, but they were certain to be missing a drivetrain here, a carburetor there. He came across an Oldsmobile. As he peeled off the tarpaulin, he beheld the power of a Rocket 88. It had a burgundy body accented in black. The interior was burgundy leather. It had a detachable fiberglass hard top, a little gift to private industry from the brainiacs at the War Department. It boasted a Hydro-

Matic transmission. It was beyond classy. It was a car from the future.

"Nice, huh?"

"Mighty nice," Elliot said. "Almost too nice."

"Some blues singer come up wit' two shit-kickers from da Chicago Outfit usin' dis one to cavah his nut. Tol' Izzy to take it or leave it."

"Izzy took it?"

"Just took it and said beat it. He ain't tha same, Elliot. This rat fuck callin' himse'f da Turk has him fak'd up in the head. It's good you're back, babe."

"I'm not back to work for Izzy, Amos."

"Don't matta. It's just good youah aroun'."

The scars on Amos' face twisted into a look of concern.

"You think he'd mind if I took this one?"

"Let's get some of dese boats oudadaway so we can get her in the garage. Turn up da idle, like da old days."

"Yeah," said Elliot. "The good ol' days."

After Amos worked his magic, Elliot started her up. The sound under the hood roared like a Midwestern thunderstorm. First, the loud clap. The rolling crackle. The consistent hum that sounded like a soft rain on pavement. Eight horses, all running in unison. Amos nodded in approval. Though he only tinkered for his own amusement, his handiwork was still the best around.

"Gah 'head."

Elliot barely touched the accelerator. She leapt forward like a hungry beast. Elliot hit the brake. He had to catch his breath.

"Too much?"

"Hell naw!"

He took her through a few donuts in the dirt before speeding off the lot and out onto the main drag. He could feel she wanted to go. He geared her into park, took a deep breath, counted to three, threw her in drive and floored the pedal. He drove fast cars before, yet this wasn't just speed, but power he felt so little of since 1945. He aced all the Army's tests. That earned him the right to choose his own field designation. His college experience may have even earned him an officer's path. Instead, he chose the tank corps—sweaty, stinky, stifling, dangerous. Elliot got to ride around in a death-dealing monster that was impervious to bullets. Easy peasy.

He returned to the shop. Amos grinned ear to ear. The man found joy working on cars, as opposed to working over people.

"Oh, mama," Elliot said, laughing wildly. "She's true blue!"

"I was worried for a secon', deah."

"Ah, I'm out of practice. They had us colored cops drivin' rusted boats. A fella tries makin' a run for it, you didn't chase 'em. You'd just shoot 'em."

"Whaddya say, fifteen?" Amos said, wrench in hand.

"Fifteen would keep me from killin' myself. Say, you got any touch-up paint?"

"Deah's a buncha cans o' enamel on da she'f."

Elliot chose taxicab yellow. He found a fine-tipped brush soaking in a can of thinner. When Amos was done, he walked over to watch Elliot scrawl the name "Lucille" on the wheel well.

"Who's that?"

"She kept a bunch of us safe in Europe," Elliot said, as he added three exclamation points.

"She pretty?"

"Big. And ugly. Once you needed her though, she was a real beauty."

"Was it bad, fightin' in da war?" Amos sounded almost tender.

"Not as bad as coming back," Elliot said. "Part of me wishes we were still fighting."

CHAPTER 7

He parked Lucille at the corner. He checked his reflection in the rearview—hair, teeth, tie, collar, all tip-top. He was showing up, hat in hand, to Mikey Rabinowitz up on his offer. His self-accusing spirit plagued him with guilt, but the thought of his uncle in bed in that flophouse made him the worst kind of desperate. His principles were long out the window. The best he could hope for is, whatever job he'd get, Mikey Rabinowitz would pay him enough to make the self-betrayal worthwhile. If he was lucky, maybe he'd get to keep the suit on.

Elliot opened the door to find Mike yelling into the phone. Elaine pleaded with an older white fella seated atop her desk, compress held to his bloody forehead.

"Smitty, now you're our only server."

"I'm sorry, Miss Elaine," Smitty said. "I like you plenty, but—"

"What if you had some backup?"

"Backup? I ain't a cop."

"How about next time—"

"Next time? Wouldja look at me?" Smitty removed the compress. Elaine pushed his hand back to his forehead.

"Just…keep it there," Elaine said. "Michael, hang up the phone."

"Maybe I'll come down there myself. I'll serve you. Right up your ass!" Mike slammed the phone down on the receiver. "I got a mind to call Amos. He'd bite his goddamn nose off."

"Hello?" Elliot said. Everyone finally noticed he was standing there.

"Elliot, right? Elaine Critchlow. I'm Attorney Robin's paralegal."

"And his old lady," Elliot said as he shook her hand. "I was outside your place yesterday."

"You were?"

"Got a haircut. Say, if it's a bad time, I could—"

"It's not a bad time. It's a great time." Mike paced the floor. "You got a gun on you?"

"Michael. Calm down."

"Uh...not at the moment. What's goin' on?"

"We have to serve a court order on the manager of an A&P by today," Elaine said.

"Said manager gave Smitty what-for." Mike snapped his fingers at the bloodied process server. "Smitty—"

"What?"

"You told him you were an officer of the court?"

"I told you I told him."

"You told him you were serving him?"

"Before or after the can of peas hit me in the goddamned head?"

Elliot tried not to snicker.

"You couldn't get it in his hand or shove it into his fucking apron?"

"Michael, stop berating him. He's been through enough," Elaine said. "I'll call you a doctor."

Elaine reached for the phone. Smitty laid on his back across the desk.

"I'd have liked to give you a better orientation," Mike said. "You up for starting work a little early?"

"I've never done this before," Elliot said.

"There's nothing to it."

"From the looks of Smitty here, seems like there's plenty to it."

"If we don't add him to our witness list by the end of the day, we won't have enough to push for trial," Elaine said.

"A&P won't settle without the threat of trial."

"We're not taking a settlement."

"We are most certainly taking a settlement. Unless the NAACP is finally paying us a retainer."

"We spoke about this." Elaine crossed her arms. Smitty groaned.

"It's Green Stamp redemption, Elaine. We're not taking the cause of free toasters for Negroes all the way to the Supreme Court."

Elliot raised his hands in surrender. Mike and Elaine looked at him as if he was calling them to order. That always happened—Elliot took control just by being present. He hated it.

"So what? I gotta get this fella to sign somethin'? I drag him back here?"

"Just hand him the court documents. Let him know he's been served before you record it in a ledger. If he doesn't come to court, they'll put a bench warrant on him."

"So why couldn't Smitty do that?"

"Asshole didn't let me get a word in," Smitty said. "He saw that I had papers in my hand, grabbed me and pushed me right out the back. Then the jagoff threw a frickin' can of peas at me."

"I take it you don't like peas."

Elaine frowned. Mike chuckled.

"How many other guys you have serving process?"

"Just Smitty," Mike said.

"Not anymore," Smitty said.

He walked out of the door. Mike didn't protest. Elaine audibly sighed.

"It's the race cases," Mike said. "Nobody wants to get involved."

Elliot wasn't sure if he himself should get involved. He could have told them he wasn't up for a hassle, but he needed money.

"You say there's nothing to it," Elliot said. "I can give it a go."

"First things first," Mike said, just before he opened the door to his office. Elliot followed him into the small, purposeful space. A worn desk. Old filing cabinets. Stacks of corrugated boxes all over the floor. On the wall hung his diplomas from the University of Illinois. The glass in the frame of his *juris doctorate* was cracked.

"Close the door, will you?"

Elliot did so. Mike stood behind his desk, took off his glasses, and rubbed his eyes. Elliot braced himself for either the big hello, or goodbye.

"Obviously, I'm in a bind."

"Yeah," Elliot said. "But that's not what we're talkin' about right now, is it?"

"Why aren't you a cop anymore?"

The way Mikey pursed his lips when stressed reminded Elliot of Izzy. He couldn't tell if he found it threatening or comforting.

"You said yourself I still am. For the time being, anyhow."

"C'mon, Elliot..."

"Truth is, I never really took to it."

"Were you—"

"Dirty?"

Mike shrugged. Somewhere inside his heart, Elliot found some truth to tell.

"May I sit?"

Mike gestured to a chair. The two of them in a squat office, both raised by the same man. Elliot as a soldier. Michael as a sire. Brothers, of a sort. The Jacob and Esau of Southville.

"Did you want to fight?"

"In the war?"

Elliot nodded.

"Not as Izzy Rabinowitz's son, I didn't. I was angry, same as every other Jew," Mike said. "But the armed forces were full of anti-Semites. The old man told me not to be fooled. That the goys weren't fighting for us."

"They didn't much like colored folk neither."

"So I'd imagine."

"Most of us figured things would be better when we got back. In Europe, I'm respected for my part in the fight. Go where I want. Do what I want. Walk arm in arm with a white woman in broad daylight, if I want."

Elliot clutched at his hat. His jaw tensed.

"I come back here, I have to take off my class A on the boat and stuff it in a sugar sack 'cuz peckerwoods are stringin' up colored men in uniform. Fellas survive the German front, just to wind up swingin' from a tree here at home."

He realized he was lost in his own thoughts.

"After that, I just couldn't go back to pickin' string beans."

"Or collecting vigorish for my father," Mike said. "I could see that making you angry enough to make a play for yourself."

"I did what most colored guys did, Mikey. I went to the big city and got a good government job. I got ahead because my skin is lighter than a paper bag."

"I imagine your time at Bradley didn't hurt you, either."

"You know what CPD calls a half-nigger who went to college?"

"What?"

"A half-nigger who went to college."

"The word is you were dirty."

"That's the word, huh?"

"I've also heard you were an informant on other cops."

"Well, you didn't ask me."

"I got the feeling you wouldn't come clean on your work history."

"I wasn't dirty."

"So you were a mole."

"Depends upon how you look at it."

"Look, Caprice. We got enough trouble around here because of —"

"The race cases. Yeah, yeah. We of the colored masses thank you for your sacrifice."

"I can't have anything from your past coming back on us."

"Mikey, you offered me a job, not the third degree." Elliot shifted in his seat as he fought through his obvious exasperation. "I wasn't a dirty cop. I haven't broken the law. Mostly."

Elliot stood.

"You don't want to take my word for it? I'll leave now. If you hurry up, maybe you can catch Smitty."

"Got me by the shorthairs, hmm?"

"Call it what you wanna."

"Just...be professional, please," Mike said.

"You're askin' a lot of a fella on the first day."

It was late afternoon. Most would-be shoppers were picking up their children from school or home making dinner. Elliot walked up to a checker sporting reddish hair. He was pock-marked with acne.

"Roger Cullen?"

"That's the manager. You here to serve him some court papers?"

Acne smirked. Elliot grabbed him by the collar.

"Call him."

The kid picked up the intercom.

"Manager to the counter." His pubescent voice cracked.

Roger emerged from the rear. He had a burly frame packed of the fat that comes when a man makes too much money for work that is beneath him.

"What the heck is it now, Chip?"

Elliot glanced at Chip. The kid nodded confirmation. Elliot made out the globe and anchor of the U.S. Marine Corps tattooed on Roger's left forearm.

"A devil dog, huh?"

"The first. Guadalcanal. What do you know about it?"

Elliot side-stepped the ex-marine. Roger reached for him, but only grabbed air. Elliot threw a chop to his throat, followed by a knee to the minerals. Roger doubled over onto the floor.

"I know you assholes thought you were fightin' a different war than the rest of us."

Elliot shoved the papers in his apron.

"You've been served, tough guy."

Roger lay writhing in pain. Elliot walked over to Chip, who ducked under the counter. He snatched a stack of S&H Green Stamps off the counter for good measure before he briskly walked out.

The next several weeks were like returning to college. Elliot spirited Lucille all through the rural counties of Illinois, the Quad Cities, and even Missouri. Everyone was properly served. Only a scant few avoided appearing in court, if only because the crazy mulatto would come back.

Elliot learned about the ins and outs of case law from Mike and Elaine. What made a person a good witness; why a respondent would want to avoid trial; how estates were challenged. He could see where laymen were at a disadvantage to attorneys, how they could be lost forever in court processes that would bankrupt them if the meter was left running. He thought of the mountain of debt he still had to climb. Perhaps there was a loophole he could exploit. He felt smart again. He started early and worked late, sometimes crashing the Castro couch in Mikey's apartment.

He loved their dynamic. Elaine ran hot. She was possessed of the primal anger that burned in the hearts of freedom fighters. Angry as a woman in a man's profession. Angry at her own people's refusal to take a colored legal professional seriously.

Mike, on the other hand, ran cold. His calculating demeanor made him appear indifferent. His mouth said he cared, but his eyes said he had a plan. He had as adept an understanding of the angles as Izzy, yet used those abilities to thwart the rich, not join them. Elliot wondered if Mike wanted to spite Izzy, or just become a more legitimate version of him.

At night, when work could be deferred, they loved as powerfully as they worked. It was dazzling how quickly Elaine shifted from earnest professional to woman in love. Mike Robin was cold-blooded in his profession, yet in the arms of his lady, he melted. In a world of hate, love made them vulnerable to each other. To witness it made Elliot feel lonely.

One afternoon, Elliot asked Mike about the unlikelihood of their union.

"Ever had a woman have your number, Elliot?"

"Maybe once, but that funny business back in Chicago made it all go to shit."

"Well, you got off easy. You can have it all figured out for yourself. Maybe you're not the same race or one of you is already married. You're poor. She's rich. You're a Jew. She's Catholic. None of that matters if she's got your number. There's nothing you can do about it but give in. If you're lucky, she won't eat you alive. I see it all the time."

"Yeah?"

"Take this bit of probate business."

Mike took a file from a stack.

"Here you have a maid working for some rich joe less than a year. Everyone loves her. The wife. The adult kids. His mother they keep locked up in the attic."

"Typical."

"Except the rich joe's wife dies in some stupid boating accident up in Waukegan. A few months later, he's calling me over to their estate to change his will because he's getting married. He's running around like he's in his twenties again."

"Not the maid."

"Of course the maid. Claims he hadn't had eyes on her until after she responded to his grief. I'm supposed to believe he wasn't giving it to this betty the entire time. Money bagged, blue-blood like that, tossing it all in on the maid? She had his number."

Mike pulled a bottle of bourbon from his drawer, plus two glasses.

"I'm tryin' to stay straight," Elliot said. "Let's hear the rest of the story. I'm intrigued."

"You know what happens next." Mike tipped up his pour.

"The old man dies?"

"The old man dies!"

Mike slapped the table. He had his father's laugh. It made him seem a bit sinister. "Drowns in the goddamn bathtub! The driver finds him after they were late heading out. You can't make this up!"

"Was the will changed?" Elliot's cop mind had taken over.

"About six months prior. They got married real fast the month after. He's dead five months after that. I met the gal. A Brit. Real polished. Gorgeous. Refined. If she was colored, I might have been tempted."

They howled in laughter. Elaine shouted for them to keep it down.

"Was she present on the boat during the accident that took the wife?"

"No," Mike said. "What are you getting at?"

"She wasn't around when the wife bought it. She wasn't around when the old man bought it. Now she gets everything. It's too pretty."

"Right now, she's getting nothing."

"What do you mean?"

"The estate is going into receivership at the end of the month. All parties named in the will aren't accounted for."

"Wouldn't their cuts just go to a trust?"

"When one plans their estate, they can make sure that everyone gets what's coming to them or the whole thing gets tied up in probate. Keeps relatives from killing each other."

"And the maid-wife isn't seeing her money fast enough."

"It's been a year."

"Damn."

"He named a multitude in the will. Friends, business associates, caddies at the country club. The help. Everyone got something. The old man felt guilty he was born into great wealth."

"Pity the rich."

"Even bequeathed money to the Urban League to help Negroes. I don't think he even knew any Negroes. Anyhow, everyone was good about responding when contacted. Except one."

Elliot's stare went blank as he calculated.

"The driver."

"Same one what found the coot dead in the bathtub."

Mike finished his bourbon.

"Christ on tha cross. How does someone take that?"

"You can ask her."

Elliot noticed that Mike handed out assignments in the same manner as Izzy: after providing some unsolicited tutelage in the ways of the world. It wasn't the first time he displayed a provincial attitude.

"Get up there when you're able. Have her sign the receivership documents. No sign, no allowance. The entire estate is going into trust. His obligations will get taken care of. She'll get a pension every month, get to stay in the house. Her lifestyle won't change at all. But until someone either finds that driver or confirms he's dead, the control over the estate lies within the power of a board comprised mainly of his adult children."

"I'm betting they don't like their new stepmother," Elliot said.

"Well, you think you can see right through her." Mike shrugged. "It's a shame. Now it's just more work for us for less money. We get a cut when the estate is satisfied. Now I'll be stuck recording meeting minutes and hearing complaints from the Duchess' every month when her check is late. Ah well, can't have everything."

"Apparently not! I'm going home," Elaine said.

"Coming," Mike said. He grabbed his jacket and hat.

"So take that file with you. Try to get up there before the week is out. You in tomorrow?"

"Gotta take care of Caprice business. Unk has an appointment with Doc. After, it's to the bank."

"Well, a sign painter is coming. Your name is going on the door."

"No kiddin'?"

"It was Elaine's idea."

"Oh."

"I told her you would rather be the invisible man, but she insisted."

"I don't know what to say."

"Say you won't find another job, so I don't have to change the fuckin' door again."

Mike laughed. After he walked out, Elliot sat alone in the office. He was utterly transfixed on the file. All those zeros. So much wealth handed down from generations prior. Were it not for the missing chauffeur, the bulk of it would have gone to a savvy broad that managed to run the right game, at the right time, on the right old fool. Her proposed monthly maintenance payment was nearly three times what Elliot needed to reclaim the farm. He wished he could blow off the meeting. He hated Margaret McAlpin's guts already.

In the hall, he touched the space where his name would go on the door. He didn't want it, partly because he didn't feel totally comfortable for carrying water for the son of his old boss. Mostly it was because he didn't want the responsibility, even if it was for show. Mike was funny actin', perhaps not on the same level as John Creamer, but Elliot wasn't quite sure if Mike didn't have that same white savior's mentality. He didn't need someone else in his life imbuing purpose. He already had one, and he didn't feel any closer to achieving it. Here he was again, serving. Helping others instead of helping himself. His uncle was right. Other people's business would one day be the death of him.

CHAPTER 8

Uncle Buster and Percy were in the lobby having a game of dominoes. A few other tenants were huddled around the television. There was no sign of Miss Betty so Elliot felt safe to watch the action. Percy was only a casual player, as he was mainly attracted to pastimes that involved losing modest amounts of his sister's money. Buster, however, never sat down to do anything where he was willing to watch it go wrong. He hated losing, a trait passed down to his nephew. Elliot remembered when Buster and Shapiro would enjoy a card game. Doc was calm and affable, yet he plotted. Buster was coarse and deliberate. It wasn't a real game without smack talk. Opposites attract.

Buster threw stitches and gleefully recorded his score. He was slaughtering Percy, no matter if the desk hound didn't give a shit.

"You ain't doin' nuthin'," Elliot said. "Lemme g'on whoop this old man for you." Uncle Buster cracked his aching knuckles. Percy retreated to the booth. Elliot turned over the dominoes. Buster scrubbed the pot. Elliot noticed his old uncle wince, but didn't say anything. As they pulled bones from the yard, their coded banter started.

"How's work goin'?"

"*Are you still employed?*"

"It's goin'. These race cases are really heating up."

"*Yes. It's stable.*"

"Cain't be good for bidness."

"*Are you getting involved in other folks' affairs?*"

71

"Mike and his ol' lady make it work alright."

"*No.*"

"Figure that's good work."

"*How are we faring on the debt for the farm?*"

"It's six in one hand, half-dozen in the other."

"*Not close.*"

This was their dance. It could take an hour of tenuous verbal maneuvering to produce consensus on something as basic as what to have for dinner.

"They put me on a thang up in Kenilworth. Got me takin' meetings now."

"Kenil-wha?" Buster put out a 5/5 as the center bone.

"North Shore, Lake Michigan. Where the snots live. Rich folks' squabbling over a dead fella's money." Elliot started a new line: 5/3.

"That's a little close to Chitown for you, ain't it?"

"Na. Up there is like a whole 'nother world. I'll be alright," Elliot said. Buster dropped a double-three for a score.

"That was quick."

"You want a lesson?"

"Play on," Elliot said. He played a 5/1 off the center tile 5/5.

"Some chippie that married well got a lot of money comin' to her, but the family don't wanna give it up. I gotta get her to sign off on some allowance agreement."

"Must be nice," Buster said, as he pondered what to play.

"I dunno. She wanna fight for all of it. Them fat cats ain't g'on give it up."

Elliot watched as Buster played a 5/4. Elliot quickly played a 4/4 as a branch. Buster was forced to draw another tile from the boneyard.

"Good play."

"How much is enough, ya know? What we owe the bank for the farm, it may as well be a million dollars. I might be able to find that in this woman's couch cushions. She's rich. I'm poor. But we're both needy."

"Everybody has a hole in 'em need fillin'," Buster said. He played an ace/deuce, leaving the ace dangling. Elliot dropped snake-eyes. Back to the boneyard Buster went.

"Want me to slow down on ya?"

"Sassin' ya elders. I raised a peach."

"Figured we'd go to the bank tomorrow. Try to set up some terms."

"Dem people want dey money, not no song and dance," Buster said.

"I want to keep my face in the place, so they remember you ain't by yourself. Folks like to do you wrong when they think you're by yourself."

Buster played a 4/6. Elliot had boxcars, the shutdown of all shutdowns. Just before he could play, the last voice he wanted to hear called out from behind his back.

"See here, Elliot Caprice."

"What thatcha say there, Miss Betty?" Elliot kept his face in his dominoes to avoid eye contact.

"I remember you tellin' me this was a temporary arrangement."

Betty Bridges herself, all five feet one inch of her, was dressed smartly. Her mannered green skirt set lent her the impression of a PTA president, rather than a reformed working girl turned hotelier. She used a straightening comb and enough Aqua Net to push her considerable mane back into a bouffant as wide as it was high. Elliot used to tease her that it looked like a skunk.

"Ain't nuthin' changed."

"Two months ain't temporary."

"You gettin' your rent on time?"

"That ain't the point!"

"What is the point, you old bat?! I'm sitting here playin' dominoes wit' my uncle, not grab-ass with you!"

Elliot and Betty were like bulldogs and hounds. That she was one of Buster's longer acquaintances made no difference to either of them.

"I finally got all the trouble out of this place. I plan on keepin' it that way. Your uncle is tops in my book, but you the devil's own."

"Stop talkin' at me as if you've seen the inside of a church this century."

Betty took a swipe at him. Elliot jumped out of his chair. Buster stood up.

"I'm sorry, Betty," he said. "He's been havin' it rough at work is all."

"Only reason he still here is we go back, Nathan." Betty pointed at Elliot. "I'm countin' the minutes 'til yo' red ass is outta my road house!"

She kicked the card table. The dominoes fell to the floor. Uncle Buster exhaled.

"How's about somethin' ta eat?"

"I'm starvin'."

In Sugartown, every day was Fat Tuesday. Each night was Mardi Gras. None of the buildings was more than three stories tall. There was Pitt's Place, a juke joint with a sawdust floor. On weekends, they the most popular blues artists. One day, the Chicago Outfit's coin-op man brought in a jukebox that played 45s of popular music. He was run out of town on a rail.

Games of pool could be found at Murray's, where you still had to check your weapons at the cashier's booth or you wouldn't get a table. Dice was played out in the open, but the bets on the ponies were taken in the back by Murray's son, Miles. Betty told Percy if she caught him there she'd kill him, so a runner retrieved his bets at the road house.

More than a couple pawn shops littered the landscape, but the best return always came from Majestic Loans. They even kept hours on Saturday and Sunday, which offended South-ville's Jews and Christians alike.

Mamie's Grub And Git offered the finest peasant food for

the best price. Her eight tables and counter seats were never empty. There was no chance getting in during the dinner rush, so the Caprices would have to take their chances at Duffy's Tavern, where they'd likely order the gigantic corned beef sandwiches and colcannon. They enjoyed the wild tales spun by raucous patrons at the top of their lungs, like an old Dublin pub. Or they could watch brawls. Sean Duffy only stepped in when real blood was spilled, otherwise, all he did was buy the winner a round. Generally, the sheriff wouldn't venture inside, but stood outside the vestibule, which was a good place to arrest whomever stumbled onto the pavement.

They parked Lucille at the top of the strip to walk the boulevard, partly to enjoy the cool night air, but mostly so Buster could get in Elliot's head.

"You lucky that hag broke our game up."

"You should show her some respect."

"I pay our rent on time every week."

"The woman been survivin' this world longer than you been in it," Buster said.

They walked a little farther until they had to stop for some drunks in the sidewalk.

"I think you visited upon ol' Betts at some point in your youthful meanderings," Elliot said.

"She wasn't always so bitter."

"Before or after the continents split?"

"You ain't the only one seen ugly, boy."

"That old battle-ax has never missed an opportunity to give me hell."

"To be fair, you wuz a bad kid."

"What's that say about you?" Elliot gave Buster the side-eye.

"Says I reached my natural limit."

Across the street, a ruckus spilled out of Le Chateau Du Paree, the burlesque house on the row. The name of the place meant nothing in French. Suddenly, a customer barreled out the front door. Another was thrown out by George. He slammed the perpetrator into the side of his cruiser's door. His buddy bolted down the street.

"You got nuthin' on me, spook! I was mindin' my business!"

Misty Munroe, a regular performer at Le Chateau, approached.

"Every night this week, this asshole comes in here gettin' all grabby!"

"Bullshit," the drunk said.

"Shut up!" George leaned his body weight on the drunk, whose foul breath left his lungs in a huff. A bouncer walked over expecting far more respect than his job afforded him.

"He's been warned twice tonight, Sheriff. You need to do something about these hillbillies from the next county."

George tried not to focus on the indignity of it all. The drunk got squirrelly.

"That's enough!"

"Get stuffed, nigger sheriff. Figures this piece of shit town would have a coon as the law."

He spat in George's face, which finally provoked his wrath. George pulled a blackjack and rapped the man on his left temple. Before the drunk could fall to the cobblestone, George took him by the lapels. He kneed him in the ribs. Even Misty was shocked. Elliot ventured over to help when he noticed the first man returning, this time with a double-barreled shotgun.

"Georgie! On your right!"

George looked up, threw his coat back and pulled his revolver. Before he could get a shot off, a blast rang out from the opposite end of the alleyway. The man holding the double-barrel went down like a sack of potatoes. Misty ran back into Le Chateau. George spun around to see Ned Reilly holding a twelve-gauge.

"I was around back."

George felt the heft of the pistol in his hand. His adrenaline slowly dissipated. Even in self-defense, the ease with which he drew his weapon on a bigoted white man frightened him. Ned walked over to the first man and kicked him.

"Not what you'd thought you'd be gettin' in Sugartown tonight, huh?" Ned held up the shotgun for George to see. "Rock salt."

Buster and Elliot walked over.

"Ned. Nick of time, huh?"

"Heard you were back," Ned said, without eye contact. For his elder, he smiled.

"Mr. Caprice."

"Youn' fella? How's ya mama?"

"Old."

"Ain't we all."

George was silent while he cuffed the drunk. The gunman was still moaning on the ground a few feet away.

"Christ, shaddup! You'd think I shot you with lead."

Uncle Buster observed Ned's handiwork as he cuffed the gunman. He lifted him off the pavement. Elliot helped George put the unconscious drunk in the back seat of the cruiser.

"How you doin' there, Preacher?"

"I hate this job."

"It ain't a job, Georgie. It's a calling."

"Third night this week," George said. "Hell, every week. I don't know how they expect only the two of us to get it all done."

"They expect you to go along to get along."

Ned dragged the first man over to the cruiser.

"This one is gonna need Doc Shapiro to come by," Ned said. "He ain't bleedin', but it's better to be sure."

"He drew on the law. He's going to Stateville."

Uncle Buster walked over brandishing his silver flask. He took a swig and handed it to George.

"We wuz just headed to Duffy's for a sangwich," Buster said.

"I'll get these bums to the jail. You gotta call the state boys," Ned said.

"I'll scoot by on the way home." George smiled as best he could.

Elliot patted George on the shoulder before they walked off.

"Ned Reilly don't like you," Buster said.

"Aw, he's sore at me over all the shit I gave him when we were kids."

"Why wuz you mean to that boy?"

"He was the onliest one of the gang whiter than me."

Elliot and Buster walked into Duffy's when it was in a mood. Somber murmurs of conversation revealed the passing of Johnny Calloway, an aged veteran of both world wars. Elliot took off his hat out of respect. He knew what it meant to be too faithful. To give too much.

They took their seats in the rear. Not that anyone discriminated in Duffy's. It was more due to how people care to socialize themselves. If you walked in looking for a colored fella, you'd most likely find him at the tables in the back. If you wanted to be alone, you took the end of the bar by the door. If you were a regular, you grouped around Sean. He was a happy drunk. If he imbibed enough, he was certain to buy rounds. Sean's daughter Molly worked in Duffy's at least a few times per week. She was shortish, with a long neck and smooth, pale skin. She had tiny freckles underneath her deep-set eyes. Whenever she received compliments on them, her standard reply was "Oh, what these Irish eyes have seen here in Southville." She'd put a slight lilt on the phrase for added affect. The only effect was that it made the men all swoon.

Elliot caught a crush on Molly the first time he saw her in Doc Shapiro's office. Sean's wife Molly, after whom his daughter was named, died of exposure shortly after she was born. When Little Molly's womanhood came calling, Sean immediately rushed her to St. Margaret's for counsel from the Sisters. Molly was so horrified at their edicts, she nearly belted one in self-defense. Once Doc entered the picture, he kindly filled in the gaps in Sean's understanding. From that day, Elliot and Molly were tight.

They were enjoying their sandwiches when Elliot decided to go to the bar for a Coca-Cola.

"My flask is empty," Buster said. "Brang me a whiskey."

Johnny's memorial had lightened considerably. Molly was up to her neck in pours. As he waited patiently for her attention, he heard a familiar voice behind him.

"Elliot Caprice. I'll be damned."

There are men in the world for whom a nemesis in the strictest sense exists. For Elliot, Chester Williams was that nemesis. As dark as Elliot was fair-skinned, Chester was the first taste of an enemy Elliot had in his life. The two had plans to kill each other going back to the schoolyard. Elliot managed to avoid any awkward homecomings his two months back. Now the conditions were right for one to happen, in spades.

"Never figured I'd run into you," Chester said. His grin revealed a gold tooth in the upper left of his mandible. He had a mustache that was trimmed so thin, it looked penciled. He was dressed in a black pea coat and matching derby. A large bear of a man in identical dress stepped behind him. He was equally dark complexioned. He wore the same dress. The uniformity reminded Elliot of the Nazis.

"This our man?" asked the big fella.

"Him? Naw. This here is Elliot Caprice, one o' Soufvil's finest. We go waaaaay back. Elliot, this here is Gimp."

"Gimp, huh? Ya mama give you that name?"

"High yella here is a joker," Gimp said.

Fightin' words. Elliot took off his hat and laid it atop the bar. Molly motioned to Sean. Elliot noticed her tremble. He added that to his long list of reasons to kill Chester.

"Some folk named for what they do. Farmer this. Skipper that. You wanna guess why they call him Gimp?" Chester said, smiling. Baiting. Gimp looked Elliot up and down.

"This the Jew's nigga?"

"Oh, not no mo'. This one here come home from the war, go on the straight and narrow. Ain't that right, Elliot Caprice?"

Elliot took a step toward Chester.

"Collectin' for The Turk, huh?"

"You of all people know how good the work pays."

"That's rather civic-minded of him. Hirin' straight out the penitentiary."

Elliot grinned. Chester didn't. Everyone knew he always had been inside more than out. It was a sore spot.

"I figure after all your trouble in Chicago, you'd learn a thing or two about puttin' ya mouth on the next man's bidness."

Elliot balled up his fists.

"It's out on the wire, is it?"

"If'n you know who to ask."

"You wanna see what else I learned in Chicago?"

"Shol' do."

Elliot lunged forward at the same point George Stingley stepped between them. He was still wearing his badge. Elliot remembered the blackjack.

"Chester. Not your usual place to have a drink, is it?"

Chester smiled wider, feeling validated by the show of authority.

"Naw, Reverend Sheriff. I'm here on other bidness."

"Perhaps you want to get to it," George said. He looked over to Gimp. "Unless you and your big friend want to continue your conversation down at the jail?"

"Alright, Georgie. Alright."

Sean motioned over to Chester. Chester walked to the bar. Sean handed Chester an envelope. Molly watched, sadness written all over her face. Elliot and George watched Molly. Chester returned, still grinning with that one gold tooth.

"If you were anglin' to go back to collectin' fo' the Jews,

you're too late. Hear he's gettin' out of money lendin'. Take care of yourself, light-skin."

Chester and Gimp disappeared as Elliot and George watched.

"Sorry about the wait, boys," Molly said. She eased her nerves by wiping the bar. "What can I getcha?"

"Bourbon," Elliot said, holding up three fingers, sideways. It would be the first of far too many that night.

The next morning, Elliot vomited once in the shower before he walked to where he had left Lucille parked in Sugartown, where he vomited again. He cursed himself for allowing Chester to push old buttons. Such is the hazard of leaving small towns, for when a man returns, it is usually to the old self he tried to leave behind.

He stopped at Mamie's for coffee to go, but she took pity on him. She gave him a bicarbonate. Once she saw he could keep it down, she served him a light breakfast of eggs, a biscuit, and tea. Elliot grabbed an old newspaper, put it over his face and napped for at least thirty minutes, right there in his booth.

He ached so bad, he hated everything. He put on a pair of mirrored sunglasses he kept in the glovebox to prevent the daylight from harming him further. His drive wasn't to the bank, but Kenilworth.

She had no way of knowing, but Mrs. Margaret McAlpin was in for one hell of a meeting.

CHAPTER 9

To avoid Chicago, Elliot headed north to Rockford. From there, east through unincorporated townships until he was safely fifteen miles away from the city. It was worth the extra hour on his commute to ameliorate the risk of being spotted. He had wondered if anyone cared anymore what happened. Folks die all the time in Chicago, even policemen. Perhaps, in all this time, he could be the only one still keeping score. How much distance would one need to put murdered cops behind him? Better to take Sheridan Road down to the McAlpin Place and enjoy the Lake Michigan shoreline. The drive was pretty enough.

Before the turn of the century, a household oil man named Sears visited the English countryside and fell enchanted by its beauty. And snobbery. When he returned to Chicago, he acquired two hundred thirty acres of undeveloped wetlands, woods, and pastures on which his beloved Kenilworth would be established. Even the town's moniker was appropriated from the title of a historical novel written by an English baronet. None of the residents seemed to care that the book was replete with inaccuracies. Elliot could understand how folks in this town would be taken in by a proper-acting limey broad. It fit their illusion of themselves. Cobblestone streets. Gilded gas lamps. Quaint cottage shops. Restrictive covenants.

Along roads lined with oak, hickory, and butternut trees, Elliot passed multi-building estates, trussed up in pedimented-stone window heads. There must have been a run on marble columns. Coach houses and seven-car garages took up more land than the domestic help could ever afford to live on outright.

Indian summer lent everything an idyllic tint as if it were filmed in Technicolor. Wild blackberry bushes were a staple in every yard. The top down, Elliot could smell their fall ripeness as he cruised down streets named Abbotsford and Warwick. He finally reached Essex Road, hung a left, and coasted up the main drive that was nearly as long as the farm where he was raised. The joint was so big, to get anywhere on time, one would have to leave ten minutes early just to allow what it took to get off the property. He stopped Lucille at the end of the private cul-de-sac next to a large fountain at its center. This was once the home of the late Jonathan McAlpin, one of the Midwest's wealthiest swells. Now it belonged to the luckiest frail that ever lifted the family silverware. The one time Elliot had seen wealth like this up close, he was on a police guard detail at a ball at John Creamer's Prairie Avenue family mansion. He wondered if they were friends with the McAlpins. His stomach sank at the thought.

The first thing he noticed was the two-story domed rotunda. It had windows so large they seemed to reflect every ray of the late morning sun. The grounds were so large, the lawn had a lawn. Sculpted hedges lined the perimeter at each arched window like sentries on guard.

Elliot rang the front doorbell but soon realized he forgot the leather document envelope underneath the passenger's seat. As he walked back to Lucille, he noticed he was being watched by someone peering out from the far end of the grounds. He couldn't make out a face. His vision was still blurry. His hangover had him off his square.

When he arrived at the door, he was greeted by the current maid of the McAlpin household, a youngish colored woman named Sally, which was embroidered into the lapel of her uniform.

"Hey there, darlin'. Margaret McAlpin home?"

She was dressed not as if she was a trusted member of the household staff but on duty cleaning rooms at a hotel. It was little details such as those that Elliot took as tells. The new boss woman couldn't be bothered to remember the name of the gal she hired to do her old job. She welcomed him inside. Sally was just his type: big-legged, deep brown skin, a bright smile that just had to be straightened by an orthodontist. She had kind eyes. Her thick coarse hair was dressed in a smart bun. He wondered what she looked like when she let it down.

"You need to use the service entrance," said a similarly complexioned fella, medium build, in a dark blue maintenance uniform. He walked in from a side door. Elliot noticed his name was not sewn on the front. He was dressed for harder work but wasn't dirty, except for grease on his shirt. He was clean shaven. He wore his hair high and tight, like a military man. Or someone used to harsher institutions.

"Do I seem like a servant?"

"Chauncey. This man is here for Missus McAlpin."

"*Chauncey*, is it?" Elliot smirked in a manner the handyman didn't appreciate. Chauncey's disdain for waiting on another colored man was apparent.

"What's your business?"

"Look here, Sally'," Elliot said. "What's say you let Mrs. McAlpin know that Elliot Caprice is callin' on behalf of Attorney Michael Robin. See if that gets her down to the foyer, hmm?"

"May I take your hat? Perhaps something to drink?"

At least Sally was all manners.

"I'll hang on to it, thank you. And no thanks. Had more than enough last night."

Elliot winked. Sally gushed ever so slightly, which further agitated Chauncey. She sashayed off to her task. Once she was out of sight, Chauncey shut the rolling doors that separated the foyer from the receiving area.

"As Master McAlpin has passed on, we've seen our fair

share of callers. A young woman comes into a huge inheritance; she's bound to encounter con-artists."

Whether it was the use of the term *master* or the references to *we* and *our*—as if the house boy somehow had a personal stake in things—Elliot immediately detested Chauncey.

"Glad you're on the case, Cap'n. What else do you do around here when you're not the guard dog?"

"I throw out assholes."

Chauncey was angling for a toe-down. Elliot was surly enough to oblige.

"How long did it take you to learn that Mid-Atlantic accent, Chauncey?"

"Come again?"

"Did you recite it from a book or follow along with one of those records you send away for? Ya know, they keep stuff like that in prison libraries. For the personal betterment of inmates."

"Nigger, watch your mouth."

"Nigger, huh?" Elliot snickered. "What, they let you live in the coach house? You get to eat in the kitchen once the main course is served."

"You wear a suit to work, yet you smell of cheap liquor."

"That would be good liquor, poured by a white woman."

Sally opened the sliding doors. Chauncey stepped back.

"Chauncey, would you please show Mr. Caprice to the recreation room?"

The handyman was silent as he led Elliot through the silent labyrinth of wealth. Portraits of McAlpin family members lined the walls. Even pets were rendered for posterity, yet nothing of the newest Mrs. McAlpin.

They arrived at the recreation room. Chauncey opened the large double doors. The first thing Elliot noticed was the rich wood paneling. A picture window draped in red velvet was background for two large red leather chairs arranged around an antique pedestal table. A matching large sofa sat along the far wall in front of a long sofa table. Handmade Turkish area rugs covered the hardwood floors. A stuffed head of an eighteen-point buck was mounted over the fireplace. Elliot would bet his balls *the master* didn't have the stones to kill it himself. Maybe Chauncey did that for him too. A billiards table and a snooker table stood at opposite ends. Elliot wondered what the hell was the difference. Trophies for various accomplishments in rich people's frivolity stood on Italian trestle tables. Elliot was discomfited in that setting—why show off the trappings of the rich to Mike Robin's messenger? What was her gambit?

"Wait here. Don't steal anything."

"Please don't mind Chauncey, Mr. Caprice. He's not used to receiving guests."

When she appeared out of nowhere, all the air rushed from the room. Margaret Thorne McAlpin stood around five-foot-eight. Her strawberry blonde hair didn't come from a bottle. Her tits stood at attention, like soldiers guarding that lean athletic frame. She had alabaster skin, deep green eyes and lips that took up no more room on her face than necessary. At the center was her slight aquiline nose that bore a barely noticeable scar on its bridge. Either she wore glasses or once took a shot to the face. It was fall, yet she wore a summer dress that looked as if she poured it on herself like a fine lotion upon stepping from the bath.

"I've had to furlough some of the staff while this estate business is sorted. That will be all, Chauncey."

"Are you sure, ma'am?" Chauncey glanced at Elliot.

"Yes. Off you go."

Margaret's manner made her rebuff sound like high praise. No wonder Chauncey forgot he was the help. This dame knew how to handle men. As Elliot watched Chauncey shuffle off, he reflected on how difficult it is for a man to be so far inside a world to which he could never belong.

"I expected you tomorrow."

"I set my own schedule."

"You're certainly not dressed like a messenger," she said. Damn her syrupy condescension. "An assistant of some sort?"

She itched him to see just how he'd scratch. It was little ol' her against that big bad board. She was intent upon holding her own, even against the attorney's man.

"I perform various services for Attorney Robin."

"Such as?"

"Today I'm delivering sensitive documents for execution."

Elliot held up the leather envelope. Margaret directed him to the sofa. She still moved like someone afraid of agitating her betters. Once she sat, she made certain to fix the hem of her dress. Perhaps she didn't want to send any negative impressions back to Mike that could get back to the trust board. He unwrapped the binding string, pulled out the contents and laid them in front of her.

"Need a pen?"

Margaret slowly reached for an elegant cigarette box on the sofa table. She offered Elliot a smoke, but he refused. She pulled a Gitanes Brunes out of the box. Using a nearby crystal lighter, it took a few flicks to yield a flame before Margaret could light her smoke.

"I have no idea why I keep that girl on."

"Well, if you want a job done right…" Elliot said.

Margaret took a drag. She gave him a cold stare. Elliot immediately regretted the quip. If she didn't sign for being pissed off, Mikey would pitch a fit. He tried small talk.

"Didn't know one could find blue gypsies here in the states?"

"One can't," Margaret said. "Your bon mot lends the impression you are privy to the"—she interrupted herself to produce a plume of exhaust— "complexities of my legal situation."

She took another drag. Margaret examined Elliot's face as if it was the cover of a worn book. She pointed her cigarette at him. Her hair cradled her face. Elliot tried very hard not to find her beautiful.

"You're rather cheeky." She exhaled again, blowing smoke in his direction.

"I apologize. I've been nursing a headache."

"Under the weather?"

"Under a bottle. Ran into an old acquaintance last night. Things got out of hand."

Elliot's admittance of his hangover was deliberate, intended to put Margaret at ease. She rose from the sofa, walked over to a marble bar, and pushed a recess etched in the wall. A panel opened to reveal an extensive collection of spirits.

"Pick your poison, Mr. Caprice."

"Not while I'm on duty." He wondered why he felt like a policeman.

"Everyone knows the best thing for a hangover is a stiff drink. Chop chop."

Oh, that syrupy voice. Elliot examined the selection. Seems as if he judged the late Master McAlpin a bit prematurely. The man hoarded a bevy of rare spirits. He either had a drinking problem, or problems that required a lot of drinking.

"I'll have a single-malt."

"Top ball. Speyside, Islay or Skye?"

She was taking him out of his depth, on purpose.

"I'll trust your tastes." Elliot smiled. He told himself to stop flirting.

She scanned the bottles for Talisker thirty-five-year, produced two crystal rock glasses.

"Two of your fingers, or two of mine?"

"One of yours and one of mine."

She winked at him as she poured both their drinks. It was her subtle invitation to let his guard down.

"Bottoms up, then."

Do dheagh shlàinte," Elliot said, almost at a whisper. He breathed in the aromas. After a small sip to savor its details, his hangover started to dissipate. Over the top of his glass, he watched Margaret gulp half her drink. She used the back of her hand to wipe her mouth.

"Used to drinking amongst the Irish, are we?"

"I heard my mother was Irish."

"My mother was from Surrey. My father from Cornwall."

"*Sowena dhys.*" Elliot smiled.

"I'm impressed."

"A few Brits joined our company during the war. They liked their liquor." Elliot took another sip. Margaret knocked the rest of hers back. "There's a lot of idle time in-country. Holding positions. Waiting out the enemy. Fellas make conversation about anything just to take their mind off what's comin'."

The scotch loosened Elliot's tongue, but he wasn't embarrassed about opening up. Something in the way she couldn't take her eyes off him seemed to pull his true self forward. Margaret offered to pour him another, but he put his hand atop the glass and shook his head no. She refreshed her own glass and capped the bottle.

"Yeah, the limeys weren't a bad bunch of joes. Didn't mind we were colored one bit."

Margaret's eyes went up.

"Couldn't tell, huh?"

"Can't say I could, Mr. Caprice."

"Oh, I'm no mister."

"Elliot." Margaret smiled. Elliot noticed her subtle cheek freckles. They were the size of Molly's.

"I've been called swarthy, olive-skinned, red, mestizo." He chuckled. "Confused for everything from Moroccan to Sicilian to Cuban. Not by Negroes, tho'. Colored folk obligate me to be colored."

"It must be maddening to be taken for the lesser," said Margaret.

"Yeah," Elliot said. "I hate when folks think I'm white."

Margaret laughed. She replaced the bottle in the cubby.

"Wealthy men devise such clever ways of hiding things." The secret panel went click.

Of Kenilworth's two hundred fifty-two acres, the McAlpin Estate must have stood on most of them. Elliot and Margaret walked the grounds until they reached a secluded rear garden. Shrubbery as tall as a man was arranged in long rows. Along the shale pathways stood beautifully sculpted marble benches, each bookended with magnificent topiaries.

"What else do you do, Mr. Caprice?"

"Nothin', if I can help it."

"I didn't expect to be meeting someone possessed of such—" She pondered the right word. "Gravitas. It means—"

"One of the original Roman virtues. Pietus, dignitas, virtus, gravitas. Density of character or personality, though you may have that part wrong."

Margaret looked impressed but embarrassed.

"Bradley forensics team. Go Braves."

"I didn't mean to suggest—"

"I'm used to it," Elliot said. "I noticed you speak received English."

"My, you are full of surprises." Margaret caressed his shoulder.

"Boarding or finishing school?"

"Boarding, for a while. My father was something of a diplomat back in Britain until Ferdinand was assassinated. Daddy fell from grace when he expressed he saw no point in honoring the Treaty of London. Thought it antiquated. That didn't help the war profiteers, you know. To prove his loyalty to the aristocracy, he joined the front, as an officer. He was dead within a week."

"That's war."

"He was no warrior, I assure you. Apparently, neither was my mother. She fell off the deep end. Men were in and out of our lives, taking advantage of us. By the time I was twelve, I was cleaning houses so we could survive. By the second war, I was here in the States. Still cleaning houses."

Margaret stopped walking. She gestured to a bench. They sat and, for a moment, did not speak. A light lake breeze wafted through the maze of hedges.

"Did you love him?" asked Elliot, wondering where that came from.

"I beg your pardon."

"Your husband. Did you love him? Or was it about all of this?" Elliot gestured to the expanse of wealth around them. Margaret sighed.

"I loved the idea of him loving me. I resisted at first. The age difference. The circumstances. Eventually, I fell for him. It wasn't about his money. Or maybe it was."

She turned away from Elliot. He didn't know if she was sincere or if he was being played.

"You must think of me as they all do. That I'm some gold digger."

"I doubt you had that much control."

She turned back around and looked Elliot in the eye. The fine scotch was already wearing off.

"What did you do before?"

"I'd rather not say."

"You'd rather just air out my dirty linen. Pity. We were getting on so well. Back to the house then." Margaret stormed off. "I won't be signing any papers. Chauncey will show you out."

Elliot abruptly stood. "I was a cop."

She turned around. They met at the center. He didn't know what was happening inside of himself, but he knew he didn't like it.

"In the city?"

"Chicago, yes."

"But it went bad." Margaret's concerned gaze made Elliot

91

want to vomit, but the lump in his throat wouldn't let him.

"Tragically bad." His voice trailed off. "A friend lured me into things that were questionable. When it was over, I wouldn't let it go."

"You're still paying for it, aren't you?"

She reached out to touch his face, but that's where Elliot drew the line. He took a full step back. A stronger breeze blew. Margaret wrapped her arms around herself. The rustling foliage delivered an unheeded warning. Elliot took off his jacket and placed it around her shoulders. He may as well have sealed a covenant.

"Do you think you could find him?" Margaret asked.

"The driver?"

"His name is Alistair Williams. He's from Brixton. It's an area—"

"I know where it is," Elliot said. "What is it with this town and limeys?"

"We were once an item. He's was so smart. Driven. When I first met him, he was studying nights and weekends to become an accountant. Some mornings, I would find him asleep in the garage, books open, papers strewn about." Her voice trailed off again. "You see, Jonathan and Esme were good people."

"Esme was his first wife."

"Second. They didn't regard the help as automatons. They had Alistair take me places, help me meet people, become part of the community. We fell in love. It was harmless, really."

"Until the wife died. That when McAlpin took a shine to you?"

"I never felt that way about him in all the time he was my employer, but once tragedy struck, he didn't seem so powerful. He was helpless without her. He refused guests. He didn't attend to his business affairs. Oft times I would find him sobbing alone in her closet. One day I knelt down to help him off the floor. He just seemed so lost. So sweet."

"It's gotta burn a guy up to put his time in on a gal, just to lose her to the boss man."

"I wanted to be discreet. Wait until a good time to tell Alistair, but Jonathan was insistent he would have it sorted. At first, it seemed to be fine. Chauncey took over the duty of driving me so Alistair wouldn't have to be burdened. This place is so vast, it was easy to avoid each other. Shortly thereafter, Jonathan dies."

"And your Alistair makes a run for it."

"No, no, no. He stayed. He stood by me, even though I broke his heart."

"Oh, I bet he did. His girlfriend just came into half the money in the Midwest."

Margaret stared off into the clearing, her memories transporting her back in time. Tears streamed down her face.

"A few months passed. I failed to resist his overtures. We spent time together in secret. Chauncey suspected us once Alistair began driving me again. He won't admit it, but I knew when Jonathan's children came around, he told them what he saw. That was the start of the trust board's hostility."

"Can you blame 'em? You've gotta know how that looks."

"I've never cared about the money. I just wanted to honor Jonathan's wishes."

"Bet it was killin' ol' Alistair."

"He couldn't understand. He knew nothing of money or status. He was naive to think we could just be openly involved."

"Spoken like a diplomat's daughter."

Margaret yanked off Elliot's jacket. It fell to the ground.

"I'll pay you five thousand dollars." Margaret's back straightened. Her tone, terse.

"To do what?"

"To help me fix this probate mess."

"You think dragging him back here is going to fix your problems? This is old money."

"I know full well of old money. Once Alistair is accounted

for, I'll take what Jonathan meant for me to have. The wolves can have the rest."

"What about Alistair?"

"I haven't thought that far ahead, I'm afraid."

"I figured you hadn't."

Again, she was near tears. Elliot's mind raced. Five large would be more than enough to reclaim the farm. He could start restoring it. Except this broad was playing at his convictions. That made him nervous, which meant he already decided somewhere inside himself to do it.

"I'm gonna need you to sign off on these papers I brought over."

"Why would I do that?"

"I read through 'em a few times. There's no risk to your claim on the estate, as long as you can produce Alistair. Matter of fact, if you don't sign 'em, they'll likely get one of their judge buddies to yank everything into probate. They'll starve you out. Get you desperate enough to give up. Take whatever they slide you to go away."

"And you wouldn't want to see that happen, would you?"

"I work for Mike Robin. He'd like to see this matter closed. That means I'd like to see it closed."

"I see."

"You sign the papers, I'll take a third up front. I get another third when I have news to report. Pay me the rest once I've brought him back to you."

"There will be a good bonus in it for you once you do."

"Bonuses are nice. Sign the documents."

They stared each other down. Another stiff lakefront wind blew. Even the gods would have their say.

"Very well."

She signed each in his presence. When Elliot replaced the documents in the leather envelope, she asked him to show himself out. There was no trace of the help. The house felt like a mausoleum. When he closed the door to the McAlpin estate behind him, he could feel the harsh chill of a Chicago fall. As he opened Lucille's driver's side door, he pretended he didn't notice Chauncey watching him from a window atop the rotunda.

CHAPTER 10

Willow Ellison of 4802 N. Broadway Avenue in Chicago was a mutual acquaintance of Margaret and Alistair. She was of the social set. On nights off, they occasionally attended her Bohemian get-togethers. He knew the address off the top, as it was the same as the Green Mill Cocktail Lounge, a place he twice met disgraced police Lieutenant Bill Drury. At their second meet, Elliot exhorted him to keep a lower profile. Stop pushing it, if not for his own sake, for Elliot's, yet Drury wanted the life. He wanted the notoriety. He remained active, even after he was tossed off the force. He was determined in his bitterness to wreak the most havoc. And he did. He just hadn't foreseen his murder. Elliot hadn't foreseen the death of his entire world.

Most likely this Willow gal lived in one of the apartments above the Green Mill, or she may have even been a prostitute. Maybe the lounge was where she received her calls. Either way, it was the only lead Margaret could provide. She didn't even have a photograph of Alistair, which wasn't particularly odd to Elliot, as he himself had no use for picture taking. What stood out was, Margaret's only angle was a woman. Why did Alistair's play involve another frail?

Elliot couldn't trust Margaret. She wasn't naive. If anything, she tholed the stigma of the suspicious widow for far too long. Her resentment was palpable. No way she'd allow the entire ordeal to be a trip for biscuits. This Alistair seemed like a dandy. She wouldn't likely abide one in her bed. Not without an agenda of her own.

Something else stunk. How was it the family allowed one of the help to be the linchpin? They didn't care about the money. Power and influence were their aims. As long as no one found ol' Alistair, the board remained in control, so if his pieces weren't feeding Chinook out in Lake Michigan, why was he still alive? Did he have something on the McAlpins? Were they hiding him to bring down their father's wife? The whole affair was a tangle.

Elliot returned to the office. The sign painter's work had been completed. Strips of vellum, taped to the glass, protected where Elliot's name was set. He walked in to the sound of soft snoring coming from behind Mike's office door. He looked inside to find Elaine seated in the large leather chair, leaned backward, her feet on the desk. She was fast asleep after another all-nighter. Elliot closed the front door quietly. He turned his attention to the stacks of file boxes along the walls. Careful not to wake Elaine, he found the McAlpin file. He quietly closed Mike's door and got to work.

Jonathan McAlpin's life read as a schizophrenic mess of reneged decisions. Almost every child in the family had been written out of his wills at least once, just to be written back in on several conditions. Amendments were filed in response to simple marital discord. At the slightest disagreement, it was *call the lawyer. Make certain she doesn't get anything.* Protect the family. His wives' wills, however, weren't present in the files. Either they had their own preparers or, more likely, they didn't have wills at all. Why would they? Their world was on loan from the McAlpins. Elliot remembered Uncle Buster's warning: "Folk what change they mind all the time will white on ya, sho' as the day is long."

Jonathan McAlpin was certainly a creature of his family's intentions. On paper, he seemed soulless. Change orders involving women and children. Amendment after amendment about personal affairs. He went through the front of the file to find the earliest document. Esme Ross McAlpin was not his first wife—that was Diana Kostopolous, a foreign national of Greek extraction. The first will on record detailed how Diana and their son, Jonathan II, would only receive McAlpin's personal holdings. The bulk of the estate would remain in the hands of the McAlpin family. There were additional orders to allow one Stavros Kostopolous to repurchase Jonathan's interest in a company called Costas Cartage, Limited. It was an arranged marriage to be sure. Elliot dug deeper. Jonathan II was written out of the will after the divorce from Diana. That decision was consistent, until his marriage to Esme. Jonathan II was written back in, though without stipulation. Elliot scanned the trust board roster for names. Jon McAlpin was listed as Chair, Endowments. Obviously the new wife loved the guy enough for her husband to welcome him back to the fold.

Then the switch of all switches. Esme McAlpin dies in a freak boating accident. Her personal holdings are distributed amongst her five children, stepson included. Six months later, just as Mike Robin called it, McAlpin orders a new will that gave Margaret the whole schmear, including his stake in the family estate. Mike communicated his vehement disagreement in writing. Jonathan McAlpin heeded nothing. He found the love of his life. Everyone was going to accept her, or else. Good thing for Margaret the bastard died in his own bathtub before he could change his mind again.

Elliot combed through the laundry list of ancillary beneficiaries: the children of his estranged siblings, a few old friends, a singer he admired, outside endowments for the arts, a few pennies for colored folks' charities—which made Elliot wretch. Finally the help were named. No household employee, past or present, was omitted. It went back to nannies, butlers, maids, bookkeepers, family physicians, bodyguards and, of course, Alistair Williams. He would receive a job for life, should he choose. Plus funds for the completion of his education. Rather generous. Of Margaret.

Theories ran through Elliot's mind like mustangs. He

scribbled notes. So many angles had come to him that he had to sound them out to himself.

"Studying hard?"

Elliot looked up to see Elaine standing in the doorway of Mike's office, still looking exhausted.

"Didn't mean to wake you."

"You didn't," she said. "I had been working all night helping with a brief. Mike's assisting the Ruby McCullum case."

"The colored side-piece in Florida what killed her beau?"

"The same one. I put him on the train a couple hours ago. Hope he makes it there in time."

"I gotta tell you, Elaine, she sounds guilty as they come."

"Of course she is. That's not the point. By limiting the charges to a money dispute, they're restricting her right to a fair defense, only to protect the reputation of the deceased."

"She killed the fella who kept her on the side."

"A dead white man's honor doesn't outweigh a Negro woman's right to a fair trial," Elaine said. She pointed in the air as if she was trying the case herself. Elliot felt guilty at how attracted to her he was at that moment.

"I got the McAlpin documents signed. They're ready to be recorded."

"Really? I figured she'd hold out."

"Yeah?"

"I couldn't imagine being married to a man for any length of time, just to be cast aside by the family once he died. I'd sleep in a cardboard box underneath a viaduct before I'd give in to that bullshit. What's in the file?"

"McAlpin's estate. Considering the motivations of folks named in the will."

"Mike have you doing that?"

"No. It's more of an elective."

"An elective. Sure."

Elaine turned around to give Elliot his space.

"Elaine, wait. I got Margaret McAlpin to sign off on the

condition that I'd do what I could to find Alistair Williams."

"The driver."

"Yeah. She gave me a lead. I plan to follow up on it. I figure it'll be a dead end, but I accepted her offer to find him."

Elliot stood up, reached into his jacket pocket for an envelope and handed it to Elaine.

"It's eight hundred."

"Whoa."

"That's half of my advance. If I find the guy, or prove he's no more, it's twenty-five hundred in it for the office."

Elliot sighed.

"One minute, I'm a hard ass, shoving some papers in front of her to sign. The next, we're drinking. By the time we're walking through the garden, I'm accepting an offer for more money than I need to find some fella who, if'n he ain't dead, ain't tryin' to be found."

"That's what you want?"

"I just want my uncle to be back at home where he can be happy. I won't allow it to get in the way of work."

"I know you won't."

"I do need a favor."

"Okay."

"This Williams fella is taking me back to Chicago. If I uncover a solid trail, I'll get the next third of my fee. Added to the money I have saved, I can settle up on the farm."

"What's changed about Chicago?"

"Nothin'. I'm gonna make out very lucky or very dead. If it's the latter, please protect my uncle from the bank."

"Mike's looked into stopping the easement. He thinks he can challenge the veracity of the loan. Perhaps claim coercion due to your uncle's age and circumstances."

"It has to be you, Elaine. Mike is a good man, but my uncle is old Mississippi."

"Colored to colored."

"Besides, you're good lookin'. He'll listen to you. Allow you to help him."

Elaine looked deep into Elliot's eyes. She handed the envelope back to him.

"We won't let Mike know about this just yet."

"I don't mean for you to be keeping secrets from him."

"You think our life together runs as smooth as it does because I tell Mike Robin everything?" She touched Elliot's shoulder. "So, is this what you're doing now? Investigations?"

"I'm just in it for the dough."

"You're lying."

Elaine had a way of cutting through Elliot's bullshit. He could go for a girl like her, if it wouldn't drive him nuts.

"Why do you delight in disarming me?"

"Is that why I make you uncomfortable?"

"What makes me uncomfortable is you're fine as May wine."

"I'm flattered. Why do you pretend that what you want isn't important?"

Elliot sighed.

"I'm afraid if I show how much I want a thing, the world will take it away."

"That doesn't have to happen."

"When doesn't it?" Elliot policed up the contents of the McAlpin file.

"I'll put that away. I don't need you screwing up my filing system any worse."

Elliot put the folder on the desk and silently walked toward the door.

"Elliot?"

"Yeah?"

"Friends?"

"Obviously." Elliot closed the door behind himself. Elaine stared at the space where Elliot had just stood. She searched for some remainder of him, yet found only emptiness. Elliot was naked, right down to his spirit. That spirit was screaming, yet could make no sound. A lost spirit, marooned on a hostile world.

Tired of back roads, Elliot burned up 66 back to Southville. There was still time to get to the bank to make a deposit. Perhaps negotiate terms. He had more than half of what he needed to satisfy the loan. That had to count for something. He was so determined to make it there on time, he tried not paying attention to the tail he picked up outside Springfield. It looked like a late-model Chevy sedan, black hardtop, driven by a man in a black hat. He varied his speed until he was certain he was being legitimately shadowed. Elliot dropped Lucille's hammer and tore ass. The tail gave chase, but Elliot left his pursuer in the dust. He watched him in the rearview, laughing, until he noticed a granary trailer that stopped abruptly, bisecting the stretch of highway up ahead. He hit the brakes, but at over one hundred miles per hour, he needed a quarter-mile to come to a complete stop. He hoped there was a ranch road opposite the granary where he could bank a stiff turn. No such luck. He snatched up on the emergency brake, gave Lucille enough gas to change course, and yanked the wheel hard to the right. He hit an adverse camber at the shoulder and caught air, landing in the stalks. Lucille careened into a ditch. Elliot caught a face full of steering wheel. He saw stars before everything blurred. The familiar taste and smell of his own blood greeted him. Before he could reach the sun visor to use the mirror, his eyes rolled back. Everything went black.

Without booze, sleep robbed Elliot of peace. Uncon-sciousness lowered the drawbridge that held back the onslaught of unresolved memory. Years prior, Elliot held post outside the back door that led into the kitchen of the Creamer Family's

Prairie Avenue mansion. It was the cushier part of the assignment, which embarrassed him, as his college buddy John used his influence to score him the gig. He tried to get out of it, but his precinct captain explained how it worked among the politically well-heeled in Chicago. The inclusion of a half-colored officer in the protection detail for a gala held in Senator Estes Kefauver's honor fit the evening's agenda. Kefauver's speech included a special message about the evils of organized crime as it related to colored communities. How egalitarian of him. What the captain didn't understand is the other cops put Elliot on the spot for it. He also didn't want to be around members of Chicago's Negro intelligentsia, all dressed up to pay lip service to the powerful white folks. They had stayed after Elliot for his mixed-race features, brief education, and intelligence. All too often he had to rebuff their overtures to fall in with them. He was from Southville. That made him no Talented Tenth. The common disparagement was, while he may have looked somewhat white, Elliot Caprice was all nigger. He took it as a compliment.

Later in the evening, after everyone's highhandedness was finished, he was rolled off by the captain and directed to a winder staircase that led to the third floor. He arrived upstairs to find his old college buddy smiling. Creamer embraced him. Elliot felt he was being measured up. They walked down a long hall to an atrium. Creamer shared that he had been following Elliot's detective career from his former job as assistant Illinois State's Attorney. He had a new mission, one which he tapped Elliot to join. It'd prove far more beneficial than slaving as a beat cop in Negro settlements.

In a small wireframe gazebo, Senator Estes Kefauver and Ted Wiggins, his aide-de-camp, sat at a small table. Elliot was offered no seat, or any nicety for that matter. Kefauver rushed through a well-rehearsed version of his speech on the dangers of organized crime. Elliot wanted to say he heard it all while holding post outside the dining room. Wiggins interrupted

Kefauver when he produced a file marked *Caprice, E. Southville, IL. Roseland Boys Outfit.*

From their earliest time together, John Creamer kept a record of Elliot's past. Their late-night story-swapping in the dorms was all fair game. Now, on top of the overwhelming guilt he felt for collecting vigorish from his neighbors, Elliot had to suffer the indignity joining Kefauver's salvo against the mob.

"So, it's snitch on other cops or you ruin my career."

"Career," Wiggins said, snidely. "You have no business wearing a badge, Caprice."

"You ever wore a badge, Wiggins?"

Wiggins snickered. "I went to Yale."

"It's really simple," Creamer said. "You pass to me all the evidence you can get. You don't have to testify."

"It doesn't need to be hard evidence," Wiggins said. "Just anything to help validate suspicions. The more sensational, the better. Stuff for the cameras."

"How is that legal?"

"These are congressional hearings, Caprice," Kefauver said. "The law isn't important. Only the headlines."

Creamer motioned for Elliot to join him off to the side.

"Listen, I was assigned to this by the State's Attorney," Creamer said, in a whisper. "I tried to keep you out of it."

"I bet you did."

"They're looking at Rabinowitz. Hard. They think he's a way into Lansky."

"John, running errands for him when I was a teenager doesn't put me in Murder, Incorporated?"

"Characterize it however you like, Caprice," Wiggins said. "You either help us or we tell everyone you helped us anyway. Consider it penance."

Elliot wasn't sure what hurt worse; the end of the delusion he could ever be on the straight and narrow or the betrayal of the only white boy he ever allowed himself to trust.

"Thanks for having my back," Elliot said. John's eyes turned cold.

"This isn't a hoe-down after a speech competition. You broke the law. People in high places know about it. I'm giving you a chance to make it right."

They rejoined Kefauver and Wiggins.

"Guess I'm your man."

"John Creamer will be your contact," Wiggins said.

"We'll correspond weekly, on your day off." John couldn't look at Elliot. Elliot wouldn't look at him.

"We have a budget," Kefauver said.

"You'll receive some pay," Wiggins said.

"A couple of coins to cover my eyes once I wind up dead."

"No one can know," Creamer said. "No matter what happens to your reputation, on or off the job, you have to keep this operation a secret."

"Or we will lock you away for life," Wiggins said. "And have that piece of shit small town razed."

Elliot was so angry he could feel his eyes throbbing, but no way would these bastards see him sweat.

"Anything else while you have me by the balls?"

"One more thing," Kefauver said. "Neither make nor accept any contact from former police Lieutenant William Drury."

"The writer in the crime rags?"

"He is not a friend to this operation," Kefauver said.

"Imagine that."

"Hey, boss! You alive in there?!"

Elliot's pained remembrances were pierced by the harsh rays of the western sunset. He couldn't see but the voice sounded familiar.

"I said, you okay?"

Enough of Elliot's vision returned for him to be able to look out the window. He couldn't believe his eyes.

"Frank Fuquay?"

"Yeah, boss."

Elliot blinked to focus.

"You a little far from Yazoo County, ain'cha?"

"Lucky fo' you, yeah."

CHAPTER 11

Elliot opened the passenger's side door and tumbled out onto the dusty track of soft soil churned up by a grain harvester. Frank helped him to his feet. Lucille sat atop a mound of loose dirt plowed forward by her front end. The driver's side was stuck in the ditch. The right front wheel was free-rolling. Without a winch, she wasn't going anywhere.

"Steady, boss. Make sure you got ya wits 'bout cha," Frank said.

"Weird meetin' like this, huh?"

"I picked up some day work over at the granary yonder. Was at it a week, befo' I git laid off. I was just walkin' ta the train station when I seent a car hit the ditch. Surprised it wuz you."

"Likewise."

Elliot dusted himself off, mumbling curses to himself. Frank didn't find him as quietly cool as he did when they were both stuck in the Meat Locker back in St. Louis. He looked Elliot up and down, surveying the blood stains on his dress shirt, the wild look on his face, his left eye bloodshot more than the right. He pulled the blue paisley bandana from around his neck and handed it to him.

"I ain't got scabies or nuthin'. G'on head 'n clean up."

Frank thumbed the straps of his blue overalls as he watched Elliot wipe the blood from his face. His dirty T-shirt suggested a man hard at work. That he wasn't in stripes suggested he too got out of the clutches of St. Louis County.

"You wuzn't runnin' from no trouble, wuz ya?"

"Not the kind you're thinkin'."

"'Cuz I don't want to see no parts of a cell ever again."

"Don't worry, Big Black. It's all work related. Look here."

"Yeah?"

"What's the chance you noticed another car behind mine?"

"Black sedan?" Frank asked.

"That's 'bout right."

"Slowed down, saw me hollerin' fo' ya and kept goin'."

"You see what he look like?"

"White."

"Mmm hmm," Elliot said. "See here, Big Black. What's say you help me get ol' Lucille out the ditch. I'll get you to where you're goin'."

Elliot handed Frank back his bandana but thought better of it on account of the blood stains.

"I'ont thing you wanna ride me that far, White. I'm on my way to Gary, Indiana, but I'll he'p you. You get in. Hit the gas when I say."

Elliot didn't have a clue what the man mountain thought he could do on his own, but he climbed back in through the passenger's side anyway. He started her up. Frank pushed down in the front end, hoping to give her some traction, but she couldn't dig in from the loose composition of the soil.

"Hol' up a sec! Lemme try sum'n."

Big Black scooted underneath Lucille's undercarriage.

"Listen, Frank, that's alright. It ain't worth it. We'll just call a tow."

Frank didn't listen. He was determined to clear away enough dirt to get both of the back wheels on the ground. Lucille slammed down with a slow, angry, creaking sound.

"Frank!"

Big Black's head popped up over the front hood, smiling playfully, as if he enjoyed not only being useful but scaring Elliot out of his wits. Elliot noticed for the first time that Frank had good teeth.

"Don't go takin' any more chances, unless you got another bandana."

Frank laughed gleefully and ran to Lucille's trunk.

"Okay. Give 'er sum gas."

Lucille rocked back and forth as Frank Fuquay tried pushing her forward. Elliot met him in kind by pushing gradually down on Lucille's accelerator.

"Gotta give her more than that, White. Floor it!"

Frank dug in. The soft soil was up to his knees. He put that entire bear's body of his into it.

"Go."

Elliot put her all the way down. Lucille began to creep forward.

"That's it. Keep at it!"

Frank loved the challenge. Elliot took Lucille nearly to her limit. Finally, she pulled forward, guided by Frank's effort, until she jumped out in the dirt ahead on her own power. Frank fell face first in the soft soil. He hopped to his feet, screaming victory, fists raised. Elliot turned Lucille around on a flatter patch of earth and hit the brakes. Frank ran over to the passenger's side, hopped in, and off they went back on the highway.

"Sorry 'bout tha dirt, White."

"No harm there, Big Black. And it isn't White. It's Caprice. Elliot Caprice."

Elliot held out his hand. Frank took it in his. Damn, it was big.

"So White is your—what they call it?"

"Alias."

"Yeah, alias. Like in the crime stories in the papers."

"Well, I'm no robber but that's about right."

"Pleased to meet you, Elliot Caprice. Has a ring to it. That other name o' yourn was kinda plain."

"Not as hip as Big Black, huh?"

"That was that fool Tony's nonsense, man. Ain't nobody eva called me that befo' he did. It's just Frank. My mama called me

Big Frank, but that was just 'cuz o' my daddy. I wound up big as him pretty early so she didn't wanna call me Lil' Frank. She just started callin' him Bigger Frank."

Elliot laughed aloud.

"What happened to your tiny buddy, anyhow?"

"He ain't no buddy o' mines. As soon as we got in front of the judge, he starts cryin' and carryin' on, tellin' him how it was all my idea, and he did what I tol' him to do. They musta figured he wuz lyin', 'cuz once we pleaded guilty, they gave me ninety days hard labor 'n they sent him to tha big house for a year."

"That's gonna be some hard time for a little big mouth."

"Turns out them people whose house we robbed wuz Adventists. They came down and saw me in the lock-up 'n asked me if I was sorry. I said yeah, on account I wuz. Am. Woun' up only doin' a couple months, tho' it felt good to work instead doin' bad stuff. Even if it was on a chain gang."

Frank looked down at his hands out of shame. Elliot could relate.

"You hungry?"

"I wuz only able to make enuf money fo' half a train ticket. I'm scared to spend from it."

"It's on me. Let's find a bite."

Normally Elliot could slide into most places without issues over his race. Hat pulled down, he could find a seat in the back and eat without trouble. Frank would have no such opportunity, so Elliot popped the glove box and took out his copy of *The Negro Travelers' Green Book*.

"You up for barbecue, big man?"

"Am I colored?"

They opted for a roadside barbecue pit off a bypass near Lincoln that sold sandwiches out of a stand. Frank tried being polite, but Elliot insisted he order his fill. He asked for two large pulled pork sandwiches. He also ordered collards as his mama told him to always eat some roughage. He took only water for his drink. Elliot got a brisket sandwich on a Kaiser roll and joined Frank in a helping of greens. Elliot had a long night ahead of him, so he picked black coffee to wash it all down.

They walked back to Lucille and laid their wax paper wrapped goods on the hood. Frank made the sign of the cross, said grace softly, and looked over at Elliot.

"Eat up," Elliot said, taking note of the young fella's deference. Frank tore into his meal as if it were his last. Elliot tuned the radio until he stumbled upon a number from Big Joe Turner: "Cherry Red."

Together they dined and swapped anecdotes, enjoying each other's company like old buddies. It was common for colored men to forge their allegiances through fisticuffs. The means to overcome one's own self-loathing long enough to see the actual person on the other side was the occasional a punch in the mouth. Rarely did you find a Negro whose ace boon coon wasn't first a challenger. You'd get up, dust yourself off, and before one could offer the other a drink, you'd have forgotten what you fought about in the first place.

Elliot thought Frank was young, but in the dark of the jail, he hadn't noticed just how much of a kid he was. He had a baby face. Underneath his strong brow sat very kind eyes. Once his hunger was sated, he slowed down opened up.

"If I had my way, I'd be back in Yazoo with my mama and sistuh but wuzn't no work fo' me. My daddy—he died some years back—got people in Gary. My Aunt Ruby 'n her husband. They say there's good work in steel up there, 'n 'cuz I'm so big, I might be good at it."

"So much good work up north, a colored fella can find his own way in life. My father and uncle came up from your mama's parts together. My uncle stayed in Southville, but my pap went on to Chicago. From what I hear, he worked in slaughterhouses."

"You didn't know yo' daddy?"

111

"Afraid not. Died before I was born. Big riot in Chicago. He was a fighter."

"That's where you get it from."

Elliot was a bit embarrassed. Frank grinned.

"About that, Frank. I'm sorry. Jail can be a rotten place. It's hard not to be rotten along with it."

"I had it comin'. You roughed me up real good. Figured I could fight befo' that."

"Aw, you can fight. I just know a different type of fightin' is all, Frank. The sort folks don't get to walk away from."

"You wuz in the war?"

"Yeah. Before that, I was a young criminal up in Southville. After, I became a cop in Chicago."

"That's good work, huh?"

Elliot didn't immediately answer. He just stared into his coffee, swishing it around in the paper cup, as if it were a vision pool.

"I thought it was as first. I learned otherwise."

"What happen'?"

Again, Elliot remained silent.

"I'm sorry, Caprice. Should mind my own bidness."

As reward for Frank's boundless politeness, Elliot eased the grip on his secrets.

"You know how ya buddy Tony gassed you up, got you goin' all about yourself?"

"Yeah. Let him tell it, I was gonna be sumthin'. Maybe a fighter. Some kind of tough guy."

"Yeah, well I had a friend like that, too. Liked to go on about how colored folk could have better lives. How I was in a good position to help that happen."

"I can see that. Just the way you talked to me in the jail after you put that whoopin' on me. Like you wanted to make sho' I learned my lesson. That was real kind, Caprice."

"What I'm talkin' about wasn't kind. He talked me into doin' bad, in order to do good. After it went all kinds of wrong, he left me twistin'. I wound up havin' to dangle out of Chicago. By the time we met in St. Louis, I was on the run almost a year. Couldn't get home to my uncle. Lost the family farm. I was already in prison, if that makes sense?"

"At least you and him wuz gonna help people. That's sum'n, right?"

"That's the thing. It wasn't my choice. It wasn't the choice of the people we were supposed to be helping. It was his choice. The choice of powerful people. Politicians 'n such. Take that meal I bought you."

"Fine meal, too. I really 'preciate it."

"I know you do," Elliot said. "Point is, I asked you to help me, you did everything you could, it worked out. I offered a meal. You accepted. That puts us on the same level, know what I mean?"

"You weren't payin' me back wit' a meal. You were offerin' me a meal."

"Right. You could've said no. I'd be eatin' alone."

"I could've kept on walkin', but you made me an offer, to he'p, and you give me a ride."

"Exactly," Elliot said. "We set terms. Now, sometimes folks catch you when you have no choice but to accept their help. Maybe you're sick. Or broke. Maybe you're in trouble with the law. You ain't gonna turn that help away, but if it ain't your choice, and you owe them after…"

"That's a setup."

Elliot nodded.

"The only way to truly help someone is to give them a choice and let them make it. Everything else is a hustle."

"You wuz hustled?"

Elliot considered the question as he stared down at the last of his coffee.

"I let myself get hustled."

Elliot began cleaning up the mess. Frank watched but didn't help—not out of rudeness, but wonderment. Elliot seemed odd to him. Buys a fella a meal, teaches him a lesson, plus cleans up after him? He remembered his mother telling him the story of how Jesus anointed the feet of his friends.

"Don't really matter nun how thangs turn out. You got caught up doin' bad thangs for the right reasons. Beats my trouble. I did bad fo' no reason a'tall."

Frank looked down at his feet.

"My mama raised me up right. My people are good folk. I just didn't know what to do wit' myself, is all."

Elliot went silent at how simple Frank made everything seem. He punched him on the arm. Frank looked up.

"Those who know better do better, Big Man."

Frank nodded. Elliot slapped him on the shoulder. They got in Lucille and took off.

They pulled up outside the train station in Lincoln. The colorful prairie sunset—and their full bellies—left them both quieted.

"Thanks again for helping me back there," Elliot said.

"Well, thanks for dinner, and not knockin' my block off. Wouldn't have figured you're so tough."

"That's the idea." Elliot winked. "How're you fixed, Frank?"

"Well, I'm half-way to buyin' a one-way to Gary. I was gonna panhandle for the rest. Maybe sumbody be nice. That, or I'll hop on a boxcar, try to get most of the way."

"Hoppin' boxcars will get you arrested by the railroad cops, Frank. Or worse."

"It's wurf it," Frank said. "I gotta do sum'n wit' myself, Caprice. I'm afraid I'll get myself in trouble again."

Realizing Frank was too earnest for his own good, Elliot reached into his jacket pocket and pulled out the envelope of cash. He snatched out two sawbucks—more money than Frank Fuquay had seen in his life—and pressed it into Frank's hand.

Frank couldn't believe it, but then thought better of it.

"Ain't this like what you said about helpin'?"

"Not if it's a loan. There are terms."

"Terms like what?"

"You only spend it on gettin' ahead. No drinkin' or gamblin' or anything like that. You check in and let me know how you're livin'. At some point, I'm sure you'll be doing well enough to pay me back. Deal?"

"That's all?"

"Ain't as easy as it sounds. I'm at Evergreen seven, two-three, two-four, in Springfield. Easy to remember, yeah?"

"Evergreen seven, two-three, two-four. Gotcha, boss."

"Good people there will answer the phone. You tell 'em you want to speak to me. They'll find me."

Frank smiled. Tears welled in his eyes. Elliot reached over, opened his door, and gently pushed him out. Frank shut the door and put his head in the window.

"You ever get up my way in Gary, come find my auntie. She's on Baker Street at Fifteenth. Right on the corner. I got sum cute cousins, man. They can cook, too."

"Take care, Frank."

Frank ran off to the station house. Elliot watched until he was out of sight before he headed back to Southville.

He avoided the farm because he just couldn't bear the sight of it. Every route was planned to keep it from view, to avoid all thought of the property, like a drunk on the wagon, steering clear of his old haunts. Now he stood on the access road, the gate shackled by the bank, in chains forged from his naivety. A link for each of his poor decisions once leaving Southville. "WARNING—KEEP OUT, UNDER PENALTY OF LAW" read the admonishment from the bastards from the bank. The sign was for everyone in general, but spoke to Elliot in particular. It told him don't go in. Don't go any further. He climbed over the fence. Another sign ignored.

The crunch of the gravel underneath his shoes mimicked the sound of his crumbling heart. He could see it in the distance, the small white farmhouse with an oak tree that was twice as high. When he got older, he could reach its branches from the extra half floor. It was his preferred means of escape when he was confined to quarters. As he stepped closer, he noticed the gutters were overgrown. The downspout had broken off. Tending them was his job per Uncle Buster, "You like climbin' out ya window and runnin' across the roof so much."

Some very harsh winters had passed after he left. The house lay there like a sad relative. The roof needed fixing. The house frame hadn't been primed or painted. Cracked panes of glass in his bedroom window through which he would stare out as he dreamed of freedom. In Southville, his father was a ghost. His mother didn't want him. In Southville, he was born no good. Probably would stay that way. In Southville, he traded on his lighter skin to find favor with the Jews over in Roseland. And on and on and on.

He made his way to the barn to find it relatively intact. The burnt orange of rust outlined the Dutch door, most likely from corrosion of the joists that supported the gothic roof. Elliot automatically considered the time and materials for their repair before the knot in his stomach reminded him it was all on the line. Used to be, Elliot was dragged off to the barn for beatings. Now he was finding a way in so he could stop beating himself.

There hadn't been an animal inside for years. The mule was replaced by a Farmall C series that looked relatively new. It made Elliot proud that the old man was thinking ahead, though he liked that old mule. He just didn't like his strap. He walked through the drive bay until he reached the tack room. Once there, he kicked aside old hay until he cleared away a cross ring tie. Elliot pulled it hard until the trap door released, casting a cloud of dust. He had dug it out himself, as a hiding place for the contraband he accumulated over the course of his duties to

Izzy. It was a compromise, a place to keep the items in his charge secure while conforming to his uncle's expectations. He laid down on his stomach to reach the handles of the trench safe he kept underneath. He was alone yet, out of habit, checked his surroundings before turning the single dial to his father's date of death. The tumblers gave. He opened the lid. The one photo of his parents together back in Chicago seemed to stare at him, he flipped it over. He sorted through his commendations, just to remind himself he could be brave when need be. He opened his honorable discharge letter from the War Department to check that no one else's name was on it. Finally, he came to a bindle made of his old point blanket. He unfurled it on the barn floor and took in its components: Army issue M1911A .45, three full magazines. John Moses Browning's finest design.

This particular model was manufactured by the Singer Corporation. His company commander Hap Hinshaw joked that after the war, they'd all become seamstresses. He loaded a clip, took aim and hit a galvanized pail on the opposite end of the drive bay. He fired three times. The first hit dead center. The pail leaped for its life, tumbling in the air. The last two shots hit before it fell to the ground. Skills confirmed he reached down once again into his hiding place for his duffel which held his HBTs. He put on his greens and his leather shoulder holster that still fit without adjustment. The two-buckle boots hadn't been dabbed. He himself always picked up on tells like that, but it was the best he could do under the circumstances. He had a great deal more hair than he was used to squeezing into his HBT cap. It didn't come down over his eyes enough to conceal his entire face. Best not to take any chances. No direct eye contact. No conversation if engaged. Tonight, he would play the part of the GI, just looking for a good time until his redeployment. His weapon was very useful for killing Germs in George S.'s bastard outfit of colored soldiers. It was at least good for a few more bodies should some poor unfortunates come between him and Willow Ellison.

CHAPTER 12

Lake effect fog provided needed cover. It was hard for him not to ascribe the weather to providence. Not that he felt at all worthy of God's protection. More as if the Great Absentee Landlord finally turned on the radiator.

He hung a right at Foster, walked a manageable distance and found a stretch of elevated tracks near Clark Street under which he could tuck Lucille away. That put his getaway less than a klick from Willow's location. He was still fit enough to make a run for it full speed back to the car if need be. He covered her with alley debris, patted the .45 underneath his jacket and started on his way. At the corner of Clark and Foster, he realized he was practically kitty-corner to Bill Drury's neighborhood. The thought made his palms sweat. He quick timed it to Lawrence Avenue and eased his pace leading up to the Green Mill, passing St. Boniface's cemetery on his left. It was all too ominous, even for a man comfortable risking death. The headstones in the mist. The voices in the distance. Even in the fog, he could see the neighborhood was fading. More vagrants hung about, many in old military wear. Broken men. The broken women they chased. The Aragon Ballroom up the way must've had an event. The crowd had begun to spill out onto the sidewalk toward the famed cocktail lounge in a steady stream. The marquee read "Coleman Hawkins feat. Howard McGhee." Elliot noticed beat cops across the street, so he hunched his shoulders, dropped his chin and blended in, sliding between the Good Time Charlies and Bettys that dominated the sidewalks on both sides of the street. Murmuring patrons whined over the early end to the show due to McGhee's inability to play the entire set. Something about aitch. Jazz was still in favor, but Jazz brought heroin. In Chicago, Uptown caught it worse than any other neighborhood.

He made his way to the door leading to the apartments above. When he entered the skinny lobby, he stood over a junky couple begging for change while he read the mailboxes. He scanned the names until he found "Ellison, W." handwritten above box 207. He knocked on the door. When no one answered, he put his ear near the keyhole. No movement inside. There were stairs at the far end of the hall, likely to another door out to the street, so Elliot first made certain the coast was clear. He checked the door frame molding for a key, got lucky, and opened the door.

When he walked in, the first thing he noticed was the decor. It was a hodgepodge of cultural influences: long strings of beads hung from the archways dividing the rooms, woven mats on the floor, an acoustic guitar, some bongos, poetry books. It was cluttered, but vibrant. A stained sectional couch dominated the living area. A coffee table scarred by cigarette burns held the center. A primo hi-fi system stood along the opposite wall next to four huge stacks of vinyl LPs. Dizzy Gillespie. Miles Davis. Dave Brubeck. More obscure, avant-garde artists.

He walked to the small eat-in kitchenette and opened the tiny icebox. No food inside, but she did have bottles of Pabst. Dirty dishes and crawling things populated the sink. On a small table lay playing cards, an ashtray, a scrapbook. The ashtray had reefer roaches inside. He flipped through the pages of the scrapbook. Seemed as if Willow's kink was following musicians around. She saved all her autographed show bills. She took plenty of snapshots. A few photos included a dark-haired girl with very large eyes. She liked patterned headscarves. Her nose could have made her Jewish or at least some flavor of Mediterranean. She seemed pretty, but the slight drooping of her lower eyelids suggested pain. Or narcotics. In each photo, she was pressed against one of the Negro musicians. Her smile was confident. She was one bold snowflake.

A handbill for tonight's performance at the Aragon was inside, yet to be archived. A blocky Polaroid camera was hung by its strap around one of the kitchen chairs. He went into the bathroom. Chemical bottles from Eastman sat on a credenza: developer, stop bath, fixer. A large timer that glowed in the dark sat on the sink. In the tub were trays, likely corresponding to each. A red light bulb in its fixture. A group of towels. An artist? A journalist? Likely a wastrel. Parents pay the rent. Photography covers her habits.

He took great care to leave everything as he found it. He closed the door behind him before he returned the key to its hiding place. His next move was to seek her out at the Green Mill.

The glittering marquee illuminated the tide fog. Waves upon waves of people crashed upon the concrete shore. He had no use for politeness, so he played the belligerent veteran, pushing his way through the crowd of young adults on holiday from their own cultural constraints. He entered to looks and a few sneers for his mode of dress, yet no one stopped him from entering. This was Uptown in its decline. Folks knew how to mind their own business. He stood by the bar in a pretty good spot to watch as Coleman Hawkins, likely out of consolation for the debacle at the Aragon, belted out an impromptu jazz set for a worshipful crowd of white folks. Willow had to be here, he told himself. When the first bars of "If I Could Be With You Tonight" flowed from Hawkins' tenor saxophone, the crowd leaned forward on the edge of their seats. Elliot wormed his way near Al Capone's booth, chosen for its view of both exits. He perched himself on the wall, hands in pockets. The band segued into "Soul Blues." Hawkins was now speaking Elliot's language. He nodded his head along to the standard twelve-bar rhythm. Coleman helped make it easy for him to fit in. The lights were low. The joint was packed. No one paid him any attention. He scanned the crowd to no avail, checked the clock over the marble bar and realized he had been there over twenty minutes. Sooner or later, someone was going to ask him to buy a drink or leave. He figured he could make it back to Lucille. Maybe nap until morning. Or just stand outside Willow's door until she returned. If she returned.

Those notions ended when a ruckus at a table in front of the stage gave away Willow's position. There she was, in typical dress, camera in hand, intent upon getting her shots, but she was being oppressed by a stranger kneeling down next to her. The oily haired goon was dressed in coat and tie. He had an annoying goatee that only made him appear petulant, like a beatnik crossed with a Chicago Outfit dago. Maybe he purchased her a drink or two. Maybe it was time to reciprocate. Words were exchanged as he grabbed her by the soft underside of her right arm. She snatched back in a huff. Before he could grab her again, she threw her drink in his face. The oily prick retaliated by belting her. She fell out of her chair. The crowd didn't appreciate the commotion. There was shushing and calls for the management. If Coleman noticed, he didn't let on. Elliot resisted the urge to jump in so soon.

The bouncer pushed his way through the crowd, but before he could reach them, Willow stood up, grabbed her camera from the table and gave the asshole an uppercut full of lens. It kicked off a full-blown brawl. When the oily suitor stood up, Elliot could see he was a big bastard. The band stopped playing. Hawkins called for calm. When the bouncer arrived, he was blocked by several patrons fighting to get clear. Before Willow could regroup or get away, the jerk grabbed her by her hair. He produced a blade to use on her in the worst way. He almost got her across the face, until he lost four fingers on his knife hand. Elliot watched them fly off in a spray of blood after he fired a single shot. It wasn't panic or reflex that guided his hand, but prescience. The same sense that told him the moment he took the gun from the barn it was certain he'd use it to kill someone.

He just didn't expect it would be now, here, in full view of the jazz-loving public.

Coleman broke camp with the band, leaving their instruments. The booths reserved for discerning clientele were emptied. Willow's abuser was on his knees, screaming. He scanned the floor for his missing digits. Willow looked around in a panic. The poor girl was abandoned by the musicians she worshiped.

"Willow! Willow Ellison!"

Willow looked up to see Elliot motioning for her to run to him, but she instead reached for her jacket from off her chair. Elliot ran to her and grabbed her arm, but she reared back to belt him.

"Christ, lady. I'm trying to help you!"

"I need my jacket," Willow said.

"Leave it."

Elliot yanked her up into his arms. He leapt into Capone's booth. He kicked the table over. They crouched down behind it. Willow tried to get away. Elliot grabbed her arm again.

"Enough grabbing, alright?"

"Relax. I'm a friend of Margaret."

"Who?"

"Alistair. I'm a friend of Alistair."

"Well, friend of Alistair, what do we do now?"

It was pandemonium. Screaming bodies built up at the doors. Everyone was shoving each other. The two beat cops Elliot saw earlier were outside the window looking in, nightsticks drawn. His only play involved flimsy legend. He grabbed Willow's arm, pushed the table out of the way, ran toward the bar, and flattened the bartender standing in front of it holding a shotgun. He tossed her over the art deco masterpiece of marble and soapstone, leaped over, and pulled up the spill mats.

"Please let it be here."

He finally found an old trap door, pulled it open and pushed Willow inside. She fell. Elliot then found a crude flip switch, threw it and jumped in himself. Down they went, in the large dumbwaiter that carried contraband during Prohibition. They descended into the underbelly of the Green Mill Cocktail Lounge.

"Holy shit," Willow said. "I can't believe it's real."

Everyone knew of the legend of the tunnels, but only Elliot Caprice was brazen enough to count on their actual existence in an emergency. They reached the bottom but weren't in the clear. The trap door was more than myth, but the tunnels of Bill Drury's tales hadn't been used for years. They could be walled off, or collapsed. Elliot hopped out of the dumbwaiter. He looked around until he saw what seemed to be clear egress, bleakly illuminated by pale yellow utility lights. He placed his hand on the wall as he walked. Willow grabbed him around his waist. It was a claustrophobe's nightmare. He felt her quivering hands. They walked a bit farther until the sound of scurrying rats vibrated at their feet. Willow began screaming. Elliot pulled her in close. If they were going to get out of there, she needed to calm down.

"The trapdoor was there, right?"

"Yeah...yeah..."

"These are the tunnels. Stands to reason we should be able to make it to the utility corridors. We'll wind up somewhere on the other side of the street."

"Right."

She grabbed him tight around his forearm. They trudged through the dark and stink until they reached the opposite end of the concrete caverns. A dirty, musty stairway that hadn't been used in decades waited for them underneath another weak utility light. They climbed the stairs to find the door was locked. He tried leverage, but to no avail, so he helped Willow down a few stairs, grabbed the rusty iron handrail cemented into the wall for leverage, and kicked at the door twice until it flew open. He stuck his head out of the doorway to see they were now at the far end of the alley adjacent to the entrance of the

Green Mill. He placed their distance at one hundred fifty yards, give or take. A pendant light cast them in a sickly pale green. Willow tried peeking out over his shoulder, but he held her back.

"Wait a sec."

He used the butt of his .45 to break the bulb overhead. Once they were cloaked in darkness, she was free to see three patrol cars out front. Foot cops questioned remaining patrons. It wasn't the first time the Green Mill had violent disturbances, so it was only a matter of time before the cops moved on.

"We should hide out here for a few minutes."

"Did anyone see us go down that shaft?"

"Maybe. Joint's been mobbed up since Capone. No one wants trouble."

They watched until the alley was awash in the headlights of an approaching car. Elliot grabbed Willow and leaned his back against the vestibule. He mashed her, which covered their faces, though he kept one eye open to see up ahead. A cop in a watch commander's uniform rode past them slowly. Elliot held Willow tighter. She melted in his strong arms. The cop eventually passed them in his cruiser headed westbound toward Broadway. The coast was clear. Elliot wanted to observe, but Willow yielded her mouth to him. She pressed her pelvis into his. Her soft sighs were adorable.

Elliot's mission-mindedness left him uncertain what to do about his fast-approaching erection, but before he could free himself of her passion, she took control of their kiss, her tongue leading his in a dance bordered by her pillow-soft, unpainted lips. Her hair smelled of lavender, which pleasantly masked the faint aroma of the reefer she enjoyed earlier. She took his face in her hands. He grabbed them, gently pushing her away. She cooed a soft moan of disappointment as she stared into his eyes. Elliot was immediately embarrassed.

"Sorry," he whispered. "I gotta see this."

Willow stepped back as he returned to his observation posture in the doorway. Already, the watch commander waved away his patrolmen. The bar manager was still out front, keeping the big shot cop distracted. Nothing operated without local pay-offs. He obviously wanted to know what restitution he'd be entitled to for his protection money.

"We should go now. We'll take the long way around, back to your place."

"Okay."

They stepped out into the alley, Elliot ahead of Willow. She caught up to him, taking his hand.

"So we look as if we're together."

Willow Ellison was a bravely liberal young woman. Her male acquaintances came in two colors. All of them enjoyed her. Few had made her feel safe. Only Elliot saved her life. She was his if he wanted. Elliot looked back at her, into her large doe eyes. Those sad lower lids. He noticed her tiny cheek freckles. The creases at the sides the lips he kissed. That kissed him. He found her beautiful. Immediately it bothered him that, in the entire ordeal, which involved shooting off a man's fingers in a crowded night club, taking a chance on one of Bill Drury's cockamamie folk tales, wading through a rat-infested tunnel, and narrowly avoiding arrest, only now did he feel nervous.

CHAPTER 13

Charlie Parker kept Elliot company as Willow fetched a couple of Pabsts from the icebox. Her ass was perfect. She threw it as she walked ensuring it would be the only thing Elliot could think of in her absence. They had made love in stages, their bodies coming together as if performing a musical composition—at first vibrant and passionate, inspired without control, settling into physical syncopation—fucking each other, fucking for one another, fucking each other again. He ravaged her using his tongue, his fingers, his cock, all in no particular order. It was immediate. It was deliberate. It was incredible.

She returned holding their beers. As they sipped together, she leaned against him and listened as strains of "I Can't Get Started" caressed their ears.

"You just get back?"

"Hmm?"

"Your outfit? You look as if you're on leave." She took a sip out of her bottle.

"I was in the big war. These were just clothes I had handy. I needed to see you."

"You wore a disguise for that?"

She laughed. Her eyes did a little dance in time to Verley Mills' harp strings.

"No, no." Elliot laughed. He found himself having fun. "I needed to be incognito. Too many cops."

"Cops usually show up when you shoot a guy." She nuzzled him under his chin.

"Though not when you hit a fella with a camera."

"He had it coming."

"Poor bastard will never pose for a picture again."

They laughed. They kissed as if they had known each other their entire lives.

"You're in trouble?"

"I know for sure I'm persona non-grata."

"You're too brave to be a criminal." She kissed his cheek and had another swallow of beer. "So why are you looking for a jamoke like Alistair?"

"Legal business."

"He and his chippie would show up to my sets. He always brought good shit. She was a wallflower."

Willow laid on her back and upward as she related her memories. Elliot noticed her breasts defied gravity. If her soul wasn't so old, he would have been afraid she was underage.

"She hired me."

"The limey girlfriend is now the boss?" Willow said. "How's that work?"

"Married the boss man," Elliot said. "That's what caused the rift between them. Turns out, he bailed on the job so no one has seen him. Until he returns, loose ends stay untied."

"Alistair was weird. Never knew why he liked hanging around that cold fish. She put on the highbrow, but Alistair could be wild when he got loose. He liked getting high. One hit or snort, you couldn't shut him up. Would go on and on about himself having been to this place or another. Always spoke of ships."

"A traveler?"

"Of some sort. Said he took the gig driving for those rich stiffs in order to work his way in. Means to an end. That the boss took a liking to him. We met in business school. I was in secretarial classes. Figured I'd pay my way following jazz acts by working as an office girl."

"Yeah?"

"All the big names come through here. I've met them all. I

even get down to the colored neighborhoods on the South Side. I love the Regal Theater. Ever been down that way?"

Elliot could tell Willow didn't notice his race. He just nodded his head to keep her talking, making notice of the second of Alistair's lady friends who were unable to tell.

"He was able to take the big shot's cars when I needed to travel out to catch a show that was far away. Swanky wheels. Always a different one. Sometimes friends of his tagged along. Some of these guys were rough characters, like his work friend. Charley somethin'-or-other."

"Chauncey?"

"Kind of a tough guy? Doesn't smile much?"

"Sounds like him." Willow leaned up to finish her beer. Elliot let his lie.

"At first, it was cool. After a while, Alistair always brought him along. Figured they were just runnin' buddies. When the heavier party favors came out, frickin' Chauncey got all bent out of shape. He wouldn't party."

"You keep mentioning good shit. Dope?"

"Of course. How old are you?" Willow laughed. She touched Elliot's cock.

"Old enough."

"He'd get rare shit. Hash, opium, military stuff like amphetamine. A lot of it. I put out the word I was having a party. He showed up carrying this big cake of hashish. I knew what it was because cats from New York would have it when their bands came through Chicago."

"What is he like?"

"Alistair? He's kind of a bozo. Speaks uppity. That Chauncey fella seemed like a flake. The real nervous type, talking in that funny east coast accent of his."

"East coast?"

"Yeah. Said he was from Connecticut. The two of them, sounding like Audrey Hepburn."

"Were they always together?"

"Not always. I imagine they fell out after the last time they were here together. Alistair brought over some smack. It wasn't our normal kink. First time. Anyhow, when he pulled it out of his satchel, Chauncey was livid. Started going on about how they had to be careful and whatnot. They stepped off into the kitchen, speaking all hush-hush. It seemed pretty heated."

Willow rolled over on her side and put her face on Elliot's lap. She ran her index finger up his thigh.

"So what happened?"

"There was a knock at the door. I went to get it, but Chauncey stepped in front of it. He was really afraid. Alistair was too high to care. Whoever showed up started beating on the door. Alistair begged me to tell whoever it was that they were gone. They cut out the back, I answered the door, but no one was there. It was very strange."

Elliot went to that place inside himself where he was all alone, sorting information, playing out scenarios in his mind. Willow could feel he was no longer present.

"Hey, Elliot," she cooed in his ear but Elliot wasn't home. "Hey!"

Elliot looked into her face.

"Where'd you go?"

Elliot touched her chin.

"Are you using me?" she asked, in mounting sadness. "If so, you can tell me. I can take it."

"I'm not using you. It's just this is all very important. It's the reason I came here." He held her face in both of his hands. "But not the reason I've stayed this long." He kissed her again, deeper than before. She straddled him. He hugged her tight. She sighed, wrapping her arms around his back. It all moved so fast, as did everything in his life when he wasn't careful. His erection returned. It wouldn't be long before caution once again went out the window.

"I can get it for you." She kissed him again. "Later."

"Get what?"

"The satchel. The one Alistair left here."
Elliot released his end of their embrace.
"Go get it."
"Now?"
"Right now."
He was terse. It killed the mood instantly. Willow's smile fell into a scowl.
"Fine."
She snatched one of the blankets off the floor to wrap herself. Down the long, dark hall to her single bedroom she went. As she loudly rummaged through her closet, Elliot got dressed. He was already buckling his boots when she returned to throw a leather attaché case at his feet and storm off, disgusted. He felt guilty. Perhaps he could've handled it better, but appeasement was never his forte.
"Willow, honey."
"Don't bother." She hurried back down the hall.
After her bedroom door slammed, he opened the front flap. Inside was an unbound stack of official-seeming paperwork. Included were cargo manifests from Costas Cartage, Limited, the shipping company from the senior McAlpin's dowry. Each form listed vast items delineated in rows labeled quantity, worth, agent, dealer, tariff, et cetera. From the thick cotton bond paper, to the foil stamping, down to the customs forms bearing official seals from different nations, they seemed plenty legit. He'd heard stories from cops assigned to the docks along the far South side that U.S. Customs in Chicago was fanatical. Postwar smuggling had increased a hundredfold. Washington was smart enough to distrust Chicago locals to protect the integrity of international commerce. If every scrap of paperwork wasn't tip-top, even legitimate business operations would grind to a halt. Massive investments would dwindle to nothing. The feds took months, just because they could. He spent a few minutes skimming through the forms. Recent shipments had been attested by Alistair as the agent of process. What's more,

many of these shipments occurred after Jon McAlpin met his end in his own bathtub.

Elliot returned the paperwork to the satchel. He turned it over to inspect the bulge underneath the opposite flap. Inside were rolls of small bills, no larger than a sawbuck, but what concerned him more was a foil square wrapped in cellophane, a bit less than the size of half of a brick. He didn't need to open it to know what it was.

He realized he left Willow alone. She must have thought him a jagoff. He put the contraband back in the satchel before he walked down the hall to her bedroom. She was the kind of cute he could appreciate for long periods of time. Quirky. Chatty. White, yet relatable. Plus she was great in the sack, though what attracted Elliot more was how she laid out that goon back at the Green Mill. She took no shit.

He wanted to see her again.

He opened the door to her bedroom. There she was, sitting on the floor, propped against her closet. A dropper rig lay at the base of her foot. She had shot up between her toes, which is how he missed the tracks when they were making love. His heart broke at the contradictions. A young, courageous, artistic white lady, injecting herself full of the white man's poison, all to emulate her colored Jazz heroes. Had they cared enough to tell her the truth, they would have warned her to stay off horse. He kicked the crude syringe away, picked her up, and put her in her bed. He left her apartment broken-hearted over the short lifecycle of their union. A relationship that bore the commonality of years played out in only a few hours. As he slipped out the back door, he was greeted by the faint light of daybreak. He needed to hightail it back to Southville. Part of him mourned that girl. A greater part of him wanted to kill Alistair Williams. Killing his running buddy Chauncey would be a bonus.

* * *

Elliot returned to the flop house well after the sun rose. He shambled up the stairs just as Uncle Buster was walking toward the bathroom. He was dog-tired and had that look in his eye. The old man learned through the years to let him be when his feelings were written on his face. Had they spoken, he would have asked Elliot what he was doing walking in at such an hour, looking crazy, wearing that get-up, but Buster had never understood how to reach Elliot, not even back when he was in short pants.

By the time Buster returned from the commode, Elliot was already asleep, right there on the bed, in his HBTs and boots. He softly murmured in his sleep, his face contorted. It was in those moments that Buster Caprice wished he had the words to say the farm wasn't worth more to him than the boy's well-being. That they should take care to ensure the cost to reclaim it would not be too great. Sure, the old man missed his land, though not completely for himself but for the center it provided to their tiny two-person family. The center they now lacked through the bank's shuttering of their familial sovereignty. If asked, Buster would say that all he wanted to do was take Elliot home, find a way to keep him from leaving ever again, but no one ever asked old colored men like Buster about their deepest desires. It's not necessary to understand the heart of a man to lay a burden upon his shoulders. As he watched his nephew dream, he wondered if sleep was just another life in which a Caprice was doomed for daring to live free. He wished he could enter that world his adopted baby was trapped. He'd free that little boy. Instead, all he could do was watch him suffer. All he could do was pull up a chair, light-up a hand-rolled, and wait until he returned from the personal hell.

If only they fell down dead after the first shot like they do in the picture shows. Perhaps then Elliot wouldn't have to run screaming down the middle of Western Avenue, bleeding out his shoulder like a stuck pig, firing his gun at the bastards who shot him in the shoulder and killed his friend. Rage is what fueled him. For Bill Drury's murder sure, but more because they expected to get away.

Drury was a peacock. Elliot tried to warn him away from the spotlight. Parading around as the wronged, avenging ex-cop, signing autographs for readers of his columns, snapping photos for fans outside gangland landmarks, all meant the end of him. When Creamer left Elliot out in the cold after Kefauver's committee on organized crime fell out of favor in Washington, Elliot offered Drury an inside scoop, only the idiot turned right around and handed the same evidence over to Kefauver himself. He should've known the crusading dandy of the Senate couldn't resist attaching himself to the hero of American crime journalism. They were all fools, but that didn't mean Bill Drury's family deserved to find his body in their garage the next morning. If only he had taken him up on dinner. If only he could turn back time and accept that drink. Bill wouldn't have been murdered in a place where he thought he was safe. That's why Elliot was out for blood. It was wrong. It happened in front of him. There was no way Elliot could let it go. Not even to save himself.

Since that night in the atrium with Creamer, Kefauver and Wiggins, he knew he was dancing on the precipice of doom. Yet Elliot was slick, trained by the slickest. He used his dual race to play into their affectations of grandeur. The colored political elite gossiped like schoolgirls. The white brass ate up his code-switching deference. They always underestimated the savvy of Negro cops. The more he advanced in his job—due to John Creamer's political influence—the more evidence he harvested for Kefauver. They told him not to contact Bill, which was like giving Elliot his phone number. They had gotten to know each other and even did one another a few favors here and there. Once Creamer screwed him, Elliot offered to be Bill's insider. The fame-seeker was more than happy to pay him for his information, but Elliot did it out of spite. Drury wrote some real hum-dingers for the *Chicago Herald*. Most wound up nationally syndicated. The unlikely team really shook things up. It was easy.

So easy that Elliot didn't foresee Drury screwing everyone, including himself.

The younger one that got him in the shoulder was faster on his feet. Elliot fired his first shot mid-stride, catching him with a hot one in the back, just above his left hip. It rattled around and exited out the other side of his pelvic bone. The man teetered. Elliot let off two more, catching him between the top of his spine and the base of his skull. He went down tumbling like a kite that fell from the sky once the wind stopped blowing. Elliot stood over him to watch as the last bit of life left his convulsing mortal coil. He took the man's .38 out of his dead hand before he chased down the older one. He was top heavy. Out of breath. Perhaps he hadn't figured on running anywhere while carrying a twelve-gauge. Elliot emptied the barrel of the young buck's gun into the fat bastard's thighs until he crumpled onto the thoroughfare. He crawled to the curb and used it to prop himself up as he fished through his pocket for more shotgun shells. Elliot followed the fat man's trail of crimson, walking slow, as if he had a lifetime to get there. He kicked his assassin in the chest, which laid him flat on his back, but before he put a hot one in him, Elliot beheld his face in the amber streetlight. That push-broom mustache. A high and tight haircut. The beer-barrel physique from years of sitting more than walking. A younger accomplice. Each indicated deep grooved habits. God-damn it. If he wasn't consumed with bloodlust, he may have put it together earlier. Elliot looked at the gun he took off his partner. It was police issue; standard checkered walnut grip, "CPD #8141" etched across the side of the barrel.

"Fuck me, right in the face."

Elliot bled from his shoulder at the rate of a broken spigot. His mouth was dry. Sweat poured from his panicked brow. The adrenaline rush that helped him ignore his pain had long passed. He'd have to finish the task with cold awareness. Elliot put a hollow-point from his own gun into the old fat cop's forehead, then another for punctuation, and a third out of spite. Dogs barked. Pulled shades cast light upon him through apartment windows. Sirens grew louder from the distance.

"I called the cops!" went a voice from an unseen busybody.

He had to run. He'd run ever since.

Buster carefully took off Elliot's boots. He rolled him out of his jacket without waking him. He raised the boy, yet he was forever opaque. He wanted to know what happened back in Chicago. He wanted to know what hurt him beyond being a child of fate. He'd have to ask another time, for now, wherever he was, Elliot wasn't there in that single room. He was set adrift on a sea of grief.

CHAPTER 14

"Southville County Sheriff. Deputy Reilly speaking."

"The bastard's dead," a muffled voice said through the phone receiver.

"Wouldja narrow that down a bit?"

Ned grabbed a pencil, scribbled DEAD BASTARD on the desk blotter and underlined it twice.

"Pettingill," the voice said. "S.E. Pettingill!"

Ned's stomach sank at the name. He hoped it was an accident. Farming. Hunting. Anything would have been better than murder.

"Where?"

"Up at the house."

"What's your na—" Ned said, but the line went dead.

George walked in from the car park to see his deputy hang up the phone the Ned way—dropping it from his two fingers atop the carriage, wearing a faint look of disgust. George didn't even stop. Only checked his gun and turned right back around. Ned ripped the notes from the blotter page.

"S.E. Pettingill," Ned said.

"Lord, have mercy."

"Tits-up, after all these years."

"Language, Ned."

It was going to be one of those days.

Everyone hated the Pettingills, going back to when Samuel Eugene Pettingill founded the county. Pettingill's son, S.E., was a fop and never worked a day in his life. He and his sister, Clarissa—the shut in—lived it up in the old Pettingill manse as if they were stuck in an antebellum fantasy. The family handlers maintained appearances and the status quo. Now the colored county sheriff would have to enter their northern plantation, shuffle his feet and figure out what killed the prodigal son.

They didn't speak as they drove up Main. The two were on coarse terms over the return of Elliot Caprice.

"Did you call—"

"The coroner? Yeah."

"You'll likely need to go in ahead of me."

"Buncha assholes behind that gate."

"Some things can't be helped."

"Don't I know it," Ned said, watching the road, as they turned on Pettingill, named for the family of jerks.

"We going to talk about it?"

"Nothing to talk about."

"You've had an attitude for weeks."

"I just don't like how you've been making decisions," Ned said.

Once they passed Sugartown, they could see, far in the distance, the Pettingill Manse. They were already five minutes outside of Southville proper. There was a two-mile drive to the front of its gigantic gate left to go.

"Including my decision to help Elliot," George said.

"You shouldn't have gotten us involved."

"Ned, men die in police custody in St. Louis."

Ned opened the glove box and rummaged around until he found a pad for case notes.

"You know what they're sayin' about him on the wire? That he was on the scene when two off-dutys from Chicago wound up dead."

"He's our own, Ned."

"Nah," Ned said, as he made notes of the initial report on the blank spaces of the top margin of the pad. "He's yours. And his uncle's, who he abandoned."

"You've seen Buster Caprice?"

"He's been friends with my mother since they came here."

"How is he?"

"Stuck in Betty Bridges' flophouse," Ned said. "No thanks to his nephew."

"Don't judge."

"You give me some song and dance about processing everyone we arrest, just to run off to St. Louis to help him evade the law."

"Ned," George said.

"Here comes a sermon."

"You're not colored."

"What? I gotta be colored now?" Ned waved off his superior officer.

"The life of a colored man bears its own unique problems."

"Pettingill's dead, no chance it's natural causes."

"Likely not."

"He's constantly surrounded by Negro house staff."

"What's your point?"

"Looks to me the colored people I know abandon their relations, kill their own employers and aid and abet their no-good friends." Ned shifted in his seat. "Maybe it's good I'm not a Negro."

They spent the rest of the trip in silence.

The grounds to the plantation were quiet. McWhirter, the family attorney, opened the front door. He was squat, balding, and employed a comb-over to no effect. He wore a suit that was darker than anyone should wear on a Midwestern summer day.

"I'm Deputy Reilly," Ned said. "This is Sheriff Stingley."

"The Reverend's boy," McWhirter said, without really looking at him. "Fine achievement for your people."

"Thank you. Where's the body," George said. His jowls tensed atop his shirt collar.

"Upstairs," McWhirter said. "In the bathroom."

"Always the bathroom," Ned said.

McWhirter led the two into the house. As they walked through the foyer, they could see the family's colored servants, all in uniform, milling about. They seemed aloof. As if being there was a waste of their time.

"We'll need to question everyone," Ned said.

As they climbed the large staircase to the second floor, he noticed a woman down the hall, peering out through a bedroom door.

"That means everyone," George said.

"Understood, Sheriff," McWhirter said. He visibly bristled at George's authoritative tone.

S.E. Pettingill's mortal coil lay on the tiled floor of the hall bathroom underneath a satin bed sheet. George and Ned gave McWhirter the side-eye.

"He was lying there," McWhirter said. "Naked."

"We only received an anonymous tip," George said. "We never got a call from the family."

"The Pettingill's are important people, Deputy," McWhirter said. "I have my duties."

George leaned in on the attorney. He fixed fierce eyes upon him. Ned stepped in.

"This normal?"

"He's been known to tie one on now and again," McWhirter said.

"We've fetched him from the dives in Sugartown a lot more than now and again," George said.

"There's a night shift housekeeper named Hattie." McWhirter cut his eyes. "She takes care of Clarissa Pettingill. She may know something."

"Where is she now?" asked George.

"She lives off the grounds," McWhirter said.

"Any other household staff live off the grounds?"

"No," McWhirter said. George and Ned looked at each other.

"Time to ask the staff what they may know," George said. McWhirter looked over to Ned Reilly.

"Is that absolutely necessary? Most of them weren't on duty—"

"Sheriff said to get the staff together," Ned said. McWhirter shuffled off. "Frickin' asshole."

George walked through the bathroom taking in the crime scene. He reached into the large double-pedestal bathtub and ran his finger across the porcelain. It squeaked. He rubbed his fingers together.

"Dry as a bone."

"Maybe they cleaned it after they made the master decent."

Stacks of folded cotton bath towels lay in a credenza, but none were on the floor or draped over the bath. George knelt and lifted up the sheet on Pettingill's body. His lips were blue. His eyes were wide open, staring up at nothing.

"He's supposed to look as if he'd fallen," George said.

"That your medical opinion, Reverend?"

Southville County Coroner Bobby Shaeffer walked into the bathroom. He was carrying a black medical bag, dressed in a tan linen suit, no tie, and a white handkerchief around his neck. Sweat ran down his face. He was out of breath from the stairs.

"Doc," Ned said.

"Humid as a son-of-a-bitch out there, Deputy," Shaeffer said. "Sheriff, please unhand my corpse."

George stepped away. Shaeffer walked over.

"He was strangled."

"Not until I say so," Shaeffer said.

"We need a time of death right away," George said. He walked out.

"Seems more pleasant than usual," Shaeffer said.

"This ain't the usual," Ned said. Shaeffer put on his pinch-frame glasses and waved Ned off.

Ned stepped into the hallway to see George facing the bedroom at the long end. The door cracked. A woman inside peeked out, then shut the door.

"Clarissa Pettingill," Ned said.

"We know each other. My father—"

"Right."

"Perhaps you should start on the staff," George said.

"Right."

Ned descended the stairs, where he found a teenage Negro woman in a maid's uniform in the lobby.

"Mr. McWhirter told me to fetch you to the dining room," she said.

"What's your name?"

"Dorothy."

"Got a last name, Dorothy?"

"Not around here, I don't."

George knocked on the bedroom door.

"Miss Pettingill." He softened the tone of his preacher's voice. "It's Sheriff Stingley."

He heard nothing.

"Clarissa. It's Georgie. May we talk—"

Clarissa Pettingill threw open the door and yanked him inside the room. George wasn't a little man, but she had the strength of someone off her rocker. She slammed the door as if to save herself. To George's surprise, hugged him tight. She wore a silk bed gown, although it was afternoon. Her salt and pepper hair was tousled, yet still flowed as if it was well-tended. She had put on makeup, obviously to receive a special guest.

"It's so good to see you, Georgie," she said.

"It's been a long time."

"Remember when we used to play in these halls?"

"I do. When our fathers would have one of those meetings."

"Only coloreds he'd let in the house," she said. "Remember when you would sneak me kisses, Georgie?"

George gently peeled Clarissa's arms from his waist.

"I'm here to find out what happened to your brother," he said, sitting her down on her bed. He noticed dead roses in a vase on her valet. A tray of uneaten food sat on the nightstand.

"Why are you cooped up in here?"

"It's what they do to the crazy ones."

"Crazy, like a fox," George said. He patted her hands as if he were a reverend again, calling upon the sick.

"He was seeing that colored housekeeper," she whispered. "Hattie. She's terribly mean. I know she switches my pills on me. That's why I'm..."

Clarissa twirled her finger around her ear.

"Last night, I heard bumping around in the dark. I looked out my door, as I always do. I saw two large colored boys leave the bathroom."

"Did you see their faces?"

"They were dark. It was dark. It's not safe for me here, Georgie. The house workers all hate me."

"I'll take care of things," George said. He patted her hand again.

"Town finally has a good man as sheriff," she said. She lunged forward and hugged him around his neck. "Don't you let them kill you, Georgie. They'll never forgive you for being a nigger."

George stood up

"Do come back to see me, Georgie."

George left the room, not saying a word.

Ned Reilly was questioning the staff all together as George walked in the dining room.

"Your real name," said the Deputy.

"Mister Pettingill calls—called—me Dobie," said a youngish Negro fellow, dressed in a smock.

"What's your mother call you?"

"Robert. Robert Peale. But I gotta go by Dobie at work."

Ned looked over at George.

"Pettingill nicknamed all the staff. Each one, he's callin' something ridiculous. Like they're children."

"I need to know about Hattie," George said. "When's the last time she'd been to work?"

The staff all were silent.

"A murder was committed," George said. "Speak up."

The staff all looked at each other but didn't say a word. Shaeffer walked in the doorway.

"Sheriff Stingley."

George stepped into the hall. Ned continued the questioning.

"You were right," Shaeffer said. "Definitely strangled, but I'd guess somewhere off the grounds. He was brought back here post mortem. Abrasions on his heels indicated he was dragged. Imagine he died a day ago. He certainly died in his birthday suit. There's more."

Shaeffer reached into his shirt pocket.

"I found these in his mouth."

Shaeffer produced three pennies.

"Not sure what it means," he said.

George returned to the dining room. Ned pulled him to the side.

"Her house name is Hattie," Ned said. "Real name is Merriam Robichaux. Early-twenties. She hasn't been to work in a week. No one wants to say more."

"Does anyone want to tell us about Merriam's and Pettingill's relationship?" George asked. No one answered. Ned walked over to Robert.

"We were getting along pretty good there, Robert," he said. "I'd hate to have to arrest you."

"F-for what?"

"Dunno," Ned said. "I'll figure out somethin'."

"Don't think we won't put an obstruction of justice charge on every one of you," George said.

Dorothy found the nerve to speak.

"She and ol' S.E. had a thang," she said.

"Shut up, Dorothy!" Robert said.

"I ain't goin' to jail for that heifer!"

"Why does everyone think they were involved?"

"He liked her," Robert said. "Let her live off the property. Only had to work at night. Only looked after the crazy sister."

"We all hated her 'cuz she didn't have to do no real work," Dorothy said.

"There were two associates," George said.

"Her brother is likely one of 'em," Dorothy said. "Don't know the other. They live in one o' dem apartments over the pawn shop."

"Majestic?" Ned said.

"Yeah."

"He snuck out regularly to Sugartown," said an older Negro man dressed in a white shirt and bowtie.

"What's your name," George said.

"S.E. call me Skipper. My real name is Walter. Walter Gibson."

"Tell us somethin' we don't know, Walter Gibson," Ned said.

"He been in the safe a whole lot," Walter said. "Sometimes he has me run him to the bank in the middle of the day. Take his purse when he go out at night. Usually, he back in the safe the next mornin'."

"Someone is still not telling me something," George said.

"I'll run to the jail," Ned said. "Bring the paddy wagon over."

"She got a baby. Rumor is, could be S.E.'s."

George waved Ned into the hall.

"Call the state boys. Ask for a couple of units to meet us at

144

Majestic Loans. Make sure they keep it quiet. We don't need this blowing apart the holiday."

"You can use the one in the kitchen," Dorothy said, after eavesdropping.

"We free to go?" Robert asked.

George looked at them all. It was a harsh gaze. The kind that a righteous man who had enough of the world cast upon the brazen. He walked out, running into McWhirter in the foyer.

"Sheriff?" he said.

"Fire them all. Hire white folks."

George walked out the door and waited for Ned in the car.

True to type, the Illinois State Police overdid it. Three units plus a paddy wagon. Barricades on both ends of the street. The troopers were talking through the loudspeaker up at the window when George and Ned arrived.

"What's all this?!" George said.

"And you are?" said the lead uniform. His name tag read "Sgt. Burke."

"Southville County Sheriff George Stingley." Burke blinked twice but didn't say a word. The other uniforms chuckled. Ned stepped up.

"I'm Deputy Ned Reilly," he said. "I called you, but I didn't ask for this."

"S.E. Pettingill is an—"

"Important man," Ned said. "Yeah, yeah, we know."

"We're gonna need for you to step back."

"This is my jurisdiction, Sergeant," George said. "I demand to know what's going on here."

"As far as we can tell, one of 'em is dead. Shot by the other one. There's a woman with a baby up there."

"Merriam Robichaux," Ned said.

"Yeah, well, whatever her name is, she's a hostage," Burke said.

"She wouldn't be a hostage if you didn't come in, guns blazing." George was livid. He snatched the microphone from Burke.

"Hey, fella."

"Not fella! Sheriff," George shouted in Burke's face.

"Step back," Ned said. "We know how to handle this."

"Miss Robichaux!" George said. "This is Sheriff Stingley!"

A dark face peered out from the curtains.

"The sheriff is colored?" a male voice shouted.

"I'm here with Deputy Ned Reilly," George said. The face peered out of the curtains once more.

"Deputy's white."

"This doesn't have to get any worse," George said. "I'm coming up."

"Georgie," Ned said.

George handed him the microphone.

"Give me five minutes," he said. "If I don't come down, they can come up."

George ran in the apartment building door next to the pawn shop.

"Ya know, pally," Burke said. "If you didn't need us here—"

"Shut up," Ned said.

George found the front door to the tiny single apartment wide open. By the door was an altar to Baron Samedi, trussed in cayenne peppers. A black wax candle shaped into a crucifix was burning. What appeared to be dried blood was in a saucer at the Baron's feet. In bassinet by the kitchen sink cried a baby. He or she was wrapped in a hand-knitted blanket. A large colored man—dark-complected, portly—lay prone atop a murphy bed. He had a hole in his forehead. George could hear whimpering coming from the side of the tall icebox.

"Help me, Sheriff!"

Merriam Robichaux's tear-soaked face peered out from the recess. She was the color of café au lait. She had large eyes, and wore her hair in a tight bun underneath a purple patterned head scarf. She spoke in thick creole dialect.

"He killed my brother!" she said.

"Imma kill you too, you double-dealin' whore!"

"State your name," George said.

"Buck!" said the man. "Buck Williams! And I been done wrong!"

"Mr. Williams, there's nothing left for you to do but give up!"

"You the real sheriff?" Buck said. It was all George could do not to roll his eyes.

"I am."

"So shoot this fool!" Merriam said.

"Shut up, bitch!"

"Mr. Williams, the Illinois State Police are outside," George said. "You have about three minutes before they get up here. You will not survive."

"I wanna negotiate!" Buck said. He stepped out from the recess near the ice box. He had Merriam around the neck.

"She led me on for weeks, tellin' me she had some scam to take that fat cat for all we could get."

"It was workin' fine, too," Merriam said. "Until you killed him."

"I wouldn't have you fuckin' him on my bed!" Buck said.

"Fool, you ain't got shit around heah!"

Buck clubbed her on the side of the head. The baby seemed to scream louder.

"Be easy, Williams!" George said.

"I said I wanna negotiate!"

"I'm afraid there's nothing to negotiate."

"That's 'cuz you a nigger sheriff!" Buck said.

"It's because we already know everything," George said. "You killed Pettingill in a fit of jealousy before you could finish the plan of blackmailing him over the child."

Merriam looked at George. She was contrite.

"He was nice," she said.

"He was an asshole!" Buck said.

"At least he was about sum'n," she said. "At least he wanted to take care of his baby."

"That deah is my baby!" Williams said.

"Why did you take him back to his house?" George said. "Why didn't you just dump him someplace?"

"Folk usually come around heah lookin' fo' 'im," Buck said. "That Skipper, what used to drive him around. The lawyer fella. We needed time!"

"He didn't believe the baby was his," Merriam said, as she calmed down. "Said he knew we were hustlin' him, but he didn't care. He loved me."

"He loved yo' cooze," Buck said.

"Shut up!" Merriam said. "We wuz supposed to divide up the loot and split. Buck and me were gonna go one way. Barry—my brother—was gonna go back to Baton Rouge. This idiot up and strangle S.E., right there on top of me."

"He was fuckin' my woman!"

"He had been fuckin' me, fool!"

"Put three pennies in him, like he special."

"I ain't gonna have him cursin' me from the next world!"

"You killed Barry over the money," George said.

"They wuz gonna take my cut and split. Take my baby!" Buck waved the gun around again.

"I said I wanna make a deal!"

"Buck, do you want your baby to see his daddy die, right here in this apartment?"

Buck began to panic. George spoke sincere words in his preacher's baritone.

"You're right," George said. "I am just a Negro sheriff. I can't stop those white state troopers from killing you. Both of you."

George, looking at Merriam, nodded over to the bassinet.

"All of you."

Merriam shuddered. Buck blinked his eyes rapidly as he attempted to think through the stress.

"Let her go. Give me the gun," George said. "For your child's sake. Please."

George figured he reached Merriam, but figured on Buck keeping up the fight, except he immediately let go of Merriam, dropped the gun and dove onto the floor.

"I give up!" Buck said. "Don't kill me!"

Buck looked as if a lynch-mob had come to get him. Merriam ran to the bassinet and picked up her crying child. George dove atop Buck and cuffed him. Ned Reilly was in the doorway, as white as ever.

"Don't kill me," Buck said. George finally rolled his eyes.

That afternoon, after a lunch run, Ned Reilly returned to the jail to find George behind closed doors in his office. He was having his ass chewed off by two fat cats from the bank. After all the what-for, they left. George walked out, ashen-faced.

"What's goin' on, Georgie?"

"Go to Miss Betty's, pick up Elliot."

George checked his gun before walking toward the door.

"Where are you going?"

"To the Caprice farm," George said. "Bring him there. Wear your uniform. Arrest him if you have to."

"Baby," Buster said. "You gotta get up, boy."

Elliot woke in Buster's room at the flophouse. He could see his uncle standing over him, backlit by the diffused late afternoon light, like a stained glass saint. Elliot slept clear through the morning. He still had Willow's smell in his nose.

"What's goin' on, Unk?"

"Ned Reilly is downstairs. Says he needs to talk to ya."

Elliot and Buster walked down the stairs to find Ned waiting for them by the lobby door. He stood straight in full uniform, as opposed to slouching in his farming dungarees. He was also wearing his star, which was most unlike him.

"Ned. Dressed kind of official, ain'tcha?"

"We need to get on over to the farm, Elliot."

"Wha happen?" Buster placed his hands in his rear pockets.

"I can't say just yet. George sent me here before he went up to the place. He's there now."

"Lemme get my woolen," Buster said.

"That isn't such a good idea, Mr. Caprice."

"My nephew. My farm. I'm comin'."

"I'll be okay," Elliot said. He patted his uncle on the shoulder. "Ned's just doin' his job. I'll be back. In no time."

Buster Caprice pointed a weathered black index finger in Ned's direction.

"I know yo' mama," Buster said. It was country folk code for *no screw jobs.*

On the drive, Elliot rubbed his eyes.

"You look pretty tired."

"Worked late last night."

"What work are you doin', Elliot?"

Elliot slowly turned toward Ned.

"You puttin' cop questions on me, Ned?"

"Just askin' is all. Not back to collectin', are you? Maybe took your place handlin' the Jews' business?"

Elliot turned away without answering. He watched the road, wondering if anyone saw him break into the barn. At best, it would be a misdemeanor. If the bank leaned on George to press charges, he could argue his right to his own personal property. Still, something in the way Ned maintained his distance made him uneasy. Ned Reilly was George's boy, going back to when they all were kids, and he had always been a better friend. Elliot's presence usually rendered the deputy a third wheel. Once he went away to college, Ned had George to himself. Ned followed George, listened to him, grew to appreciate the straighter path. He never tried influencing him off his square,

DANNY GARDNER

like the young mischievous mulatto had so often done. Whenever Mother Stingley chastised her baby boy, she knew two
things: Ned Reilly was innocent and it was all Elliot Caprice's
idea. Though Ned was respectful of their close bond, there was
no love lost when Elliot went away. Even still, Ned was Irish.
He cared about the community. Elliot was a fellow Southvillian.
Normally that counted for something.

"I'd appreciate the courtesy of some insight here, Ned."

"Alls I know is a bank officer took an assessor up to the
property this morning. They're close to getting that easement
from the county, so they can parcel out the land like they
want."

"What that have to do with me," Elliot said.

"Fella from the bank comes into the jail afterward reporting
something he found in the barn. Said they found the gate chain
broken. They took George into his office in private. After they
spoke, Sheriff had me fetch you to the property."

Ned glanced over at Elliot.

"Look here, Ned. This ain't what it looks like. There were
some things in there I needed for work—."

"Don't tell me anything else, Elliot. I ain't got a position on
it one way or another. Save it for George, alright?"

They made the rest of the trip in silence as Elliot pieced
together what little information he had. He left the chain intact.
Zero residual presence inside. None of it made sense to him.

Ned drove up to the open gate. Ned was polite enough to
allow Elliot to walk up the drive. When they got out the car,
Elliot kicked around the gravel seeking clues.

"I thought you wanted to walk, not disturb an area under
investigation?"

"It's a point of egress, Ned. You were going to drive through
it, so either it's already been swept or you didn't find anything."

Elliot leaned over the trespassing sign. Cut heavy-gage chain
lay in the gravel. George's cruiser was parked outside the barn.
When the Sheriff stepped out the Dutch doors, the two could

see the tension in his shoulders from a hundred yards away.

"We should get up there," Ned said.

Ned walked past George into the barn. A pool of light shone through the open grain door above.

"The hell's goin' on here, Georgie?"

"Come inside."

Elliot followed George down the drive bay to the tack room. He knew. Even before he saw the sheet over the lumped mass. He knew it when he saw it written all over George's grim countenance. From the moment he got that first haircut at Boots' place, when he dared feel the light of day on his face—dared to intend the best for himself—he knew tragedy was approaching.

"Ned," George said. He motioned toward the mass on the barn floor. Ned Reilly grabbed the front of the sheet.

"Don't."

Elliot's whispered plea wasn't just to Ned, to stay his hand so he couldn't see that which was underneath. It was also to Fate, whose infinite capacity for cruelty Elliot had momentarily forgotten.

"You need to see this," George said.

"Let me," Elliot said, his voice barely registering.

George nodded and stepped back. Elliot grabbed the sheet and pulled it gently. He swallowed his own scream as he beheld the pale, lifeless face of Willow Ellison.

CHAPTER 15

He could hear George speaking to him but paid no attention for he was already plotting Willow's revenge, focused on where to begin, and who to beat answers out of. It hadn't occurred to him that he could have been a suspect until Ned Reilly pulled out a pair of handcuffs.

"We'll get Mike Robin up here," George said. "You have rights."

"There's no way in hell you think I could've done this."

"I don't know what to think."

"Do you know her?"

"Of course I do, Ned. That doesn't mean I killed her or brought her body to my own barn." Elliot ran his fingers through his hair.

"The body makes the property the scene of a crime. This place gets tied up for months. That buys you time," Ned said.

"I'd have to be crazy."

George and Ned looked at each other in silence. Elliot felt all alone.

"It's been a rough couple of years for you, Elliot."

"Oh, fuck you, George Stingley."

"Who's the girl?" George was using his preacher's stare. The question froze Elliot in his tracks. The shock had passed. The grief had arrived.

"Her name is Willow. Willow Ellison. She's from Uptown. She's...she was a photographer. Followed jazz acts." Elliot remembered their kisses. That poor girl.

"In Chicago?"

"Yes, George. Chicago. We were together last night."

"Doing what?"

"I needed to interview her for a case I'm working on. I picked up a side hustle based on work I've been doing for Mikey Robin."

"This Mikey know you're working side hustles?" Ned fingered the cuffs.

"What difference does that make?"

"Keeping secrets isn't going to help you much now, Elliot," George said.

"When last I saw her, she was alive in her apartment. I found her on the floor, doped up on heroin, so I put her in her bed. I returned to Southville, went to sleep in my room at Miss Betty's, and that's where Ned found me."

"Can anyone other than the deceased account for your whereabouts?"

"That's not relevant until you learn how long she's been dead, Ned! Jesus Christ, do they give you assholes any training?!"

"No need to insult me, ace," Ned said. "Just want to know why there's a dead body in your barn."

"If you're working a case, as you say, what were you doing in her bedroom?"

"What grown folk do, George."

"That's real professional."

"Stuff it, preacher man. This isn't Sunday's sermon."

"You're not in control here, Elliot. I am," George said. "Right now, I'm at a crossroads."

"Oh, I bet you are."

"The farm was locked down. Maybe you assumed no one would be here for a while," Ned said. "It'd give you a place to put her until—"

"You think I would hide someone's dead body in my uncle's house? Someone I killed?"

George Stingley fixed his gaze upon Elliot. His disappointment finally came to the fore.

"I think something happened that you hadn't intended. You needed time to figure out what to do next. You counted on this place being locked up. Maybe your old pal George the Sheriff could help you fix it." George took off his glasses. "Like I helped you fix St. Louis."

"You self-righteous bastard."

"Don't make us do this nasty," George said. He pulled his revolver. "I'm still your friend."

Elliot, wounded in so many places, in so many ways, stood shocked. Everything felt like a bad dream.

"Wait a second, George," Ned said. "Look, Elliot isn't my favorite person in the world."

"Thank you for your candor, Ned."

"He says he didn't do it. It sounds to me he's making sense."

"This guy I'm looking for, he's connected to a wealthy family, and what I think is a clear case of murder. The more I dig into him, the more he seems like the type to do something like this," Elliot said.

"Fine. We'll take you in. You attest to what you know. We handle this the right way," George said.

"So the right way is leaving me twisting while some ofays from the state police figure this out? Maybe the true killer comes forward before I get the electric chair up at Stateville?!"

"What do you expect me to do?"

"Get out of the way while I find this fuck!"

"What happens to the sheriff that found a dead white girl in his friend's barn but let him go?"

"Seal the barn off, declare it a crime scene. Leave me out of it."

"No chance."

"If I wasn't hot on his trail, the dead body of my only lead wouldn't be lying right there!"

"Or you make a run for it like you did from Chicago," George said.

"Keep your mouth off that until you know something about it."

"You're too good at disappearing."

"That what this is about?"

"It's about all of it, including this poor woman."

Ned could see it was getting personal.

"I'm this close to getting at least some part of my life back," Elliot said.

"I don't see it that way."

"Goddamnit, George, where am I gonna go?!"

"If that's how you truly feel, you'll do the right thing. Ned."

Ned pulled the cuffs, but Elliot had already given up on loyalty. He rushed Ned, planted his foot inside his left heel and threw the deputy off balance. Elliot yanked Ned's service revolver out of its holster. He grabbed Ned around the shoulder and jabbed the business-end of the revolver into Ned's side.

"Oh, Christ on tha frickin' cross."

"I'm sorry about this, Ned."

"Can you see now why you're not my favorite person?!"

"Put it away, George."

"What do you think you're doing, Elliot?" George wasn't intimidated but confused. "You think this is a game?"

"No, but we're gonna play one called motive, means, and opportunity. So you found a dead white woman in my barn, yeah?"

"Dammit, Elliot!"

"Dead woman, in my barn. Tragic, but how's that make it my crime?"

"It's your barn," Ned said.

"It's the bank's barn now. Wanna be the law. Know the law. Dead girl. I knew her, so that's opportunity. My barn, in theory, so that's means. She's the last person to see the guy I'm looking for, but I just up and kill her? Where's the motive?"

"She didn't have the information you were looking for. Or didn't want to talk to you," George said.

"Oh, we talked, alright. Supposition. My only connection to the girl is through the woman that hired me to find Alistair Williams. Willow Ellison is a jilted paramour."

"Paramour?" Ned tired of Elliot's grip.

"Means lover."

"Why couldn't you just say that?"

"So, my only contact got me so mad, I'd blow the entire case by killing her in a fit of frustration, ruining any chance to profit from our association. When I'm desperate for money. I stashed her in my own barn, which fifty other people have the keys to?"

"He's got a point, George. Can you let me go now?"

"Soon as George puts his gun away and agrees to talk."

"No one in a panic thinks things all the way through, Elliot," George said. "She's here to buy you some time."

"The Illinois River would buy me all the time in the world. Bringing her here is stupid. You ever know me to be stupid?"

Silence filled the room as George considered the possibility he was once again being manipulated.

"No. Cold and calculating, but not stupid," George said. Elliot let Ned go and returned his gun.

"Now, unless you'd shoot me in the back, I'm leaving."

"C'mon already, George. It's gettin' old. I told you how you have a hard-on for Elliot when that whole Pettingill mess went down."

"What Pettingill mess?"

"Dead," Ned said.

"Pettengill's dead?"

"Dead as he wanna be."

Elliot heard the familiar sound of the long neglected wooden pasture fence creaking. He stepped out from the tack room.

"What's the matter?"

Elliot shushed George. He walked toward the Dutch doors.

The creaking continued until the sound of wood falling atop itself filled the barn.

"He never got the fence fixed," Elliot said, as he took off running. Ned followed. George's shouts to stop were ignored. As the burly sheriff was no athlete, he walked briskly to the front of the barn and held post at the doorway, hand on holster. Elliot picked up speed on the decline of the access road. After a few seconds, when they were out of sight, George could hear a scuffle.

"Ned! What's going on?"

George trotted out from the barn but, a few moments later, they walked back up the hill. Elliot held a panicked Tom Molak by the arm. He was no match for either man, much less both, so he complied. He looked disheveled. There was a long rip down the back of his tan suit jacket. Ned held his gun on him while Elliot pushed him forward. Each time Molak tried to turn around, Elliot pushed him again.

"This is?" asked George, as the men went back inside the barn.

"Someone that can make life hard for you bumpkins if you don't let me go."

Elliot shoved him again.

"Easy, you prick!"

"Good to see ya, Tom. It's been a long time."

Elliot shoved Molak into the Farmall C. He kicked the man's legs apart and frisked him.

"You frickin' spooks can't spend a little time mending the fence?"

"Where you think you are, polak? The stockyards?"

"This is an expensive suit, Caprice."

"You look dashing in all five feet of it, half-pint."

Elliot pulled a .22 caliber semi-automatic from Molak's ankle.

"This belong to your sister?"

"I'm so frickin' gonna kill you when this is over."

"Maybe you're dead when this is over."

"Again, who is this?" George was exasperated.

"This here is Detective Sergeant Thomas P. Molak from the Chicago Police Department. My guess is ol' Tom here was the one what ran me off the road outside Springfield the afternoon I picked up the case I've been tellin' you about."

"I was just tailing you. You ran yourself off the road."

Elliot punched Molak in his right kidney. He went down hard on the barn floor. Elliot sat into a duck squat.

"What you know about Alistair Williams? And don't act like you aren't lookin' for him, too."

"Been lookin' longer than you."

"You were checkin' the Meat Locker in St. Louis for him."

"How do you know about that?"

Elliot pushed on Molak's forehead. The back of his head hit the Farmall.

"That's enough." George put his hand on Elliot's shoulder.

"Yeah, you're roughin' him up pretty bad there, Elliot."

"Tom here is from Chicago, like me. He knows how we do it. So this Negro and ofay you were lookin' for in St. Louis—"

"The white guy is Williams. Word is he's in bad with some nasty characters. That's why he's on the run."

"Tell me something I don't know. The colored fella runnin' wit' him is probably named Chauncey."

"The handyman from the McAlpins. Turns out he's missin' too. The two have been makin' enemies all over. They roughed up a guy in St. Louis pretty bad over a heroin buy. We heard about it from some underworld connects."

"This 'we' you're speakin' of. That someone from the trust board for McAlpin's estate?"

"Fuck you, Caprice. You're not gettin' me to spill."

"I figure you owe me some professional courtesy."

"I figure you're green and should get work as a security guard."

Elliot hopped up, snatched Tom Molak to his feet and

clubbed him in his ear. He next dragged Tom to the tack room and threw him to the floor, right next to Willow's corpse.

"Anyone caught up in Alistair Williams's secrets winds up dead. Like this girl, whose only mistake was she got herself hooked on his heroin. Now, I'm gonna to ask you once more."

Elliot made a show of rolling up his sleeves. He kicked him in the shoulder. Molak fell out on the barn floor.

"You two are the law! You're just gonna let this happen?" Molak was cowering.

"Southville is the boondocks, Mr. Molak," George said. "We do things a bit slower around here."

"Yeah," Ned said. "We'll probably get involved after the first finger is broken."

"Now, Molak!"

"My guy's name is Costas," Molak said.

"Costas Cartage, Limited? That Costas?"

"Yeah."

"That company belonged to McAlpin's first wife. They had a son."

"Jon Costas. It's an alias he uses while he tries to get out in front of what's goin' on."

"This is about his family's shipping company."

"McAlpin never gave it back after the divorce. It was a feather in his cap. Ever heard of a fella named Nickelson? A real heavy?"

"No."

"I guess Bill Drury never talked about him, huh?"

"What do you know about Drury?"

"What everyone knows. You dropped a dime on other cops to him and it got him killed. Ya know, when I found out you were lookin' for Williams, your name rang a bell. I did some digging and got the entire scoop on you. That night in Drury's garage. Those two stiffs you left out in his alley. Turnin' over your own is one thing. Killin' 'em is another. Guess you don't bleed blue. I don't judge. Me neither."

George and Ned glanced at each other. Elliot planted his knee in Molak's chest.

"I wanna know how you know I'm lookin' for Alistair Williams."

"The wife told us! Came right out with it. The entire trust board knows. They hope to Polish Jesus you don't find him."

"No way she told you."

"Whaddya think? She's savvy? She's masterminded a plan to take the McAlpins for all they got? She's a fuckin' maid, Caprice!" Molak snickered. "Sure, she's a cultured limey broad. So what. She's just a housekeeper. All she knows how to do is bat her eyes. No amount of playin' it up is gonna keep these rich fuckers from eatin' her lunch."

"You got no angle, figure I might, so you tail me. What happens when I find him, huh? You make sure he and I take the dirt nap together? One hole, two bodies?"

"It ain't like that."

"Don't tell me what it ain't like, you frickin' jagoff. Unless you got a dead body in your barn. For all I know, you killed this girl."

"My instructions were to find Williams. When my trail went cold, I was to tail you until you got far enough to where you may be amenable to a deal," Molak said.

"Yeah? What deal?"

"Costas—McAlpin—says he can straighten things out for you at the department in exchange for Williams. He's got the connections."

"I deliver him to you so he stays missing. Margaret gets shit. Is that the thing?"

"Bill Nickelson is currently the heavy on the South Side. The Chicago Outfit runs it since they killed Teddy Roe."

"Fuck me," Elliot said. "Teddy Roe was my friend. When?"

"August."

"Go on."

"About Ted Roe?"

"Costas and Nickelson, idiot."

"Nickelson doesn't give a shit about running numbers. His bread and butter is narcotics. From what I could tell, this Chauncey character worked for him, until he met Alistair. That's how he got a job in the house."

"Nickelson put a man on McAlpin? What for?"

"Dunno. They had some dealings together, but the new wife had McAlpin reevaluatin' his life. He wasn't the same, not cooperatin'. Maybe Nickelson wanted him watched."

"Or Nickelson had Chauncey kill him."

"Not likely. Nickelson needed McAlpin for his shipping concern. You just can't replace those political connections. My guess is the guy just got drunk and took a bath. Jon Costas figures giving Williams back to Nickelson is a peace offering to get him out of his family's affairs, once and for all."

Elliot backed off. Tom rose to his feet.

"Everyone wants to bargain for this fucker," Elliot said.

"Can't see why? Real pasty fella. Nothin' too special."

"You've seen him."

"Sure I have. Costas asked me to keep an eye on the family the day his *tatus* drank his own bathwater, if you get me."

"Got a photo?"

"Nope. Not gonna do you much good, anyhow. He's underground. He ain't comin' up unless you smoke him out."

Elliot paced the tack room, speaking to everyone, but no one.

"So Nickelson has McAlpin by the short ones somehow, McAlpin gives him full use of the shipping company. The old man's clout can get anything past customs."

"Sweet setup, right?"

"No one expects McAlpin to take a powder, so Nickelson has to fill the gap somehow. McAlpin took a liking to Alistair Williams. Margaret said he was giving him a leg up."

"Stupid, I know," Tom said.

"If Chauncey is Nickelson's man in the house, he has him

lean on Alistair to keep everything goin' smooth. Williams tries puttin' it back on with Margaret, has access to files, maybe can sign McAlpin's script."

"The family didn't announce he was dead right away. Those rich stiffs don't ever want to be caught holdin'. Always gotta get out front."

"How long?"

"A few weeks."

"Alistair fudged up the documentation enough where he's now signing off on cargo manifests on behalf of the company. Which must piss off your guy to no end."

"All Costas wants is his grandfather's shipping company back."

"Even if it means putting a bullet in Alistair Williams' head?"

"He'd prefer that, actually."

"Where do I find McAlpin's kid?"

"He owns half of the Greek Delta. Walk into any place down there, you just might find him sitting down over some souvlaki. He ain't like the rest of 'em. Tough character. Made of different stuff. Even has a little accent."

"Except I can't show my face in Chicago. You probably got the word out."

"What word you think I got, Caprice? I've been out of the department over a year."

"Yeah, but you white."

"I'm Polish, which ain't that frickin' white."

"You take what I know, then get me out of the way so you can finish the job yourself."

"Christ, Caprice. No one cares that you killed those two cops." Tom said. He shook his head. Elliot was stunned stiff. It was a secret he wanted to keep from George and Ned. Now Molak let it out of the bag.

"What's he saying?" George pulled Elliot around by his arm.

"Wait," Ned said. "Weren't you on the Chicago cops?"

"I didn't know they were cops until after I killed them."

"You killed your fellow police officers?" George seemed afraid for him. Elliot felt cold. It was finally time to spill.

"I informed on the brass who were mixed up in the Chicago Outfit."

"That'd probably have you dead." Molak snorted.

"That's why I couldn't mention it in St. Louis. I was a mole for Senator Kefauver's special committee."

"No shit?" Ned put his hand to his mouth. "I read about those hearings. That was big news."

Elliot stared off into his own memories. His voice shook. His eyes watered.

"One guy was old. Probably retired from the job. The other was some kid. They assassinated my friend, the writer Bill Drury, right in front of me. One of them got me in the shoulder. Probably thought I went down, too."

"Good Lord," George said. He put his hand on Elliot's arm.

"I...I got mad." Tears fell down Elliot's cheek. "If there was any chance Bill could survive, I wouldn't have gone after them, but they opened his chest up like a watermelon at a picnic. With his family upstairs having dinner in the kitchen."

Elliot felt weak at the knees. He wanted to throw up.

"I didn't even feel my own wound. I was filled with wrath. I chased them down and shot them both right in the middle of Western Avenue. Afterward, I made them as cops. I been runnin' ever since."

The entire barn was silent. Even Molak kept his mouth shut.

"I tried to do good, Georgie." Elliot wiped his eyes. "I can't say my intentions started out that way, but once I was in deep, I tried to do good."

George didn't speak. Neither did Ned.

"So look, is that what's on the wire or not? Don't try to con me, Molak. I really need to know."

"Where do you think you were? New York, where cops all kiss each other's asses? You idjit." Molak stood up. "Look, they were dirty. Why you think the young one was off the job?"

"He was off the job?"

"Got caught dealin' aitch in Rogers Park. Didn't kick anything up to his watch commander. Axed maybe a year before you plugged him."

Elliot was stunned into silence.

"That's why nobody gives a shit, ya bozo."

"That's the word?" Elliot didn't let it show, but he was hopeful.

"Hey, you're still in deep shit for bein' a rat, but you gave up the badge. It's yesterday's deep shit."

Elliot's jaw tensed.

"Just don't buy any tickets to the policeman's ball. And stay here, in this half-horse town."

Tom Molak's high-pitched laugh was full of scorn. Elliot wanted to hit him again. He also wanted to believe him, but he wasn't that desperate.

"What do you want me to do?" George said.

"Yeah, Elliot. How can we help?"

"Well, I think this property is clearly marked no trespassing."

"That it is," Ned said.

"Seems to me this gentleman was violating the law, no doubt trying to cover up his tracks for a murder."

"Now hang on a second," Tom said.

"Ned, would you please take former Detective Sargent Molak into custody," George said.

"Oh, for fuck's sake!"

"Right away, Sheriff. C'mon, big shot. You're spending the night."

Tom Molak was struck whiter than usual as Ned handcuffed him and led him out to the cruiser.

"How long do you need?"

"Twenty-four hours. Maybe he walks back to his car. Finds it on two flats."

"You've gotten yourself into a deep one, haven't you," George said.

"You got it wrong, Georgie Boy. Things are lookin' up." An uncomfortable silence filled the space between them.

"I didn't mean what I said about—"

"Yeah, you did."

Each stared at the other.

"Thanks for keeping Molak on ice."

Elliot walked out the barn door.

"What about...?"

Elliot stopped in his tracks. There was still Willow. He took a deep breath, which he released in a tremor of guilt.

"You're the sheriff, George. You can call the undertaker in town and ask for them to store the body until someone comes to claim it."

"Right."

"They just threw you into the job, huh?"

"We need to determine next of kin."

"I'll take care of that."

Elliot jogged down the access road. He ran the entire way to Miss Betty's. No chance Willow's murder would go unanswered. No chance in hell.

CHAPTER 16

Jon II was not his daddy's favorite, yet he still wielded enough power to dictate the bread and circuses. A lesser lord, yet still a McAlpin, thus to cross him was a risk. Elliot didn't want to confront him cold, so he called Elaine from Miss Betty's and asked her to check the files for intel related to the elder McAlpin's first marriage, the shipping company, anything that could even the odds in their sit-down. Or toe-down. He needed an angle. Elliot bet it could be found in the manner of his father's death. Maybe his stepmother, too. Or Margaret's advantageous union. If Jon Costas, McAlpin or whatever, was the stand-up guy Molak suggested, that'd have to piss him off. He'd start there.

Alistair's satchel in hand, he walked into the office as it was just hit by Hurricane Mikey. Tom Molak's boast rang true. Margaret had disclosed to the trust board she'd hired Elliot to seek out Alistair. They informed their probate attorney of their severe displeasure. Mike pulled Elliot into his office.

"Who are you to book yourself out for investigative work?"

"It just fell in my lap."

"You work for us, Elliot. It's our lap. I don't want some messy business—the wife screwing the driver while the husband's body is still warm—in our goddamned lap!"

"Margaret made her intentions quite clear."

"Margaret? She's Margaret now?" Mike struck the top of his desk. "Are you and the wife schtuppin'?"

"What?"

"Are you fucking Margaret McAlpin?"

"I can't believe I need to answer this, but no."

"This is what she does, Elliot. Pouring on the charm is how she casts a wide net. She's not naive."

"Neither am I."

"A lady that looks and sounds like she does? It's the most disarming thing she could be."

"You think I don't know that?"

"I think you're under pressure to do something for your uncle. You may not see it, but you wear your desperation like a Sunday suit."

Elliot took Mike's overreach as an affront but bit his lip. He tried reason.

"I heard what you said the day you gave me the assignment. How you wanted to be able to wrap this McAlpin thing up. All I have to do is get a line on Williams."

Mike looked up at Elliot.

"Don't."

"Don't what?"

"I only want to help, blah blah blah...you sound like my father."

"So do you."

The words shut Mike's mouth, if only for a second.

"I thought we were friends," Mike said.

"Friends trust one another's judgment."

"You should have come to me."

"Stop the world from spinnin' to get your permission for what only I can do?" Elliot shook his head. "There he is."

"There's who—"

"Isadora Rabinowitz. I figured he'd show up sometime."

Mike seethed.

"You insult me, just because you took an opportunity for yourself behind my back."

"I took an opportunity for this firm, that worked for us three ways!"

"I don't need you taking opportunities. I need you doing what I need you to do!"

Elliot resented nothing more in this world than being treated as the white man's nigger. He took off his hat and held it in both his hands as a means of self-restraint.

"Mike, when I met you, I was in a jam. I may not have had it all figured out, but I was alive. I was breathing. My heart was still beating. So don't act like you saved my life by making me the guy in the office that gets things done."

"I offered you a job," Mike said.

"You offered me a gap to cover. Call it what you wanna."

"So a little gratitude is out of the question?"

"You've seen my gratitude in my work. It's about something other than that, now ain't it?"

"Fine. What's it about?"

"You're like most ofays. You think you're entitled to keep the niggers you save."

"Don't make this about me! Your name on the door wasn't even dry and you were already angling for yourself."

"Seems as if my name was on the door for show."

Elliot threw open Mike's door. He marched out into the main room toward the door. Elaine looked up from the McAlpin file.

"Elliot, wait."

"I have to run."

"Where are you going?" Mike paced after him. Elliot spun around.

"I told Elaine not moments after the offer that I was doin' it. Tried to give her the office's cut. Take it up with her. I'm in a world of shit. I gotta go."

Mike turned to Elaine.

"What's this about?"

"Get out of his face about it, Michael."

"Dammit, Elaine, the McAlpin account makes this office!"

Elaine slapped her palms down on the desk and hopped to

her feet. She pointed her finger, but just before she could erupt, she righted herself. Her tone was hot, but she kept her voice low. It froze Elliot in his tracks, as it did Mike Robin.

"No. You make this office, Michael. You. Me. Now Elliot. If we didn't have these butter-and-egg men footing the bill, we'd be able to branch out, maybe take in another attorney. Or at least a paralegal. Finally do some work that really matters."

"Here we go," Mike said.

Elliot was smart enough to not say shit. He was leaning on the wall at that point, nursing his guilt that his decisions caused such disharmony. Mike Robin was the licensed attorney, but Elaine Critchlow was his queen. She would have her way. In smooth, cold tones of a greater bearing, she spoke fierce words.

"It's time you took a risk. Look at Elliot. He's been getting by on the seat of his pants for, what now? Three years?"

"Two," Elliot said. "I like to think of it as living by my wits."

"Shut up. You're a train wreck." Elliot shoved his hands in his pockets.

"These race cases we assist would be won outright if you were out front. Instead, you write the briefs and allow the other attorneys to argue. You do the work. They get the recognition."

"I don't care about recognition," Mike said.

"I am so sick of your dishonesty."

Elaine grabbed the file from her desk and shoved it at him.

"Have you looked at the McAlpin's files? Beyond the probate issues, I mean? Have you seen how far their dirt goes? Where their influence lies? Why do you think McAlpin turned to you, a small-time rural attorney in the state capital? Why didn't he let the meter run over at Winston and Strawn? It's because he was buying you. He wanted things kept from the rest of them because they're scary. He was paying us very well to remain in our lane. I'm tired of people expecting me to stay in my lane, Michael!"

Elaine showed no signs of slowing down. Mike rubbed his

eyes. Elaine walked around the desk, grabbed his hands and forced him to look at her. Elliot wanted to leave out of shame for tracking hell through the place, but something else had occurred in the space between the three: commonality of station. Each of them, in one way or the other, was sick and tired: Elliot of the bank and fellas like Creamer, Mike Robin of his father and the McAlpin trust board, and Elaine, who was angry at American men in general.

"We're not married for the same reason we haven't expanded for the same reason we're in Springfield for the same reason you don't speak to your father. Fear."

"You think I'm a coward."

"No. You're all man. It just seems you're no longer certain of yourself. Not like you were before we started...you know."

"The race cases bring real danger, Elaine. It's only going to get worse."

"I need you to tell me that?" Elaine said.

"If we keep going—"

"There are no ifs." Elaine folded her arms. "Get that straight right now."

"We can't take unnecessary risks."

"Unless your cousin Shapiro calls in a favor."

"You're gonna give me shit over my family, too?"

"Michael, you didn't have to help the sheriff that day. You certainly didn't have to take Elliot on afterward. As soon as he walked in here you got the color back in your cheeks."

Before he could reply, Elaine kissed Mike full on the lips.

"I know the man your father is. I know why you'd want to play it safe, but that's not you. Own up to being a Rabinowitz. Take back your balls."

She kissed him again. Mike seemed powerless to resist her loving logic. Elliot stared at the floor, embarrassed to witness their intimate moment. Elaine squeezed Mike's hands tightly, forcing her way into his fears.

"One day people will find out that I'm not just your paralegal. These race cases we work on are going to come to a head. It can't just be you and me anymore."

"You're right."

"Help Elliot," Elaine said. "And you..."

Elliot looked up at her.

"You can't do everything by yourself, fool."

Elliot frowned.

"How bad?" Mike looked over at Elliot.

"Dead body in my uncle's barn bad. The driver did it. Or the estate maintenance man."

"So what if you find the driver. You think these people are going to allow that to come between them and their millions?"

"Alistair Williams isn't the point anymore." Elliot held up the cargo documentation. "Jon II. Everything ties into his family's shipping company somehow."

"So we'll start there."

"All the files are already out," Elaine said. "My notes are right here. I'll order Chinese."

For the next two hours, Elliot and Mike pored over everything. They also called the state recorder's office, the county clerk and anyone else with insight on the family empire. They hammered out theories, eliminating angles until discrepancies became clear.

"Well I'll be goddamned," Mike said.

"Got somethin'?"

Elaine walked in holding the Chinese take-out.

"Did you go over these manifests?"

"Skimmed them once before I was arrested. In my barn."

"Looks like the driver gave us a little gift. See?"

Mike pointed to line items on a ship's register. Elliot and Elaine walked over to see.

"Is that what I think it is?" Elaine said. Elliot was embarrassed. He ran his fingers through his hair.

"You would've found it," Mike said.

"Not until it was too late. You're right. I have been

desperate. It almost cost us everything. I'm sorry."

"It's like what I tell the great emancipators. Not everyone can be Thurgood Marshall. Someone has to sift through the shit."

The phone rang. Elaine answered.

"One moment, please. Call for Elliot from a Frank Fuquay."

Elliot took the receiver.

"What's that'cha say there, Frank? I didn't expect you'd be callin' this soon."

"Hey there, Caprice. Me neither. So I'm in Gary, and my uncle hep'd me get on at this pressin' 'n stampin' place what make automobile parts. 'Cept just befo' I was ta start work, union guys showed up. About a hunned or so. They lined up, holdin' signs, callin' us colored workers scabs. Sayin' the man usin' Negros as cheaper labor. One fella tried crossin' the line and all hell broke loose. I know you tol' me to stay outta trouble, but it's ugly 'roun heah, man. I dunno what I should do."

"You got any of that cabbage I gave you left?"

"Nearly all of it. Did jus' what ya tol' me ta do."

"Get yourself on the first thang smokin' to Springfield."

Elliot looked around for a train schedule. Elaine was already holding one.

"Gimme the phone," Elaine said. "Frank? Hi, my name is Elaine. Where are you now?"

"In Gary, Miss Elaine."

"Alright...there's a four-forty-five, change in Chicago. You'll have to wait, but there's a six o'clock that'll have you in Lincoln by eight-thirty."

"That's no good," Elliot said. "What's the very next train to Union Station?"

"Frank?" Elaine said.

"Yes'm."

"I want you to get the four-forty-five from Gary to Union

Station in Downtown Chicago. Elliot will be there to pick you up at five p.m."

"Tell him to wear fightin' clothes," Elliot said, already headed to the door.

"You hear that, Frank?"

"Yes'm. Heard him fine. I'll be there, fo' sho'. Nice talkin' to ya, ma'am."

Frank hung up on his end. Elaine looked over at Elliot.

"What?" he asked, knowing she was judging him.

"What's that they say about the life you save?"

"May be your own?"

"Is the one you take care of."

Elliot grabbed the doorknob.

"Mike, if I don't have to put a hot one into Alistair Williams, you're gonna have to depose him right away. So many folks want to kill him, he almost makes me feel safe by comparison."

"Be careful," Mike said.

"Careful went out the window this mornin'."

Elliot walked out the office, out the building and hopped into Lucille. He pulled the .45 from the glovebox and loaded a fresh clip. This time, there'd be no more circuitous routes back into Chicago. This time, he'd drive straight through the heart of town. Alistair Williams was his, dead or alive.

CHAPTER 17

Elliot parked Lucille just outside the giant doors of Union Station, right on Canal Street. It was a brazen move, but he was riding a wave of fatigue, fear, and fascination. He'd never admit he was loving every minute of it. By all accounts, he should be avoiding the entire city, no less its enormous public transportation hub. Instead, he walked inside the headhouse and stepped briskly until he reached the station's Great Hall. He listened to the arrival announcement came over the loud-speakers. Frank's train was pulling in. He perched himself perpendicular to the doors, his shooting hand on the .45 down in his pocket for good measure. Within moments, countless commuters streamed past him in both directions, all bathed in the last light of the setting sun that shone through the gigantic skylight that covered half a city block. Soon the boyish brute emerged. It wasn't lost on Elliot how much safer he felt.

"Hey!" Frank smiled like a kid. He was dressed appropriately: dark blue dungarees, work boots, thick, black canvas jacket, black woven skull cap. He would've seemed like a tough longshoreman, were he not so darned giddy. He took Elliot up in his large arms.

"Glad to see ya, boss."

"Easy there, Frank. Easy," Elliot said, as he writhed out of Frank's monster grip. "Let's get the hell on."

They left as fast as he entered, hopped into Lucille, and burned rubber on Canal Street south to Harrison over to Blue Island Avenue. This triangle formed the capital of Greek life in Chicago: the Delta. While the city supported tens of thousands of hard working Mediterranean expats throughout its confines, their economic hub laid firmly within that triangle. Jon Costas owned more than his fair share of real estate in the area. The county recorder listed him as a deed holder for large portions of land that were needed for the University of Illinois' Chicago campus. That made him a heavy in his own right. In the Delta, he'd have to be one steely son-of-a-bitch to hold his own.

"Glad I could count on you again, boss," Frank said. "Didn't want to be bothered wit' all dat mess in Gary. My cousins talkin' 'bout standin' up to dem union boys."

"Well, I could use someone watchin' my back right now, so it worked out."

"I'm witcha, Caprice. What's the deal?"

"There's a fat cat goes by the name Costas, lives here in the Greek part of town. Gotta see him about his family business."

"You figure it ain't gonna go so well?"

"It's six in one hand, half-dozen in the other. I crossed his man, so either he likes what I say but don't like what I did or he don't care about either."

"Don't soun' good."

"I think I have an angle on what he needs more than anything. I'm gonna go inside. Wait here."

They parked outside Jane Addams' Hull House on Halsted. Elliot left Lucille running. Ten minutes passed. Frank grew concerned, until Elliot returned to the car clutching a copy of the *Greek Star* newspaper.

"There's a banquet for the Greek Professional Men's Club at the Congress."

Elliot made a U-turn at Arthington, which sent them southbound.

"You figure he's there?"

"Sometimes I had guard duty at these per-plate shindigs. One fat cat usually foots the bill as a show of wealth."

"What you want me ta do?"

"Know how to drive?"

"A lil', yeah."

Elliot pulled over to the curb, got out, and motioned for Frank to slide over to the driver's seat. Frank felt a twinge of fear at Lucille's power.

She ain't no pick-up truck, big man." Elliot pulled Frank's skull cap off his head. "Keep your eyes to yourself. Wait in the car."

"So I'm kinda like yo' driver den."

"Sometimes ya gotta play the part."

"I ain't complainin'. So you gonna catch dis boy when he's at sum function, dressed all nice 'n whatnot. He ain't gonna be wantin' ta fight if'n he need ta be puttin' on a smile 'n such."

"You avoid surprises by being the surprise."

"I like that," Frank said, smiling.

"If I'm too long, get on, call the office and explain what happened."

"Gotcha, boss."

Elliot hopped out, tipped the doorman and asked him where to find the banquet. Inside, he entered the Pullman Room, where the soiree was in full gear. This wasn't a gala full of stuffed suits, all seated and putting on airs, but high festivity. Elliot walked around the room, watching an enormous group of Greeks dancing the *hasapiko*. Shouts of "Opa!" and the noise of shattering wine glasses cut through the music played from the bandstand. These Greeks were mercantile players. Their ranks controlled the markets for commodities of all types in Chicago. Glad-handing would come only after strong wine, good food, and fiery dance. This banquet was feting the members of one of the hundreds of mutual benefit societies in the city. Chambers of commerce were places to shoot dice. Exchanges were great for stag parties. The best bars in town were in union halls, behind doors marked Private. Sweet home Chicago.

Elliot scanned the room for the sponsor's table, where his man would most likely be present. He made his way forward to a long row of settings, which were underneath an arrangement of architectural models. A middle-aged man Elliot placed in his late-fifties was seated, passing out handshakes to well-wishers and chocolate coins to kids. He walked over, removed his hat and looked him square in the eye. No peacocking, no posturing. He learned long ago that cultural melting pots held dangers the arrogant never anticipate.

"Mr. Costas," he asked, holding his gaze firm.

"How may I help you?"

"I'm here to help you. I believe we may have mutual business."

"You Caprice?"

He simply nodded.

"Tom Molak figured you for a fool."

Elliot smirked.

"You're interrupting my community business, Mr. Caprice."

"Alistair Williams. Costas Cartage. The death of your father."

"I need more than innuendo."

"Members of his household staff were planted by the same men that control your grandfather's shipping company."

"I know this," Costas said.

"A change of heart cost him his life and Costas Cartage. Williams was playing both sides to the middle, attesting for shipments himself."

Two toughs glared at Elliot from a banquet table across the room.

"Next time you'll need an invitation," Costas said.

"Once we compare notes, I'll have enough to piece this thing together, find Williams, and help you stop your family's downfall."

A pair of pretty, dark-haired twin girls wearing traditional Grecian dresses, floral wreaths in their hair, walked over. Jon Costas smiled, handed them chocolate coins wrapped in gold foil, and offered his cheek for kisses. The girls ran off to play. Elliot felt precious time tick away.

"Mr. Costas, I'm in the thick of it."

"The body in your barn. At the family farm you're about to lose."

Elliot played it cool.

"It's time you state your interest."

Costas gulped wine from its glass, afterward tossing it into the throng of dancers. "Opa!" he shouted, rising from his chair. He slapped Elliot on both his shoulders.

"You're an interesting man, Caprice. You have a slow hand. Not at all what I've heard. Meet me at my brownstone on Vernon Park Place in an hour. If I like what you have to say, I won't have you killed."

On the way out, Elliot scanned the room, making note of all the threatening faces watching him. Opa, indeed.

"This is my associate, Mr. Fuquay."

Frank nodded his head, partly to seem tough, partly because he didn't quite know what to say to a man such as Costas. Elliot felt bad for bringing the kid to a throw-down.

Jon Costas sat behind a large mahogany desk in his study. The prick just finished speaking real tough at the Congress, but now he was just like any other fat cat, perched behind symbols of power: leather writing pad, silver cigar box, velvet drapes over the large window that overlooked his horse stable—same ol' shit. All the office needed was a bit of taxidermy and it would seem just like the recreation room where he met Margaret McAlpin. Perhaps Costas could fool the genuflecting immigrants in his presence, but Elliot knew better. This was the prodigal son left out in the cold by dear ol' dad. Jon would have his show, and his supporting cast of Greek bruisers. The one standing behind Costas was Monk. He kept his one good eye on Elliot. He was every bit as big as Frank, but his stiff body movements gave away a lifetime of hard living. Elliot figured that Jon was loyal to Monk, which is the reason the cyclops's deficit was covered by Leonidas, the younger, scar-faced tough. He wore a slick gray suit which Elliot found tacky. He also wore a gun. He sat in a chair next to the only door in or out. Jon II came off as tough, but his posture and demeanor were far too comfortable. He wasn't a breaker but a fixer. Monk's presence was the tell.

He motioned to his cigar box. Elliot waved it off.

"Drink?"

"How about we get to it."

"Not accustomed to courtesy, huh?" Leonidas said.

"You threatened to kill me less than a half-hour ago. If you wanted to dance, you could've stayed at your ball, McAlpin."

"No one calls me that here," Jon II said.

"Jon H. McAlpin the second. Son of Jon McAlpin and Diana Kostopolous. Only grandson of the great Stavros Kostopolous, Greek shipping magnate. At least, until your daddy's family swindled him out of his company as some half-baked dowry."

"Measure your words, Caprice."

Monk seemed ready to strike at any moment. Frank held firm without flinching but his heart rate doubled.

"I also do my homework, McAlpin. I'm a lot more on the ball than your boy Molak. Now, we jaw-jackin' or talkin' bidness?"

Leonidas stood up, but Elliot pulled the 1911 and pointed it at him without glancing in his direction.

"Siddown, tough guy," he said. "You startin' to make me nervous."

Monk stepped forward. Frank, not missing a beat, brandished a standing lamp within his reach.

"That's enough," Costas said.

Frank started to sweat, but he looked over to see Elliot ready for blood. The air turned electric; the fear in Frank's body felt like purpose. Elliot swung the gun in Monk's direction. Frank, on cue, turned to Leonidas, covering Elliot's flank.

"I could have you killed where you stand," Costas said.

"Now I regret not shooting you in the face when you threatened me earlier."

The two men stared one another down, until Elliot holstered his gun.

"So, any interest in what I can do for you?"

Elliot's shift to cool disarmed Jon II. He felt exposed. It was something that didn't occur often.

"Could we perhaps speak in private?" Jon said. Elliot knew Jon had folded.

"Yeah? What about?"

"About how perhaps Tom Molak wasn't the right man for the job," Costas said.

"Easy to see he would...come up short."

Both men erupted in nervous laughter. Frank finally exhaled.

"I'm sure your associate would be comfortable in the anteroom. Leonidas, get Mr. Caprice's man a drink."

"I don't drink," Frank said. "Not liquor, anyhow."

"I'll get ya a pop," Leonidas said. He winked, in reassurance they were square. Frank looked to Elliot for permission which unsettled Elliot a bit.

"It's alright, Frank. We'll be done here real soon," Elliot said. Frank followed Leonidas out the door. Monk followed Frank. It seemed choreographed.

Jon II presented Elliot his hand.

"I apologize."

"Forget it," Elliot said. Jon's grip was strong.

"I see my sources were wrong."

"I won't ask about what. Or whom."

Jon II loosened his tie. He exhaled in a long, pained release.

"It's all smoke and mirrors, isn't it?"

"Folk think they know you well enough, they'll screw you. Show 'em too little, they won't trust you. Then they screw you anyhow. It's all a game."

"How close are you to locating Williams?"

"He hasn't fled."

"How do you know?"

"The dead body in my barn."

"A message, no doubt."

"Stop seeking."

"But you're not going to stop."

Elliot paused as he thought of Willow's sweet face, dead. It made him want to kill something.

"That girl didn't deserve to die," he said. "Also, I made a commitment."

"To my father's wife?"

"To my friend and employer."

"Attorney Robin," Jon said.

"Your family's affairs have taken enough of their time. They want to lessen your influence."

"Yes," Jon said. "It is rather hard to surmount our...beneficence."

"You got it bad for your family."

Jon walked toward the window. He stared outside at his two horses in the stable.

"What I've seen of Negros, Caprice, is they love their own."

"We only appear that way in relation to white folks. We also do each other dirty. Sometimes worse."

"But you stop short of genocide."

"Go on."

"My father never loved my mother. He didn't care about her in the least. How they managed to sire me is a mystery."

"It was all about your family's shipping business."

"It was more than a business. My grandfather was the pride of Greece. Our roots are in the Aegean Peninsula."

"The Sea People."

"He assembled that company by convincing men to captain and crew for him on a promise. Just his word. No deals beyond the extension of his character. Within ten years, they controlled shipping throughout the Mediterranean."

"Gravitas," Elliot said, remembering Margaret's observations.

"The McAlpins wanted *that*. To claim that pride, that strength, for themselves."

"So why sell your company to folks like that?"

"He wanted to expand beyond the Mediterranean. Carry the promise of Greece to all places where Greeks emigrated."

"Rich man's ego," Elliot said, shaking his head.

"I never said my grandfather was perfect. Just that he had character. What started as contracts for the McAlpins became friendship, resulting in an offer to unify around a marriage. I'm embarrassed to admit that this conformed to my grandfather's old world sensibilities. He sacrificed my mother to the wolves."

"You as well."

"Yes," Jon said.

"I know a little something about that." Elliot resisted the urge to empathize. Seeing himself within a wealthy white man was just too much for one day.

"My family sees everything through a prism of lack. It drives them—us—insane. We only want what we don't possess. When we're no longer lacking, the desire runs out."

"Which is how Costas Cartage sat on bricks until it was co-opted by this fella Molak mentioned. Bill Nickelson."

"A former lieutenant of Al Capone."

"Capone had a lot of lieutenants. The guy that fetched his morning paper got to be a fuckin' lieutenant."

"Nickelson was the real thing. A Dutchman. A Viking."

"I still don't get how a gangster can squat on an entire fleet of cargo ships, owned by one of the richest families in America."

"The War Department turned to many private citizens during the conflict."

"Like those Murder, Incorporated guys gettin' paid to rough up Brown Shirts?"

"An apt comparison."

"What would they need y'all for? They have the Navy."

"Navies are used in combat, Caprice. Governments were at war, not corporations. Ford continued operations in Germany until 1942. Victrola maintained its partners in Japan, even while we were bombing them."

"Bill Nickelson used your grandfather's boats to run a god-damned charter service for captains of industry." Elliot shook his head in disgust. "Christ on tha cross."

"Patriotism over business gave us the Depression. That's the only reason Congress was prepared to keep us out of number two, Pearl Harbor be damned. Allowances had to be made."

"Good men died over there."

"Good men die everywhere," Jon II said. "Nickelson knew the seas. He also had the smuggling connections so the government put him and our family together. My father vetted the deal and took oversight. It made him feel patriotic."

"After the war, why didn't your family take the business back?"

"For some reason, my father turned his attention from it. Once my stepmother died, he fell into a malaise."

"In comes Alistair Williams."

"Then my grandfather's life's work sits at the mouth of the Calumet River, a whore for evil men. Drug smuggling. Human trafficking."

"Evidence suggests he's in too deep. Wants to get out."

"What evidence?"

"Shipping manifests. Customs forms. He figured he had leverage, but Nickelson don't care. He'll kill him out of spite."

"What's next, Caprice?"

"Get a line on either Williams or the handyman. Beat the truth out of 'em. Drag 'em back to justice. If I don't have to kill 'em."

"I don't see how that solves my problem."

"You didn't hire me to solve your problem."

"I'll triple what my father's wife is paying you."

"Seems like a bargain."

"Name your price," Jon said.

"Twenty-five thousand, plus you use your connections to have the cops' bounty taken off my head. For that, I'll get you the driver plus what you need to stick it to your family."

"Your agreement with Margaret?"

"I don't see any conflict."

"She wants Williams."

"When you're done with him, she can have him. If you're inclined to make sure there's a piece of him left."

"All that's on your agenda is money."

"I have my own motivations, and they ain't ya bidness. You keep your goons out my hair. If I see your man Tom Molak again, I'm gonna shoot 'im."

"I have reports from him that may prove useful."

"No thanks. His work is sloppy. I'll manage."

Elliot rose to extend his hand in Jon's direction.

"So, what're we doin'?"

Jon and Elliot shook on the deal.

"I've experienced my fill of betrayal, Mr. Caprice."

"You're not gonna threaten me again, are you?"

"No. I just want you to know I am far different than the rest of my family."

"Costas, that much is obvious."

Double-dipping was taboo. Elliot would have preferred to make no commitments at all. Now he had promised to track down Alistair Williams for opposing sides of the McAlpin family. That was sloppy. Still, he needed Jon's insight. If he didn't work for Costas, Elliot would be working against him. That would be stupid. Bill Nickelson made the number of parties searching for Williams and Chauncey three. Elliot controlled the interests of two, thus the odds were on his side. Bottom line: Alistair Williams would, at best, face the law. At worst, he'd catch a hot one. Disappointment was inevitable. Better for it to be experienced by Nickelson.

Elliot hung a left onto Lake Shore Drive off Congress Parkway. Frank finally spoke up.

"See here, boss," he said. "We got a plan?"

"The gal that wound up dead," Elliot said, keeping his eyes on the road that was barely visible in the downtown fog. "We're going back to her place."

"Cops ain't gonna be there?"

"Not as long as Costas keeps his promise," Elliot said. His grief was palpable. Frank feared it colored his judgment.

"These fellas what killed her," Frank said. "They wuzn't honest folk, but she ran wit' 'em jus' tha same."

"What are you getting at, Frank?"

"My mama got a sayin'. 'Jes 'cuz you tha last one to touch it don't make it yo' mess.'"

"When's the last time you spoke to her?"

"We ain't got no telephone back home, and I ain't good wit' writin'."

"You're wrong to leave her worryin'. When we finish this, we'll sit down and write her a letter."

"Soun' good to me. She shol' be interested ta heah that I was locked up fo' two months an now I run tha streets playin' cops 'n robbers wit' tha fella what beat me up in jail."

Frank laughed aloud. It reminded Elliot to stay out of that dark place inside himself. It was time to cast everything into the light, whatever the outcome.

Frank Fuquay covered the hallway for prying eyes as Elliot felt around the door frame for Willow's key. It was gone. Another bit of betrayal from Alistair.

"She got a back do', maybe?"

Elliot put a swift kick above the doorknob, cracking the frame. The door flew open. Frank down the hallway.

"Building is full of junkies," Elliot said. "Get inside."

They entered, shut the door. Elliot found the light switch on the wall. Nearly everything Willow cared about was destroyed. LPs were out of their sleeves and broken in pieces. Her cameras were dismantled and tossed out onto the floor. The speakers of her hi-fi were kicked in. Furniture was overturned, the backs of which were sliced open. Even her albums of photographs she took of her beloved Jazz greats were ripped apart.

"Somebody beat us to it," Frank said.

"This is Nickelson's shit." Elliot waded through the mess, carefully moving debris. "Alistair knew her hiding places. Hate gets in the way of the job."

"What are we supposed to make outta all dis?" Frank shook his head.

"You wanna find a person's secrets? Find the person."

"Huh?" asked Frank.

"She was an artist, Frank. All that mattered to her was music and musicians. When it came to what she loved, she couldn't be bothered to eat. She didn't clean up after herself. Most gals use their washroom as a beauty salon. I don't think she even took a piss in there."

Elliot knelt and picked up a postcard on the floor. On the front was a painted image of a farmland Christmas scene. He turned it over to see a postmark from Madison, Wisconsin. In elegant penmanship read a polite yet revealing message:

> Willow,
>
> Ma and Dad didn't want to worry you, but he's been sick. I think you should come home, partly because I miss you and because Ma needs you. Dad does too, but he won't admit it. He's stubborn like you. Please try for Xmas, 'kay?
>
> —Love, Sissy

"Nickelson is lookin' for a man," Elliot said. "Williams is lookin' for a satchel that's back at my office."

"So what're we lookin' fo'?"

Elliot put the postcard in his pocket. He surveyed everything, turning to take it in, all at once.

"A hint."

"Come a'gin?"

"Willow was bold, Frank. I saw her risk her life just to get a photograph. She was upfront. Women like that don't hide things."

"Twuzn't no reason ta tear up her flat, den."

"Nope. Willow cared about music. Colored fellas. And drugs, in that order. Anything other than that is an answer. Don't go diggin' tho'. Just look. Let it reveal itself to you."

Elliot began his search by gently moving things around.

"Rule things out. What doesn't fit? What doesn't belong?"

Frank watched him, partially mesmerized, partially inspired. He wondered if all detectives seemed this crazy. Minutes turned into over an hour. Both men were exhausted from sifting through the shattered remains of Willow's short life. Elliot found nothing in the rubble nor in any of the cabinets. He was in the bathroom searching in vain when Frank called out to him.

"Caprice!"

Elliot headed to the bedroom, but Frank met him in the hallway. He was holding a piece of clothing.

"Whaddya got?"

"You said she wuzn't big on housework, so I went through her laundry."

Frank tossed a garment at him. Elliot unfurled it. It was a tacky men's bowling shirt: black, tan plackets.

"Maybe it's nuthin', but it seemed out of place, seein' she was a girl 'n it's a fella's shirt 'n all."

Elliot was transfixed on its details, including the bit of embroidery on the pocket: Archer-35 Recreation. He also couldn't help but notice grease stains on the shirttail.

"Don't think Willow was a bowler," Elliot said.

"So we head over to that bowlin' alley 'n maybe find our man?"

"That bowling alley is in the worst part of town for a colored fella, Frank. Know what I mean?"

"But you goin', aintcha?"

"Yeah," Elliot said. "Doesn't mean you have to. Might be better for you to take off."

Truth told, the manner in which Elliot cautioned Frank frightened the Big Fella, but Elliot had been looking out for him since the Meat Locker. The fight that could've gone worse. The barrel check. The cash to get himself straight. There was no way Frank would white on him.

"Well, you did tell me to put on my fightin' clothes," Frank said.

They were stopped at a red light on Cermak when Frank couldn't take the quiet anymore. He'd rather flap his gums than shake in his boots.

"So, you figure we gonna die tonight?"

Elliot didn't respond and instead thought of the bank and their chains on his land. Thought of all the thumbs he had broken for Izzy, just for him to turn away from him at his own time of need. He pictured Drury's kids finding their daddy in the garage, head blown off. He thought of every white person, from his mother on down to John Creamer, who cared for their own agenda more than him. He thought of Willow Ellison. She was a sweet girl that hadn't hurt anyone. She didn't deserve to die the way she had.

The light changed. Elliot pulled forward. He gripped the wheel so tight his knuckles were alabaster. He spoke as if he was chewing glass.

"Not tonight, Frank. Not us."

CHAPTER 18

Occasionally Elliot worked patrols in Bronzeville, across the neighborhood border from Bridgeport. One night, when called to a domestic disturbance outside a tenement, he quelled a severe beating carried out on a Negro teen by his father. It had spilled out onto the street for all to see, so Elliot was obligated to cuff the man until he was calm. He asked him what the boy had done. The father said he caught his son returning from Bridgeport.

"You know they'll kill a nigga all the way dead," he said. "I figure, if I only beat 'im half-dead, I'm still savin' his life."

Elliot uncuffed the man, then told the boy to listen to his father, or else he'd arrest him.

They parked Lucille directly outside the stairway that led up to the second-floor home of Archer-35th Recreation, home of the Petersen Classic, the biggest, most crooked bowling tournament in America. Twenty-two steps into hell. Twenty-two steps Elliot and Frank took, side-by-side, until they reached the threshold where they were greeted by the stench of stale cigar smoke and spilled beer. The stares were immediate as patrons interrupted their precession into the bowling room to turn to each other and ask the obvious question, "Did you see those two niggers?"

"You weren't lyin', were ya, boss?"

"Let 'em stare."

As they passed the saloon, Elliot recognized it as one of the speakeasy locations on Bill Drury's list. It was a Capone-era outpost for distributing booze. Elliot finally hated Al Capone, much in the same way a long-suffering wife could finally have enough of her husband's bullshit.

He held the bowling shirt in his hand as they walked over to the counter where Murray, the night man, was sorting scoring sheets. When they saw the team board, Elliot realized it was public employee league night making them as safe as ice cubes on hot asphalt.

"You the manager?"

"You're causin' a scene," Murray said. He likely thought himself decent for delivering the warning.

"A scene, huh?"

Elliot stepped toward the counter, but Frank stepped in front of him. He leaned forward, sticking out his butt, which moved Elliot back.

"Say, boss," Frank said, laying on the poor country boy act extra thick. "We'z lookin' fo' a few friends of ourn, said we wuz s'posedta have a meetin'."

"You're in the wrong bowling alley, fella," Murray said. Elliot followed Frank's play after he decided to chew him out about it later.

"Our friend Chauncey said he had it all arranged," Elliot said.

"Niggers don't handle business here," Murray said, now eyeing them both. "Chauncey keeps the pinsetters runnin'. That's it."

"Our mistake," Elliot said.

"Thank ya anyhow," Frank said. He grabbed Elliot by the arm and made toward the door. Elliot snatched away to turn back toward Murray.

"Say—"

He shoved the bowling shirt at him.

"He left this in my car."

"Leave it on the counter. I'll give it to him when he's on his break."

Once Elliot and Frank were back on the street, Elliot started in on him.

"What the hell...!"

"Boss, I'm sorry," Frank said. "But you lookin' crazy."

"He's here. I'm dragging him out."

Elliot turned toward the stairs. Frank quickly sidled in front of him. He stared meekly at his shoes but didn't move.

"Goddamnit, Frank."

Frank didn't look up. He shrugged his massive shoulders. The contrast between Frank's size and his deference gave Elliot pause.

"I know you wanna make this fella pay," Frank said, almost at a whisper. Elliot checked his flank to make sure the natives weren't lining up.

"We know he in there. He don't know we out here," Frank said. "They got a problem wit' colo'd folk comin' in through the front."

Elliot walked to the corner and Frank followed. When they made it to the alley, they both saw the fire escape.

"Let's get our man," Elliot said. Big Frank yanked the ladder release. They climbed up and found the fire door propped open. Elliot closed it behind them.

The noise of the automatic pinsetters was deafening—motors and gears, all working together to collect the hardwood pins, inserting them, one at a time, into the slots on their carriages.

It was a busy night at Archer-35th. All eighteen lanes were in operation. The floor was slick with sooty dust and grease. The faint utility lights produced ominous shadows. Elliot stood facing the service aisle, which was only narrow enough for single-file travel. They saw a head peer out from an adjoining recess. They were spotted.

Elliot proceeded down the tight corridor. He and Frank had to angle their bodies to move forward. Elliot pulled his gun, but only to affect, as they needed Chauncey alive. The metal monsters at his side churned. A retaining wall jutted out along the corridor. Elliot went first, creating a blind spot. When he emerged from the cubby, he felt a hard thud on his forearm, followed by dull pain. Chauncey, holed up in a tool cubby, had emerged brandishing a large Stillson wrench. Elliot sympathetically fired the 1911 on the way down to the floor. The bullet ricocheted off the machinery, decoupling a pinsetter's arms from its gears. The mindless monster continued its function. Chauncey meant business. He turned to face Elliot, wrench in striking position, but before he could get another blow off, Frank Fuquay was upon him. He hooked one of his large arms through the space between Chauncey's neck and shoulder, forming a half-nelson that must've felt like an iron yoke. His free hand had Chauncey's left wrist. He yanked down, loosening the wrench from his grip. It fell to the floor, about two inches from Elliot's head. Chauncey put up a fight, but Frank saw fit to break his neck.

"No, Frank! We need him!"

Elliot picked up the .45, rose to his feet, and raised the gun waist high. Chauncey continued to struggle against Frank until he took a face full of wall. He collapsed to his knees. Elliot shoved the business-end of the 1911 in his chin.

"Nice or nasty. Either way."

Frank kicked Chauncey in his back for good measure. The concussed handyman nodded his resignation.

Frank was now in front. Elliot marched Chauncey, gun in his back, forward through the tight space back to the fire door, only to find it was now stuck closed.

"Lock's broken," Chauncey said. "That's what the brick is for."

"Guess we're goin' out the front."

"Like hell we are." Elliot rapped Chauncey in the back of the head.

"When I wanna know somethin' from you, I'll put a bullet in you."

Frank pressed on. Elliot put the gun back in his holster.

"Don't make me show you how fast a draw I am," he said, punctuated by another slap on the back of the head.

As they entered the bowling room, all eyes were on the ragged trio. Elliot's clothes were dirty from his fall. Frank was just big and black. The bloodied maintenance man was overkill. They stepped out of the bowling room and into the main lobby. Murray saw the three headed toward the doorway. He noticed the blood on Chauncey's face, grabbed a baseball bat he kept behind the counter, walked over and stopped in front of the foyer, blocking their exit. Frank turned around to notice a large group of white men advancing from the other direction. The one at the center was a youngish beefcake. He walked like he wanted everyone to notice he lifted weights.

"You alright, Murray?"

"These guys came in here earlier looking for the handyman."

"Seems like they're lookin' for trouble," said Beefcake.

"Me and this fella got bidness," Elliot said. He put a tight hold on Chauncey's collar. Three more of Murray's cohorts showed up, which brought the total to eight.

"Yeah? What business is that?" said Beefcake, rolling his shoulders.

"The kind I don't need help mindin'," Elliot said. He pulled the .45.

Two men tried muscling Frank, but he broke away. Back to back, guard up, this was now the scrap that Elliot told Frank to suit up for. Encircled by bigots, one would think Chauncey would help, but it appeared he reserved his worst for his own kind, though he had enough sense to stay put. A younger man lunged toward Frank and swung a pool cue. Frank raised his left forearm to block the strike, which broke the cue in two. Frank cold-cocked him. Elliot had enough. He fired at Murray, splintering his baseball bat. Their attackers froze in their tracks.

"You got enough bullets for all of us, halfie?!" said Beefcake. The easy answer was the hot one Elliot put right at the top of tough-guy's man-breast. He went down hard. Elliot figured the muscle-head could take it.

"The cops are on their way, nigger!" Murray was kneeling behind a bench.

"I am a cop, ofay!" Elliot shouted it instinctually. Frank wasn't sure what to think of it.

"Bullshit," yelled someone from the crowd.

"Oh, I'm the law, which means I can kill about half of you ofays right now and get a fuckin' medal for it. Now back the fuck up!"

Elliot fired another shot in the wall behind the mob, the whistling heat from the large caliber slug rushing past the faces of two cocky goons. One bolted. The other threw his hands up and backed away. The rest followed suit, except for two. They helped Beefcake to his feet.

"He needs a doctor."

"So get 'im one!"

Elliot held his gun on them as they helped their buddy down the stairway. Frank dragged their quarry down the stairs. Elliot remained, covering their flank for a moment before he ran down the stairs himself. Frank and Chauncey stood by Lucille. Within moments, Elliot saw mortal terror in the handyman's eyes. He turned to see three sets of Buick headlights headed toward them.

"Nickelson?"

"I'm a dead man," Chauncey said.

Elliot opened the trunk, threw Chauncey inside, and tossed Frank the keys after he slammed the hood over the handyman.

"Get her goin'!"

Elliot aimed the 1911 toward the first car. He squeezed off three shots. The left headlight of the lead sedan blew out. All three cars skidded. The sound of sirens grew louder. Bowling alley patrons found the nerve to run down the stairs to witness the action. Frank threw Lucille into reverse and got out of the way. Elliot jumped into the driver's seat and floored it.

He pulled a donut, ran atop the curb and destroyed a newspaper machine before he pushed Lucille, full throttle, eastbound on 35th Street. The first squad car began its pursuit at Ashland Avenue. They met the second at the intersection of Morgan and 35th when Elliot swerved to avoid the second car's reckless attempt at blindsiding them. Frank held onto the sides of his seat.

"They're calling in our positions," Elliot said, as he remembered his police training. If they didn't change their course, they'd soon hit armed roadblocks. Wild evasive maneuvers weren't possible, as they were hemmed in by throngs of jovial pedestrians strolling from nearby Comiskey Park. At Wallace Street, Elliot slammed both feet on the brakes to avoid plowing into a crowd of jaywalkers. The Chicago White Sox must have played that night. Neighborhood fans flooded the streets to head home or adjourn to nearby taverns. One of the men they nearly ran over slammed his hand atop the hood, shouting "niggers"-something or other. Elliot noticed the man wore a Minnie Miñoso jersey before Lucille's back window blew out.

"Head down, Frank!"

"Who you tellin'!"

If Lucille's hull didn't hold up, Chauncey would wind up dead before he could be of any use. If Elliot didn't do something drastic, Frank Fuquay's first trip to the big city could wind up his last. He jerked the wheel hard to the right, floored the gas, and Lucille leaped onto the sidewalk. He leaned on the horn, speeding down the pathway, screaming for everyone to clear out. The multitudes scattered for safety, rendering the intersection complete pandemonium, thus ending the chase. Once he passed Normal Avenue, he turned right back onto the road, hit a left, plowed through a wooden fence, and crossed over into the Illinois Central rail yard that served the freight lines south of downtown. Elliot cut off Lucille's headlights. They drove slowly as they crossed tracks, avoiding stacks of pallets and railroad ties. Soon they could exit farther south, at Pershing Road, where they would have a straight shot into the relative safety of the Kenwood neighborhood. Frank chewed on the air. Elliot realized he had to give the Big Fella a break so he turned right onto Langley Avenue. A left onto Oakwood Boulevard led to a darkened unpaved alleyway across from the DuSable Hotel, the Waldorf-Astoria for colored folk in Chicago. It sat in a position of prestige in the Drexel Square area where the streets were lit like springtime in Paris. The fast-house hotel. The Mocambo Lounge at the corner. A Powers Cafeteria that stayed open all night up the block. It was one of the few places where colored folk could be left alone to play big shot. No police searches for them would make it that far south. Elliot shut off the engine.

"You okay?"

Frank nodded in the affirmative but soon went about as green in the face as someone so black could get. He exited the passenger side to vomit whatever he had for lunch onto the gravel. Elliot got out, walked over, and handed him back his bandana.

"I washed it," Elliot said. Frank shook his head in disbelief.

"Shouldn't we keep on movin'?"

"Let's find out where we're goin'," Elliot said. He knocked on Lucille's back bumper. Frank stood at the ready in case Chauncey got squirrelly.

"Let me the fuck out of here!"

Elliot opened the trunk. Chauncey spilled out onto the gravel, coughing. Elliot said nothing, only staring death into him.

Frank couldn't help but look over at the DuSable, well-dressed colored folk streaming in and out, loud, wild, carefree. Expensive cars pulled up, driven by people the same race as the valets. Women were dressed loud and spoke loud. Everyone lived loud. He turned back to Elliot and Chauncey, two more colored men, one angry enough to kill the other. He was a long way from Yazoo.

"Let's get him in the car."

Frank pulled Chauncey off the ground, Elliot opened the rear passenger side door and Frank threw him in. He slid next to him and wedged him against the door. Elliot got in the driver's seat, pulled the .45 and held it at Chauncey's chest.

"Which one of you killed her?"

"Killed who?"

Elliot smashed Chauncey atop his head.

"Willow Ellison. Which one of you did it?"

"I didn't know she was dead!"

Elliot shoved the barrel into Chauncey's sternum. Frank feared Elliot would kill him right there so he threw a shot to Chauncey's temple. The side of his head hit the window.

"The man asked you a question."

"Alistair went back there to get his satchel," Chauncey said. "Maybe something happened. I wasn't there."

Elliot raised the barrel of his gun so that it hit Chauncey's chin and pushed his head back.

"That's all I know."

"Williams."

"McAlpin has a boathouse in Jackson Park."

"That's city property," Elliot said.

"Donated by the McAlpins. It's the only house in the harbor. He's there now."

Elliot handed the gun to Frank.

"If he tries anything—"

"Shoot 'im," Frank said. He shoved the business-end of the .45 in Chauncey's gut. Elliot pulled out of the alley. Off they sped, to find Alistair Williams, once and for all.

CHAPTER 19

Elliot's mother was once a student here, walking Midway Plaisance, basking in the Beau-Arts architecture, its powerful statuary and gigantic limestone buildings which seemed more built for the gods than man. Perhaps that was the point. The fat cats of Chicago didn't see themselves as the meat and potato, strong-arm politicians they were. They wanted to be more so they built more and acted as-if. When that didn't work, they consumed. Food. Objects. Wealth. People. All in the name of girth. All in the desire to meet their gods at eye level.

In the aftermath of the World's Columbian Exposition, when Chicago put its most audaciously majestic idea of itself forward, these parkways, walks and monuments stood as reminders that it was yet a modern paradise. Crime seeped in over time. No matter the rules against miscegenation, the blurred lines between the neighborhoods produced strange bedfellows, of which Elliot was a product.

As he piloted Lucille toward Jackson Park, he could see the University of Chicago to his left. He wondered what she must have looked like, carrying her books, perhaps walking alongside other students, discussing high-minded ideas about life, class, and race. He wondered if she knew she'd meet his big, black daddy. If she knew she'd have his child. If she knew she would leave him in Southville or first considered raising him herself. Leaving Elliot to a life in which, to compensate for his alienation, he minded other people's business instead of having his own. Even now, as his new best friend held his gun on a dope-pushing charlatan he kidnapped in full view, he still wondered if it all was about some emotional response to being pulled from her teat too early. Perhaps Elliot's troubles were formed of the self-doubt all young colored men experience when they exist in a world that births them to eat them. Perhaps it didn't matter where his mama was or that she didn't want him. He looked up at the sculptural details along the flattened roofs covered in polychrome tiles. He could've sworn the chimeras were laughing at him.

"You're gonna let me go, right? I'm risking a lot helping you," Chauncey said.

"You're helpin' yourself. Stupid to think you could steal the syndicate's aitch and fatten up."

"It's not about the drugs. Nickelson has three ships full of contraband he can't bring into port because they won't make it through customs."

"No more connections," Elliot said.

"Before he died, McAlpin made Alistair the agent of process. Called it a promotion."

"McAlpin wanted to get rid of his new wife's old beau."

"Nickelson's haul this time out is just too big. He can't sink the boats because of his partners. His only chance is to get Alistair to attest to the manifests," Chauncey said. "We figured we'd hold Nickelson up for money. Take advantage of his desperation."

"And get the entire Chicago Outfit up your ass. Smart, Chauncey."

"We collect on the score. Alistair signs. We fade."

"You don't disappear from problems this big, Chauncey."

Frank nodded, knowing Elliot spoke from experience.

They crossed Cornell Avenue into Jackson Park onto a plot of land likely unknown to most, situated between the lagoons and the Museum of Science and Industry where tall stalks of wetland vegetation hid a quarter acre from view.

"Up here, past this marsh," Chauncey said, as they came to a short arched bridge that passed over the small inlet between the

East Lagoon and the reflecting pond adjacent the Japanese gardens. Once they reached the other side, Jackson Park Harbor in the distance, they saw the rundown wooden structure that was the McAlpin's boathouse. It was decrepit, beaten down by the harsh Chicago weather. It could have tipped over on its side into the inlet. It sat two stories. It could have been lifted from the banks of Cape Cod. Another blue-blooded conceit by the less than worthy Midwestern elites.

"You shol' played the white man's nigger, didn't ya, Chauncey? Commandeered the boathouse 'n everything."

"Not me. Alistair. He was their boy. I'm just the help's help. You're gonna let me go, right?"

Elliot drove onto the bird trail. Passing through an open gate, he noticed a red glint from his taillights coming off something on the road. He stepped out the car to see cut heavy gauge chain in front of the gate, same as at the family farm. He returned to the car, turned off the ignition, and cut out the headlights.

"McAlpin is dead. So is his end," Elliot said. "Nickelson loads up one last score—a big one—figuring it's on Alistair Williams's neck. He attests, it all comes into port, and Nickelson is in the clear. As long as you two are dead after."

Elliot reached in the back seat to yank Chauncey forward.

"Which one of you had the bright idea to extort a fuckin' mob boss?"

Elliot socked Chauncey hard in the mouth.

"Boss!"

"Alistair." Chauncey spat blood on himself.

"Which one of you decided to hide the goods in Willow Ellison's apartment?" Elliot punched Chauncey again.

"Alistair." Elliot pulled him forward, nose to nose.

"Which one of you killed her when you found out she gave them to me?"

"I did." Chauncey's voice sounded like a snake's hiss.

Elliot snatched the 1911 from Frank's large hand. He exited

the driver's side, opened the rear door and snatched Chauncey out onto the ground. He kicked him hard in the back.

"Get up."

Chauncey rose. Elliot grabbed him by the back of his collar. When he jammed the barrel of the gun in the back of Chauncey's neck, it sounded as if a vertebra snapped.

"Walk."

Stunned, on wobbly legs, Chauncey complied. As they walked forward toward the house, Frank got out of the car.

"Boss, wait!"

"Stay in the car, Frank."

"Caprice, please. Just…"

Elliot continued Chauncey's death march forward.

"All I wanted was the satchel," Chauncey said. "Alistair didn't hide it well enough. She found it. Started using the aitch."

Elliot kicked Chauncey's legs from underneath him. He tumbled down a short embankment.

"She got to talking about you in that drugged slur. Elliot Caprice this. Elliot Caprice that. Same as Margaret. I just wanted the goddamned satchel!"

Elliot raised the .45 and took true aim.

"Those manifests were the only thing keeping us alive! She just kept…laughing…as if she got one over on me. I held her mouth closed. Just to get her to shut the fuck up, about you. Must've squeezed too hard."

Elliot and Frank watched Chauncey take on a sly grin. His eyes seemed cold.

"You put her in my barn."

"I needed to cause you some trouble. You had gotten too close."

"How did you find out where I live?"

"I followed you." Chauncey rolled over. "Hell, there were times when you stared right through me."

"Bullshit."

"That old man at the road house your kin?"

Elliot kneed Chauncey in the center of his forehead. He fell back, laughing, onto the gravel.

"No one expects the dark-skinned handyman to be smart. To have a plan. I'm invisible. You light-skinned ones are easy to handle. Always so much to prove. Always so disappointed. Me, I'm just supposed to be content to exist. Yassuh, Master McAlpin. No, ma'am, Missus McAlpin. Even the maid fell for it."

He was right. Elliot perceived Alistair to be some diabolical white dandy. He took Chauncey—dark-skinned, servile—as inconsequential. The white man's nigger. His own prejudice blinded him.

"Though, I can tell you hate them, same as me, no matter how much of them you have in you." Chauncey rose to his feet. "You were in the war, Caprice. The first time you killed a German or an Italian, you didn't realize you could have been killing whites all along?"

On the way to the bowling alley, Elliot listed out his reasons for his anger at the white folks in his life. Chauncey in front of him, he could only ponder the good fortune. His mother could have tossed him into Lake Michigan. That gave him Doc Shapiro, eventually leading him to the small firm headed by Mike Robin, where he had come to what arguably could be the best work of his life. Men like Chauncey were twisted by living in a world that had no place for them but needed them all the same. Perhaps such men learn to sneak and cheat, connive and murder, when their lives are bereft of grace, the one element Elliot's life possessed, in abundance.

"That's where you're wrong, Chauncey. I don't hate them." Elliot lowered the 1911. "I just wish they'd try harder. Frank."

"Yeah, boss?"

"This one is goin' back in the trunk."

Frank reached for Chauncey, but he scooted back from the Big Fella. He raised his hands. He walked to the car on his own, looking straight ahead, chin up. Elliot held the gun on him for good measure, but he knew he wouldn't need it. When Frank opened the trunk, Chauncey climbed in. He silently stared at them both until the hood was closed over his face.

"Damnedest thang," Frank said, legs weak from relief.

"Not really," Elliot said, his voice trailing off.

"Choices," Frank said.

Elliot headed toward the boathouse. Frank followed.

"I shol' thought you'd kill 'im, boss."

"That guy's dead already."

They found the front door of the boathouse unlocked. When they walked inside, the smell reminded them of the Meat Locker. It was an acrid stench—rotting food, human waste, kerosene. Quaint furnishings reeked of mildew. They moved slowly through the living room.

"You get the satchel?" came a voice from the next floor. Elliot silently motioned to Frank to follow him up the rotting stairs.

"Well, c'mon, didju?" went the voice again in a South London accent. At the top of the stairs, Elliot and Frank ventured down a long hallway. Old, decaying photos in dusty frames lined the walls. The floor was tilted to one side giving the place a surreal quality that befitted the entire sordid affair.

"Chauncey, you fuckin' tosser," came the voice again. "What do I have to do..."

At the end of the hall, the pale ghastly face of Alistair Williams popped out of a doorway. Once he saw his pursuers, he stepped backward in a panic and tripped over his own feet, falling hard to the floor.

"Alistair Williams," Elliot said. The door slammed.

"You don't look like Nickelson's men. The McAlpins send you to kill me?"

"No. Margaret sent me to find you."

"Margaret? That tart! She's the same as the rest."

Elliot pushed against the heavy door, but it wouldn't budge.

"You one o' her boyfriends? A new playfing?"

"Open the door, Alistair. It's all over."

Frank took off toward the door, throwing his shoulder into it, but it didn't budge.

"Piss off! That's solid oak!"

Elliot jammed the barrel of the 1911 in the keyhole and pulled the trigger. It shattered the rotting wood around the doorknob allowing him to kick the door open. It figured Williams would be holed up in the master bedroom, camped out on the canopy bed, sleeping atop stained bed linens. The end table was where Alistair cooked his high. There was an adjoining toilet past a door. The room smelled worse than the swamp outside.

"Don't kill me!"

He was gaunt. His eyes were jaundiced. A man of average height, he now weighed all of ninety pounds. He stank to high heaven. Here, in the rotted bedroom of his betters, Alistair Williams wasted away hoping on a turn of fortune. For such an elegant dandy, he had descended into a self-condemned hell.

Elliot walked toward him. Alistair panicked, fell to the floor, and scurried under the bed.

"Goddamn it, haven't you had enough of smellin' your own shit?" Elliot said. Frank covered his nose.

"Margaret sent you?" asked Alistair.

"Yeah. Margaret, and Jon Costas."

"Where's Chauncey?"

"You have your own problems, Alistair."

"You're the private copper, yeah? Elliot somefing or other. Here to do her dirty work, are you?"

"Getcha ass from up under the bed, man."

"I'm not goin' anywhere. Where's Chauncey?"

"In the trunk of the car," Frank said. "C'mon, stinky. Let's go."

"What's she payin' you? Because I can get you more. I have an arrangement with Bill Nickelson. You heard of 'im? He's an important man."

Elliot had enough. He seized Alistair by the ankle, pulling him hard across the floor. His bones rattled on the hard wood.

"What are you gonna offer me, junkie? What can you give me to make up for the lives lost from your stupid con?"

"Get your hands off me, you fucking shitskin!"

Once Elliot beheld Alistair's face in the light, he noticed something familiar. He knelt to get a good look at him. There it was, plain as day. Frank could see it as well.

"You gotta be kiddin'." Frank managed an age's education, all in one night.

"Your mother or your father?" Elliot asked.

"The fuck are you on about?"

"Which one of your parents is colored?"

Alistair was visibly shocked, as if a doctor told him he had six months to live.

"I bet it's his mama. C'man. It's your mama, isn't it?" Elliot smirked. Alistair looked away in shame.

"Me mum."

"You didn't know your pap, did you? That's why you were stuck on McAlpin. Why you bought his bullshit."

"He said I had potential."

"To be his fall guy," Elliot said. "What you figure? You and Margaret would get married in McAlpin's big ol' yard? A royal wedding? Then you and her make some quadroon babies? Within a generation, you'd get all the nigger out of your bloodline?"

Elliot looked over at Frank.

"Folks wonder why I don't try to pass."

"Mmm hmm," Frank said.

"McAlpin knew, didn't he?"

Alistair looked away.

"I figured. All this talk of him takin' a shine to you. Givin' you a leg up. A rich, guilty white fella ain't gonna do that for another ofay. Naw, they reserve that for special nig'ras."

"You obviously never had the chance to pull yourself up the ladder."

"This, from the junky who couldn't see that rich old man's con. He set you up for a fall. All you could do was dope yourself up."

"I had a plan."

"That's the problem, Alistair. You think you're so clever, but you won't get your hands dirty."

"Fuck you!"

"You couldn't even stand up to him for taking your woman."

"I killed the bastard!" Alistair sat up. "I found him in that bathtub, scrubbin' up all proper to take the maid out on the town. The two of them, gaming me all along. I grabbed the old tosser by the back of the neck."

The gravity of Alistair's admission filled his body.

"I held his head under the water. He didn't even struggle. It was as if he wanted to die."

Alistair looked up at Elliot, perhaps hoping to trade on mulatto commonality.

"And no one else cared. The man of the house goes tits-up in the bathtub, no one could give a toss. Especially not Margaret. She just went through the paces. I wasn't even questioned. The police never came. The family lawyers handled everything. Even let me keep my job. Shadowy characters, that lot."

"How'd you skate?"

"Chauncey helped me clean it up. That night, we both went to see Nickelson to make him the deal."

"That went wrong, too."

"Nickelson was looking for a way to get rid of us both from the start. I had attest authority, but he could forge that if he had to. Chauncey was of no use."

"Tell that to Esme McAlpin," Elliot said.

"Chauncey told Nickelson I did Master McAlpin in. He held it over my head. Threatened to drop a dime. How do you take on a bloke like that when you're li'l ol' me. I snatched manifests for leverage."

"Plus some aitch for your pleasure."

"We got by on selling it." Alistair traced the needle tracks on his pockmarked arms with his index finger. "Then I got bored."

"So you killed your surrogate father," Elliot said. "All for some con artist broad's hustle."

Somewhere inside Alistair was a bundle of rage. It rose from his belly until it exited out his throat. "He told me it didn't matter!" Alistair was so angry his heels pattered on the hardwood floor. "That being a British nigger—"

"Is better than a nigger from here?" Frank said. "Never mind, boss. Shoot this one, too."

Elliot could do no such thing. Empathy prevented him. His disgust toward Alistair dissipated. Versions of the same spiel were used on him by Izzy, Creamer, and even Bill Drury. Circumstances that led to their fated meeting would have never happened had he not been just as gullible.

"Got you to think that bein' half-white is better than all black, huh? Sounds good, until they get tired of you. After that, once they do you dirty, it's on to the next fair-skinned, high-minded, self-important nigger."

"That's the hustle," Frank said.

"C'man. You and your potential have a meeting to get to."

Elliot grabbed him by the collar. Alistair rose on his wobbly legs.

"Who am I meeting?"

"Jon McAlpin the second, aka Jon Costas."

"Costas is a McAlpin?"

"Unlucky for you, yeah."

"You don't know what you're dealing with, do you?"

"McAlpin's attorney has the satchel, Alistair. The jig is up."

"I don't care what you found in that satchel, it won't do a bit of good."

"That why Chauncey killed Willow for it?"

Alistair froze in horror.

"Chauncey killed Willow? No. He was just supposed to get the satchel back."

"She gave me the satchel. That's why your buddy choked the life out of her."

Alistair collapsed into a pool of heroin-laced tears.

"They told me it didn't matter," whispered Alistair, perhaps telling himself or God or no one at all. Elliot knelt and touched Alistair's shoulder.

"It always matters," Elliot said. "When they say it doesn't, you know it matters plenty."

CHAPTER 20

The sun rose over Lake Michigan. Their exhaustion was bathed in a sticky haze of unseasonable humidity. Elliot found a payphone, called Mike Robin collect, gave him Jon Costas' address, a list of documents to bring, and a suggestion to depart immediately. It took a few more dimes to reach the Kenilworth Police Department. The mention of McAlpin and murder in the same sentence reached the top brass. Finally, he called Margaret to say he located Alistair, but she'd have to meet him at Costas' brownstone to see him. Playin' all sides to the middle.

Alistair joined Chauncey in the trunk. No way that filthy junky was stinking up Lucille's back seat. They drove to The White Palace Grill at Canal and Roosevelt, a stone's throw from Jon Costas' brownstone, to wait until Mike arrived. Most rail workers from the nearby yards were already on duty so the place was empty. Elliot walked over to the waitress seated at the long white lunch counter. He ordered two basic Chicago breakfasts consisting of eggs, potatoes, sausage, and coffee. She spun around on the red leather stool, saw two Negroes, and eyed them as if they were crazy. Elliot tipped her a sawbuck, raised his finger to his lips, and led Frank to a short booth, far in the back, near a side door. By the time the cook, an older colored man wearing a paper hat, brought out their plates on trays, Elliot had nodded off in his seat. Frank was half asleep. They didn't speak as they made short work of their meal. Elliot was finishing his coffee and enjoying a hand-rolled when the manager, an old Polish fella, walked over. Perhaps he had something to say to the two brazen Negroes, but their hardscrabble appearance and droll, exhausted expressions likely warded him off. Elliot's shirt sleeves were rolled up. Frank could see where bruising set in on his forearm from the wrench blow back at the bowling alley.

"That's gotta hurt."

"It just looks bad on account of me bein' so light," Elliot said. "I always seemed tougher than I actually was growin' up as the bruises showed so well."

"Maybe that fool broke it. You might need a doctor."

"Only doctor I have is back home. It'll have to wait."

"Is it nice?"

"Where? Southville?" Frank nodded. Elliot thought to himself for a moment, wondering how to answer. "No. Nuthin' nice about it. It's crooked. Yet honest. There, a man knows where he stands."

Frank stared down his plate.

"What is it, Frank?"

"You think I could do this work you do? Witcha, I mean."

Elliot took a sip of coffee.

"We been doin' it, haven't we?"

"Well...I ain't 'specially smart."

"You're not?"

"I mean, I'ont know a lot of facts 'n figures 'n words 'n such."

Elliot put down his coffee cup. This time, instead of emulating Doc Shapiro or Izzy Rabinowitz, he was a bit shocked to hear himself sound just like Uncle Buster.

"Why would I hire you if you're stupid? What good are you?"

"Well, not stupid. Just...I dunno...not so smart."

"You found the clue that put us on Chauncey's trail."

"I just dug it out miss lady's laundry."

"You had the plan to go in through the back."

"I see the way you think 'n act 'n all. How you walk 'n talk it." Frank stared downward, through his plate, into the depth of his self-doubt. "I just wish I was mo' smart."

Elliot rapped his knuckles on the table. Frank looked up.

"Those uppity bastards we kidnapped? The two of them think they're geniuses. You and I, together, might make up half an idiot."

Elliot waved his cigarette between his fingers as he spoke.

"That's what you get when you think you're smarter than everyone else. Locked in the trunk of a lesser man's car." Elliot put out his cigarette on his plate.

"Don't ever put yourself down to me. I don't want to hear that mess, yeah? Find out what you're made of before you go runnin' your mouth about what you ain't."

The big fella nodded. Once again, Elliot Caprice put Frank Fuquay in his place. This time, it made him feel good.

"Are they all this hard?" asked Frank.

"What?"

"Cases you work on."

Elliot shrugged. "First one."

"You kiddin'?"

"Nope."

Frank put his face in his hands.

"Probably my onliest one." Elliot laughed.

"So, I might could do it."

"It's ugly work, Frank."

"Mo' ugly than a chain gang?"

Elliot remembered how slim chances to do right are in this life. How difficult it is to avoid wrong. How it takes effort—the kind you put into a young screw-up needing inspiration to keep himself straight. Doc did it for him. Now he was doing it for Frank. Carrying forth.

Elliot checked his watch.

"We better get on."

He put a tip down on the table. Frank followed Elliot to the men's room. The big man tended to his bladder as Elliot washed his face, fixed his hair, and did what he could to address the soil on his clothing.

"Gotta keep some duds in the car," he said to himself. Frank marveled at his mentor's sense of pride. Even when beat up and dog-tired, he wasn't gonna allow himself to look like a bum.

"Ready to do the dance...again?" Elliot asked.

"How's it gonna go?"

"Either bad or real bad."

"Bad would be good," Frank said.

"Shit. Right now, bad would be perfect."

Taken in total, Alistair was a pawn in a much bigger, more dangerous game. McAlpin manipulated him, as did Margaret, Nickelson and finally, Chauncey. Costas was mistaken about Elliot. He would never deliver a fellow colored man for slaughter, especially not to some fat cat behind a big desk. It didn't take the poor bastard's head to resolve everyone's situation. Better to let justice have her due.

In Costas' study was Mike, leather folder in hand, and Kenilworth Police Chief Tom Benefer. Flanked by Monk, Elliot and Frank brought in Alistair to collective befuddlement since he was barely recognizable. Elliot helped Alistair to a seat on a long leather couch along the east wall of Jon's office before turning to address the hanging committee.

"Gentlemen, I give you,"—he turned to Alistair—"what's left of Alistair Williams. You must be Chief Benefer. I know this all seems—"

"Insane?" The chief didn't take Elliot up on a handshake. "Is this some kind of mistake or a con job?"

"Oh, it's no con. Attorney Robin," Elliot said, "I can legally attest to the presence of Alistair Williams, currently employed by the McAlpin Family Trust as the personal driver to Mr. and Mrs. Jon McAlpin, Sr."

Mike approached Alistair, whose countenance was ghastly. He pulled Elliot to the side.

"What in the shit—?"

"Brief him so we can close out the damned probate," Elliot said.

"He's a drug addict, Elliot."

"Just tell him what he has comin' to him."

Mike began discussing Alistair's end of McAlpin's will as if he'd receive it. Alistair, a near zombie at that point, openly wept out of guilt.

"How does this concern me?" Benefer asked. "And the Village."

"First things first, Chief. Attorney Robin, did you receive Mr. Williams' attest?"

"Barely," Mike said, as he sealed the papers. "I honestly don't know if it'll hold up in court. Mental capacity."

"Don't think it's going to matter much. The estate is now closed?"

"Closed."

"Chief, I'm Assigned Detective Elliot Caprice of the Chicago Police Department. The McAlpin family, of which you are in the presence of via Jon McAlpin II, have been some of your village's longest residents."

"I thought you said your name was Costas," the chief said. Jon ignored the statement.

"It's my duty to inform you that Alistair Williams here confessed to me the murder of Jon McAlpin, Sr. My associate, Mr. Fuquay, was a witness."

"I heard 'im," Frank said.

"Now hold on a moment!" Jon approached Elliot. Frank intercepted him. Monk intercepted Frank. At that moment, Margaret McAlpin was escorted in by Leonidas. She was dressed like the fair maiden: smart yellow dress, white gloves, clutch purse, flower in her hat, as if, afterward, she was hosting a tea for the Ladies' Auxiliary.

"Alistair!" The ghost of a man looked away from her.

"I told you not to cross me," Jon said, seconds from reaching for Elliot's throat. Frank and Monk were in a bonafide toe-down. The chief and Mike Robin rose to quell the disturbance. Elliot raised his hands in surrender.

"The man admitted to killing your father, for God's sake."

"You're no longer a cop."

"Technically, he is," Mike said.

"My resignation letter is being drafted."

"This is not what we agreed to, Caprice!"

"I agreed to get you what you need to reclaim your family's shipping business."

"I fail to see how you've done so!"

"Give it a minute," Elliot said.

"I need to hear it from him," Benefer said, pulling a note pad from his jacket pocket. Frank walked around Monk, took hold of Alistair by his forearms and gently propped him up.

"Just tell 'im what you tol' us."

"Is this true? Did you murder Jon McAlpin?"

Alistair nodded while looking down at the floor. Margaret seemed stunned, but it could have been a con.

"You need to say it, so I'm asking you again," the chief said. "Did you murder Jon McAlpin?"

Alistair looked up into Benefer's eyes.

"I killed him. I drowned him in his bathtub."

Margaret dropped her clutch purse, put her face in her hands, and sobbed. Elliot couldn't help but notice the honesty in her grief. He almost felt guilty about what would come later. Chief Benefer cuffed Alistair and told him his rights.

"By the way, his accomplice is in my car. The estate handy-man helped Alistair cover it up. He also murdered Willow Ellison of 4802 N. Broadway Avenue in Chicago."

"I heard that, too," Frank said.

"Lord," Margaret said. Thunderstruck, she ceased her crying. Turned off the waterworks, just like that.

"And, if you twist his arm hard enough, you're certain to find out more about the death of Esme McAlpin. But maybe that's too much for one morning." Elliot smirked.

"You're going to have to help me sort this out," the chief said.

"Guess I'm doin' everyone's job," Elliot said to Mike, who gave him the side-eye.

Elliot handed Frank the keys. He followed Benefer out the door.

"If it's any consolation to you, Mrs. McAlpin, the matter of your husband's will has been closed," Mike said. "You are now the inheritor of his estate."

"I don't care about that."

"Sure you do, Margaret," Elliot said. "Anyone would."

"I hired you to bring Alistair back to me."

"I did. Can't help the rest."

Jon Costas slammed the palms of his hands atop the leather writing pad.

"Perhaps now we can revisit the fucking reason,"—he kicked the chair behind him—"we're all here in my house in the first place?"

"Margaret, now that your inheritance has been released to you, one of the assets under your control rightfully belongs to your husband's son, Jon," Elliot said. "Have you met, by the way?"

"Don't be cheeky, Elliot Caprice." Margaret took a seat on the couch. She finally took off her gloves. "What's more, I know his deceitful intrusions into my life. Particularly the bugger he hired to weasel around."

"I knew my father was a fool, but how he wasn't able to see through you is beyond me," Jon said, now standing in front of his desk.

"How 'bout we cut out the insults before you realize what you can do for one another," Elliot said.

"I agree. I'm waiting to know myself," Mike said.

"Jon here is going to make Margaret an offer to buy back Costas Cartage, Limited. Margaret is going to happily accept that offer. As they both now occupy seats on the board, that'll be, what, Mike, two members from quorum?"

Mike Robin smirked. "I'm sure at least two will follow suit."

"Not a bad way to start your ascension to power, Margaret," Elliot said. "Fixing one of your husband's most egregious wrongs."

"Why would I want do that?"

"It's the right thing to do," Elliot said.

"We disagree," Margaret said, rising to leave.

"Nineteen forty-one," Elliot said.

Margaret stopped, but didn't turn around.

"What about nineteen forty-one?"

"Attorney," Elliot said.

"Don't let me stop you?"

Mike opened the leather file and handed Elliot a sheet from the ship's manifests found in the satchel.

"According to the work sponsorship papers on file, that was the year you came to the States, right?"

"What are you implying, Caprice?"

Margaret pulled a cigarette case from her clutch. Leonidas gave her a light.

"I just want to establish that fact before we continue."

"Am I on trial?"

"Not by me," Jon said.

"Thing about cargo ships, Margaret, is that when they're on the open sea, they can do pretty much anything they want. If they want to land? Man, oh man, do they get their skirt looked up."

Elliot handed her the page. Margaret scanned it, not certain what to make of the scrawls.

"Every entry on and off the ship, at all times, goes in a ship's log. Every passenger, too."

When she realized what it read, she handed it back without looking at him.

"M. Thorne, picked up from a drowned ferry off the coast of Brighton and Cove. Perhaps you boarded in Surrey, after seeing your dear mum one last time. Except, this says 1939. Over one year earlier than you told the McAlpins."

"That's someone else's simple mistake," Margaret said, and she exhaled smoke, as if to cast a spell about herself. "It doesn't prove anything."

"A lot of folks were leaving Britain during the war. So what you hitched a ride on one of your future dead husband's cargo ships." Elliot walked toward her. "So what your ex-boyfriend drowned him while he was enjoying his booze in the bathtub. The family board won't care. They won't use it as a reason to de-legitimate your claim. They won't plot against you. They'll just leave you alone."

Margaret coldly stared through Elliot.

"Leave you to enjoy all their old money."

Margaret walked toward Jon, slowly realizing what was happening.

"I had nothing to do with your father's death, Jon."

"I have no reason to care whether you did or didn't, Margaret. I just want what's mine. He was supposed to return the family shipping company to my mother's family long ago. Instead, he let foul men use it to do wretched things."

"Like cause Alistair's heroin addiction," Elliot said. "And Willow's murder. It's one big rotten mess, Margaret. Selling it to Jon puts everything back in its proper place, including little tidbits such as cargo manifests. Y'all family now. I'm sure he'll be happy to use the fullest discretion."

"I would," Jon said. "I could also use an ally on the family board."

"So, you gonna do yourself a favor? 'Cuz trust me, by the time I make my next move, you will not want to own that shipping company." Elliot sat in one of the chairs in the office, his utter exhaustion finally showing. Frank walked back in.

"Five hundred dollars," Margaret said, her gaze steely. "That's what passage on that rat-infested skiff cost me. I'll write off the weeks your drunken sailors molested me, day after day, as if I were some Singaporean whore." She took another drag from her cigarette and exhaled, slowly, deliberately, in Jon's direction. "It's the principle, you understand?"

Jon extended his hand. Margaret took it in hers. Leonidas handed her an ashtray for her cigarette butt, where she extinguished it. After tucking her clutch purse under her arm, she put on her right glove.

"May I assume you'll be calling upon me for the balance of your fee, Mr. Caprice?" she asked, without looking at him.

"At a date and time convenient for you, Mrs. McAlpin," Elliot said. He rose to shake her hand. Margaret slapped him hard across the face, turned and sauntered out of the room. Leonidas showed her out.

Elliot was finally attracted to her.

"Well, if we have no other business, gents," Mike Robin said, laughing. "I can make it to the county clerk to file these on the way home. Damned fine work, Elliot." He shook Elliot's hand, their mutual respect assured.

"I need a favor from you," Elliot said.

"Sure."

"Look after Frank until I get back to Springfield."

"Where you g'on be?" asked Frank.

"Doin' something only I can do."

"It'd be my pleasure," Mike said. "See you at the next board meeting, Mr. Costas?"

"Attorney Robin," Jon said. Mike and Frank walked toward the door led by Monk.

"Frank," Elliot said.

"Yeah, boss?"

"You're hired."

Frank smiled.

"Tough interview?" Mike laughed and slapped Frank on the back.

"Mr. Robin, you don't even know."

Jon and Elliot were alone, free to discuss the consequences.

"Impressive gambit, Elliot." Jon sat atop his desk. "Yet, what do I do about Nickelson? He still has possession of the company. Granted, without my father and Alistair, he's finished."

"Men like Nickelson ain't finished until they've spread the pain around."

"I imagine I can contact our friends in the government."

"That'll help the family legacy a whole lot."

"Am I in crime school?"

"You don't know evil, Jon."

"My father was evil."

"Your daddy was a schnook. If he ever had to earn a nickel on his own, he'd had grown some gumption. Like you."

"You have a solution?"

"Solution for you. Problem for me." Elliot thought to himself. He paused before speaking. "Nickelson still has ships out to sea. They're coming back in carrying real nasty cargo."

"Go on."

"If, when those ships returned, the FBI was at the docks—"

"You're insane."

"You're statin' the obvious."

"They'll pick everything apart. I'll be totally exposed, as will the McAlpin family."

"Sooner or later, through no fault of mine, someone is gonna discover your pap was a war profiteer. In these times, you'll be lucky for exile."

"This doesn't fall back on me?"

"You walk away the unaware victim of a fraud, perpetrated by a gangster upon your kind, patriotic father."

"This will cost me more money, no doubt."

"No. I denied you Alistair. I feel obligated."

"It's tempting."

"C'man, Jon. I've been up for days. I need the go-ahead."

"None of this is your business, really."

"It's wrong. It's happenin' in front of me. That makes it my business." Elliot extended his hand. Jon Costas shook on the decision.

"Just be prepared to act bewildered when the press comes callin'. The guy I'm involving will likely make it big news."

"Seems as if I made a friend in all this."

"Shit. Now I'm in trouble."

"I'll reach out to my contacts in the Police Department today."

"Let 'em know I'm retiring as of now. If anyone gives a shit. May I use your phone?"

"I'll give you some privacy."

"No need. We got enough dirt on each other to be cousins."

Jon Costas laughed. Elliot walked over to the phone box and opened it. He breathed deep before dialing the devil.

"Nathan White calling for John Creamer."

CHAPTER 21

The Palmer House was touted as "The World's Only Fire Proof Hotel." When your claim to fame is that the joint won't burn down around you, it tells you what kind of city you're in.

Elliot looked like shit. May have smelled worse. He was in pain and exhausted, so he resolved to ignore the concerned stares from the employees as he darted through the luxurious lobby. *Must be lookin' colored today*, he thought as he attempted to distract himself from the pangs of nervousness in his gut. Of course, Creamer would pick this place: frescoed ceilings, gilded fixtures, Art Deco ambiance. He was too elegant for Bradley, too rich to be a state attorney, and far too privileged to be loyal to the mulatto farm boy that came to trust him. There he was, seated alone at a back table in the Lockwood Restaurant, making the same squint that suggested he was too important to be bothered. Yet John Creamer left Elliot out in the cold because he had no more use for him because kissing Estes Kefauver's ass didn't pan out. They were both desperate men, only different kinds of desperate. Creamer needed something. Elliot needed Creamer.

Elliot marched up to his old friend's table where he was headed off by a waiter suggesting better accommodations elsewhere. The guy was so polite Elliot almost didn't mind the bigotry. He pulled out a sawbuck to get rid of him, but John Creamer flashed his badge. The waiter found someone else to serve.

"Always sticking up for yourself," John said.

"Not always," Elliot said, as John poured him a cup from a

silver pot on the table. A small dark drop fell onto the perfectly white tablecloth.

"I have to say, I was surprised."

"So surprised you put a man on me?" Elliot nodded toward an agent seated alone underneath one of the gilded angel statuettes that hung from the walls. "Brown suit, black tie, cheap shoes. What'd you think, Creamer? I was gonna shoot you?"

"I didn't know what to think." John took a sip of his coffee as he stared into Elliot's eyes. "Where'd you go? After St. Louis, I mean?"

From they met, John made Elliot feel exposed, so it was no surprise he was aware of Elliot's movements. Still, it was unnerving, like realizing one's spouse knew all along they had a beau on the side but let them perpetrate their tiny deceptions anyway. There was no play. Creamer always came sideways; Elliot played it straight.

"I went home."

"How is life in Southville? And your friend, the loan maker?" John placed his cup atop his saucer, then folded his hands across his lap. He'd seemed to finally accept his bearing.

"Southville is Southville. I hear Izzy is having a tough go, but I wouldn't know for sure."

"In everything you uncovered for us, you never linked Rabinowitz to the Chicago Outfit?"

"Nothing definitive."

"Biggest loan broker in the Midwest, but *nothing definitive.*"

"Strange things sometimes happen, John. Like how a fella puts his life on the line but his calls don't get returned. Strange."

John Creamer leaned back in his chair, discomfited by the turd Elliot laid atop his toast plate. The waiter returned, but he waved him off.

"I'm not proud of what happened, Elliot."

"You don't seem ashamed of it, either."

"Kefauver's committee was handed some nasty defeats. The press gave him a beating. His prospects for keeping his seat, much less going on to greater things, were dwindling."

"So you cut me loose. Help him primp himself for election. You knew the whole thing was a hiding to nothing."

"I believed in him, same as you. We all got burned."

"Yeah, but I'm colored and I don't get any second prizes. Do I, *Special Assistant* Creamer?"

"Special Assistant in charge of press relations," John said. "A nasty bit of schadenfreude courtesy of the Deputy Director."

"My uncle is dying in a flophouse. Everyone thinks I was a dirty cop." Elliot slammed his fist atop the table. "Fuck you and schadenfreude."

"None of that makes me happy, Elliot. We're friends."

"Friends, huh? I'd still be in jail were it not for my true friends. The ones I shitted off, for my fake one."

"I never asked you to do that."

"You never asked me to do anything. You just held the American way over my head."

"I knew you had your own reasons to reach for it."

"Doesn't mean that you didn't have a responsibility to see me through."

"Maybe I would have. You could've come in. Debriefed. Served the effort."

"After that, what? I get to be your driver?"

"No one asked you to sell evidence to Bill Drury so he could write more of his articles. The crusading former Chicago police lieutenant fired for getting too close to the mob. Oh, brother."

"Anything I gave to Drury, I did so at my own risk, for nothin'."

"Well, he sure sold you out. Especially on that last one. The mob lawyer, Sidney Korshak. That's what got him killed, you know. You gave it to him. As soon as you turned your back, he gave it to us, and—"

"I know what happened," Elliot said, the anguish in his

heart searing the rest of his insides. "Drury was a fuck up, but he was a friend. He didn't deserve to die."

"You should've let it go."

"You should've finished what we started!"

Behind him, Creamer's man rose from his seat to approach the table. Elliot shoved his hand in his jacket.

"Get ya man."

John saw the rage in his eyes. He signaled to his shadow to stand down.

"Get rid of him. I'm not lookin' over my shoulder for you anymore."

"You're crazy," John said.

"He takes a walk or I do. Believe me, you want what I'm holdin'."

John knew Elliot wasn't one to bluff. He sent his guard away. For a moment, the two sat in silence. Finally, John Creamer threw a jab.

"What can I do for you, Elliot?"

"I'm here to do you a favor. What you know about Bill Nickelson?"

"I know he's nigh untouchable right now."

"That's because he is yet aware of his current predicament."

"Go on."

"Up until about an hour ago, he was sittin' on Costas Cartage, Limited out by the mouth of the Calumet. He made some contraband runs for your government during the war. As if no one knew he wouldn't stop there."

"Nickelson has friends in high places."

"You mean, other than the McAlpin Family who no longer care to be associated?"

"You know this how?"

"I caught Jon McAlpin's killer. We're like this now." Elliot crossed his fingers.

"Good Lord."

"So what's Nickelson served on a platter worth to you?"

"You have evidence?"

"When I know I'm delivering it to someone willing to prosecute, I do."

John scratched his chin.

"I just can't open an investigation for something this big. I don't have that authority."

"You must know the McAlpins personally. The late master wasn't up at your Prairie mansion? Dining on caviar or squab or whatever you fat cats eat?"

"My family knows them."

Elliot reached in his jacket. Creamer reared his head back.

"Relax, ya bozo."

Elliot produced a stack of manifest documents. He slapped them on the table.

"Three ships coming in carrying cargo for the Chicago Outfit. There's no one to attest to the shipments. They're sitting ducks. I have more evidence when you're ready to put Nickelson away for good."

Elliot stood up.

"Leave your phone open. I'll call you with the play. You fuck me on this, you only fuck yourself."

Elliot turned to leave.

"And go fuck yourself."

Elaine found work for Frank to do at the office. Although he was dog tired, he dove into it without hesitation. There was something about her that made Frank's back straighten. The way she spoke to him, as if he was just the right person for the job—whatever job it was—inspired him. It challenged his notion of himself as a big, dumb coon. Mike Robin asked Frank about his ideas of his future as a Negro in a rapidly changing America. Frank was amazed he had answers. He spoke of how he could never understand what white folk thought they could do to keep things just the way they want them, all the time, forever. That control costs money, time, blood. If they were smart, they'd see there was more to be had by sharing than dolling out the crumbs. Only weeks ago, he was a big, dumb nigger stuck on a chain gang. Now he was living adventurously, involved in the travails of powerful people. Attorneys, businessmen, smart and mighty Negro women who stared them down. He watched Elaine at work and thought of his mother and sister. How he hoped they'd meet her one day. His head spun. He didn't know life could be lived on such levels. When Elliot arrived to pick him up, he was all talked out, which for Frank Fuquay was saying something.

They arrived at Miss Betty's. She and Percy were in the lobby. She was berating him again.

"What's that ya say there, Miss Betty?"

"What you want, Elliot Caprice? This ain't you bringin' me another body for a single room, is it?"

"You got an extra room for a week?"

"I might," she said. "If'n you got cash."

Elliot pulled out a money clip and squeezed off fifty dollars. The old hustler in Betty suppressed her excitement.

"Two rooms, for a little while longer. The remainder is for looking after my uncle when I was away," Elliot said, as he handed her the money. Miss Betty gave him the once over.

"G'on take it before I change my mind."

Betty slid it into her brassiere, likely out of habit but essentially to keep it out of Percy's mitts.

"What yo' name is, boy?"

"I'm Frank Fuquay, ma'am."

"Percy. Move Frank here into 207 across from Buster's room."

"Bob Collins is already in 207," Percy said.

"Mister two weeks late on the rent Bob Collins?"

Percy scuttled over to the booth, found the key for 207 and ran up the stairs. Buster Caprice passed him on the way down to the lobby.

"What ya know good?"

"Unk, I'd like you to meet Frank Fuquay. He's,"—Elliot realized he hadn't given him a title—"my...associate investigator. Yeah."

Frank frantically shook Uncle Buster's hand.

"Pleasure, Mr. Caprice," Frank said, eyes wide.

"Frank here is joining us from Yazoo?"

"No foolin'? City or county?" asked Buster, side-eyeing Elliot, not sure what to make of it all just yet.

"County, suh."

"I knew some Fuquays back in Yazoo County. A Ruby Fuquay."

"That's my auntie! It's Ruby Gibson, now. They live up in Gary."

"How she doin' up that way?" Elliot could feel their Yazoo connection.

"Fine, suh. She and my Uncle Paul, dey got a nice house. They rent rooms to colored folk workin' in steel 'n auto parts 'n such."

A loud argument broke out atop the stairwell.

"Guess your room is ready, young Frank," Betty said. "C'mon. I'll show it to you. It ain't much, but we ain't got no vermin runnin' around. Folk here know to keep their nose clean."

"I ain't particular, ma'am," Frank said. He looked back at Elliot. Elliot smiled and nodded his approval that he go on.

"He needs to stop doin' that."

"Big fella," Buster said. "Kind o' young to be followin' you around, ain't he?"

"I was young."

"No, you wuzn't."

"I have the money, Unk." Elliot put his hands on his old uncle's shoulders. They met eyes as pounds of pressure lifted off them both.

"There's still dem bastards at the bank."

"It's enough to either take care of them or start over some-place else. It's a lot of money, Unk," Elliot said, nodding as he counted the stacks in his mind. Buster forced a smile. Frank returned from atop the stairs.

"Not much, huh?" asked Elliot.

"Don't need much," Frank said. "So, Mister Caprice? When did you leave Yazoo?"

"Back in the top of the century. And it's Buster. All that mister talk soun' like I'm stuck at the bank."

"I gotta make a call," Elliot said. That would allow Buster and Frank to get acquainted. He dropped a dime into the pay-phone.

"What's to it, Sheriff?" he started. "Yeah, I'm back. Took care of that thing."

Elliot pulled the postcard from Willow's apartment from his pocket. He stared at it until he could smell her. He could taste her beautiful young skin upon his lips. He looked over at Buster and Frank, jawing over the card table. Again, joy and remorse, side by side.

"Want to meet up at Mamie's? I haven't eaten since forever. I'm on my way over there now."

The trio spirited over to the lunch counter. When they arrived, the Southville Sheriff's Department was already seated at a table. When Mamie saw Elliot, she brought over another. Elliot grabbed an extra chair for Frank. Just hours before, they were accusing one another and pulling guns. Months prior, they were fist-fighting in holding cells. Years before, Elliot dreamed of escaping the clutches of his old, ornery uncle. Now, they sat, ate smothered chicken, greens, white rice, drank sweet tea, laughed, sighed. Even Elliot and Ned. After all that strife, over all that time, they easily fell back upon how regular folk do.

As the meal wound down, Elliot slid the Willow's postcard across to George. He tapped on the return address. George nodded. Frank knew, but didn't say a word.

"You mind I come along, Sheriff," Elliot said. "I think I should be there."

"That'd be just fine."

"On one condition, though. You gotta do the drivin'. I'm so doggone tired of bein' trapped in a car, you don't even know."

Frank tried to suppress his laughter to no avail. "Good Lawd, you do a lotta drivin'!"

"Figure you live in a car, myself," Ned said, sipping his tea.

"How about when he stole my tractor and figured he'd drive away," offered Buster, as Mamie brought over cups of her famous banana pudding.

"My mama looked out the window to see this scrawny, high yella, curly-haired ghost in his nightshirt, driving five miles per hour, thinking he's getting somewhere," George said, in his gleeful baritone.

Elliot just shook his head. Soon he laughed with them. He could take it. In fact, it was the best he'd felt in years.

CHAPTER 22

George was nice enough to give Elliot's roommates a ride back to Miss Betty's.

As he pulled into Roseland, Elliot tried to ignore the pit in his stomach. His sit-down was vitally important, so he tucked 'em in.

It was Friday night. An old Shabbos goy like Elliot knew to take the alley walkway up through the rear of the house so no one would see him. There was Izzy seated at the large wooden picnic table across from where Elliot once carved his initials in the wood.

"I remember when you docked me for that."

"Rebecca told me to fire you," Izzy said. "Said your life was hard enough without you takin' to the street to make a dollar. I told her, 'That kid is a born killer. He just don't know it yet.'"

"Well, I know it now," Elliot said.

He sat down and looked around the backyard. The fountain that never worked. The wooden swing set Izzy made Elliot and Amos assemble that took forever.

"It's a hard thing you do to yourself when you think you're a better man than you are," Izzy said. He folded his hands atop each other.

"I need information," Elliot said.

"Gettin' right to it, huh? We had this conversation, kid."

"I have a feelin' you'll want to discuss this. Bill Nickelson."

"Foreign shit he has covered by his lonely. Narcotics especially, though he occasionally deals in really dirty trade."

"People?"

Izzy nodded. "Used to be. He could get someone in the country without papers. Even carried a few displaced diplomats. Now it's just unwashed masses. Broads mostly." Izzy adjusted his sweater. It was Indian summer, but he was cold. It was a tell. "So now you got me talkin'."

"Black market guys are usually pariahs."

"It's a racket for shitheels."

"So," Elliot eased the words out, not fully believing them himself. "No one would miss him?"

"No, he'd be missed. Everyone needs someone that'll do the dirty work."

Elliot took off his hat and placed it on the picnic table. He ran his hand through his hair and exhaled long and slow.

"What are you figurin' on?"

"I just ruined his shipping operation."

"Ruined?"

"Farkakt." Elliot drew his hand across his neck for emphasis. Izzy rolled his head back.

"Whoa, kid. That's gonna get ugly."

"That's why I got to put a lid on it," Elliot said.

"Your kind of lid or mine?"

"I was hoping my kind."

"CPD ain't goin' anywhere near Nickelson."

"I'm thinkin' feds."

Izzy stared a hole through Elliot's forehead.

"You went barrelin' into this, didn't ya?" Elliot nodded. "Mikey?"

"Just me."

"You mention feds," Izzy said. "How'd I get so lucky?"

Elliot shifted in his seat.

"I get ahold of a thing. Something that implicates you. I scrub it out. The fat meat goes to Kefauver. He titillates the press."

"Always figured it was a racket."

"One of the biggest," Elliot said. "And I got fucked in it."

"Guess I owe you a favor."

"Oh, you owe me more than one."

"Bullshit."

"Skokie." Elliot smirked. Izzy's eyes went so wide the wrinkles smoothed out. "Don't worry. He had a hard on for the dagos. And your buddy Lansky."

"The money is boring. The muscle is what makes headlines," Izzy said. "So what do you want, kid?"

"I have the money for the farm, but the bank won't give it back to me unless they can't sell it. We need that easement revoked. I'm not tryin' to trade talents. I'm askin'. Respectfully. Please help me."

Izzy had never seen Elliot like this. Absent was his defiance. No piss. No vinegar. No haughtiness.

"You cherry-picked evidence for me," Izzy said. He almost sounded grateful.

"I would have done that for you, regardless."

Elliot averted his gaze. Izzy stood up from the table, walked around to Elliot's side and patted him on the shoulder.

"Tell your uncle I'm glad he has his land back." Izzy walked toward his back door. "I'll look into your Bill Nickelson problem."

"I'll keep Mikey out of it."

"Don't bother. You two need each other."

Izzy walked back into his house. Elliot rose from his seat, looked at the swings that sat still and empty, and went out the way he came.

No children played here anymore.

They approached the farmhouse. In the daylight, it looked terrible. Peeling paint. Bulging porch floorboards that, when stepped on, sounded like the cries of someone dying. Buster thumbed through the key ring and searched for a match to the large padlock the bank bolted on the door. He had the shakes in his left arm. Elliot's ache of guilt was a reminder to cease leaving the things he loved, to go off to fight battles he could never truly win. He reached for his Buster's hand, smiling.

"Here, Unk. Let me do that."

In the past, Buster Caprice would have slapped his nephew's hand away or made some crack about him minding his elder. It was the colored man's providence to be the lord of his own tiny manor. Now he put up no fight. His boy was home.

Elliot opened the door. Their second-hand hat rack still stood. Unopened mail from months of deliveries was piled up on the floor. Buster walked in first followed by Elliot. He depressed a light switch. No results.

"Yep. No service," Buster said.

"I'll get 'em out," Elliot said.

He raised the window shades in the living room. Dust particles passed through rays of sunshine. It gave the room an elemental shimmer. The Caprices took pride in how they kept their house and it pained them to see the thick layer of dust everywhere. Workboot footprints were tracked throughout, a sign that either a disposal company or Goodwill had been called by the bank. At the top of the walls, where they met the ceiling, were water spots from the untended gutters. Several windows were cracked. A few were broken. Stones laid on the floor in broken glass.

"Kids, prolly," Frank said.

"Folk been bustin' out my windows since I dared buy this place long ago."

"Remember when you would wait until mornings when other folk were workin' their farms to get the glass man to come out?" Elliot laughed. "He'd pay in cash so everyone could see we had the money."

"Remember the glass man's name?"

"Mr. Mimms. Nice fella."

"Yeah, Mimms was good people."

"One of the few white folk that didn't mind a colored man ownin' his own land."

Elliot searched the kitchen pantry for a broom. Frank followed.

"Underneath the sink should be a pail," Buster said, as he walked in. "There's cleanin' vinegar and rags in there too."

Elliot rummaged through the old cabinets, pausing several times to think, laugh, or frown. Sometimes he turned away from what he'd find and mumble to himself. Frank watched without intruding. He thought he may have seen Elliot wipe away a tear, but perhaps it was only dust.

Hours blended together. They labored to bring some sense of order to their home, breaking only to go to Mamie's for carry out. They swept, mopped, dusted, washed whatever windows were intact. They worked up such a fierce sweat, they had to open the windows to let in the cool fall air. Dusk had turned to night. Elliot lit a fire.

Frank had performed the heavy lifting all by himself, moving all the furniture back in its proper place. The last thing he moved was the sofa, which he collapsed upon from exhaustion. His long legs hung off the edges. He wanted to continue working out of gratitude, figured he would only catch a breather, but in seconds, he snored softly. It was a quiet murmur of comfort, his dangling feet not cousin to hands draped across prison bars, but brother to young legs swaying off a porch swing.

Elliot and Buster sat in front of the fireplace in their twin velvet easy chairs, one of their only bits of extravagance.

"What're we doin' wit' that big one over deah?" Buster took a nip of bourbon from his flask. He passed it to Elliot.

"Figure he'd be comfortable in my old room." Elliot took a swig.

"Where you gon' be?"

"The covered porch out back. Probably finish it off so it doesn't get so cold."

Elliot took another nip. The old man lit two cigarettes and

handed Elliot his own. They both took drags, which soon had Elliot coughing.

"Ya know, I never wanted to smoke until the war. They sent us GIs all the best cigarettes for free."

"Makin' customers," Buster said.

"Sittin' around, watchin'. Waitin'. Never know when it's comin'."

Elliot took another deep drag. Frank caught himself from falling off the couch, turned over and quickly fell back to sleep.

"We should giant-proof the house," Elliot said. White smoke eased through his mouth as he chuckled.

"We takin' 'im in?"

"Figure he'd be helpful as we get the land ready for the freeze. You think you got it in ya?"

"To do what?"

"Adopt another of the young and restless?"

"Is that what I did?" Buster tossed the butt of his cigarette into the fire after the last drag. "Seems like I was your jailer."

"You were pretty rough on me, man."

Buster took back the flask. The final sip went down hard.

"We were rough on each other."

Elliot rolled his cigarette between his thumb and forefinger, staring at it.

"I was a bad kid. I know it."

"You wuzn't bad. You wuz just uneasy. Like yo' daddy. You get your brains from yo mama."

"What'd I get from you?" Elliot smirked.

"My worry."

Buster grabbed a poker. As he broke up the ash, the fire roared, its flames flickering in his old, knowing eyes.

"Naw. You ain't nuthin' like me. Which is good, prolly."

Elliot looked up at Buster.

"I was young and stupid."

"Young, maybe. Never stupid. You wuzn't meant for me, is all. Not me, this house, this town."

"Must've been hell on you."

"At first, when I thought I wuz tha boss. Once I got wise, I let you run yase'f."

Buster stretched his legs out and massaged his old knees.

"Seem like any word from me just made you run harder. It's funny, but once you took up wit' the loan shark, you finally learned sum'n 'bout consequence. So I turned a blind eye to you runnin' wit' tha Jews."

"You sent me to the Jews."

"I sent you to my friend Shapiro, who hep'd birth ya. You fell in wit' his cousin the criminal. Still, you turned out alright."

"Did I?" Elliot sat forward on his haunches. He pressed his elbows into his knees as if prostrating. "Lord, Unk. I've made so many mistakes."

"Who hasn't?"

"I've killed men."

"Who hasn't?"

"You haven't."

"You can think that," Buster said. He folded his arms, partly as something to do them, partly to conceal himself. "A man is capable of anythin', given the circumstances."

"I don't want to know."

"I don't wanna tell ya."

Elliot stared into the fire. He wanted to ask Uncle Buster everything, while he still could. He eventually settled upon one question.

"Why did she leave me?"

"She left you here."

"Don't make her sound noble, man."

"She didn't haveta come here. She coulda stayed in Chicago. Did her bidness in a back alley someplace. She tried. You figure a gal like dat don't have much try in her, but she gave it a shot."

Elliot looked to the mantle at an old decaying photo of the Caprice brothers in their younger days back in Yazoo. They were dressed in matching suits and hats, vaguely smiling. Jefferson had a wild look in his eye. Buster seemed spent, as if following his older brother around exhausted him. The fire had died down to the embers.

"I'm glad I'm home," Elliot said. He looked at Buster across the dying light. Buster stared back at his nephew and patted his hand.

"This thing I did ain't done, Unk."

"Naw?"

Elliot shook his head. Buster looked at the floor. He made a deep sigh. His scratchy vocal chords sounded like distant thunder.

"Well, just do what you gotta, then let that be that." The old man rose from his seat and stood over him. "I can't worry no' mo'. I'm old."

Buster patted Elliot's cheek. Elliot nodded. Buster walked slowly up the stairs to his own bed for the first time in more than a year. Elliot remained, watching the embers fight their last before dying out.

The sound of the ringing phone woke Elliot. He leaped from the chair. It rang again. He stumbled into the kitchen. At the third ring, he answered.

"Caprice residence?"

"How's the old place?" Izzy said.

Elliot rubbed his face, partly to wake up. Partly in disbelief.

"Needs work. How are we—?"

"I had your phone turned on. Listen, kid. That thing we talked about a couple weeks ago?"

"Yeah," Elliot said.

"They got in. Understand?"

Elliot's heart nearly jumped from his chest.

"How?"

"Rerouted through Canada. Must've bribed someone up

there. Right now, he's comin' in through Great Lakes Naval Base. They dock tonight. Sorry, kid."

Izzy hung up. Elliot stood stiffly in one spot for so long, the busy signal screamed through the phone. He thought of his options before hanging up and placing a call himself.

"Georgie. I need to talk somethin' out. Meet you at the jail?"

"You don't know anyone on the cops you can call?" George Stingley poured coffee in two cups.

"Chicago PD at the Calumet River will be in his pocket," Elliot said. George handed him his coffee. Elliot sipped it without regard for its temperature. George sat atop his desk.

"Go higher," George said.

"I got a guy in the feds that's ready to move, but he needs a reason."

Elliot walked over to the counter to refill his coffee.

"There was a bootleg liquor distributor in unincorporated county. They paid in to Sheriff Dowd so no one could touch them." George sipped from his cup. "One day, we get a call from the county fire department. Three alarm. We arrested everyone that didn't die in the blaze. The folks that started the fire were the next to pay off Dowd."

Elliot slowly turned toward George. He couldn't believe the preacher's suggestion.

"You don't just pay off the authorities," George said. "The deal is that you keep everything on the level. If not, everything is fair game."

"I take back everything I said that day in the barn," Elliot said. "You're one corrupt son of a bitch, Georgie Boy."

"I've just seen a lot."

"I was a rat for the feds inside the Chicago Police Department. I ain't never seen no shit like that."

"I go where the sin goes," George said. "Only thing is, this gangster likely paid enough to have them look the other way."

"My man in the bureau will bring the act-right. They all get there at the same time, and—" Elliot clapped his hands together for emphasis. George handed him the phone receiver. Elliot dialed and waited.

"Nathan White for John Creamer." Elliot listened. "Yes. Please let him know it's tonight. He should expect some guests to be wearing blue. There'll likely be fireworks. My apologies for the late invitation. Yes, that's the message."

Elliot hung up the phone.

"You said you can't trust Creamer."

"I can trust him to be an opportunist."

"When do we leave?"

"What you mean, we?"

"I had to explain to a young woman's family why their daughter from Madison, Wisconsin, wound up a corpse in Southville, Illinois." George's voice was resolved. "This sin chain linked all the way to my little town. I'm going."

"I go where George goes." Ned Reilly walked in through the back door.

"Ned, I don't think—"

"Save it. If he's goin', make room for me."

Before Elliot could get another word in, the front door opened. In walked Frank Fuquay followed by none other than Amos Doyle.

"What we talkin' 'bout?" Frank asked. Elliot threw up his hands.

"What're you doin' here?"

"Izzy figured you wah gonna do sumthin' stoopit. Tol' me ta get ovah to ya house," Amos said.

"You wuzn't there, so Mr. Doyle spoke to Uncle Buster."

"Christ on tha cross," Elliot said. He sat down. "You're not riding on this one, Frank. You need to look after the farm."

"Uncle Buster said don't come back wit'out you." Frank pushed his hands down in his pockets.

"Fuckin' old man," Elliot said, under his breath.

"Amos," George said. "I can't allow you to—"

"Izzy says ta tell you ta remember which side youah bread is buttahd, Sheriff."

The room fell silent. There he was, in trouble again, but this time he would drag his friends into it. This time, his death would be the death of his Uncle who had waited so long for his nephew to finally come around to the idea that home isn't a prison, but a place for respite and in between home and death was the space to maybe do some good. That's how two and one-half Negroes and two and one-half ofays conspired to bring the FBI to the doorstep of a syndicate associate bearing a grudge. Elliot rose from his seat.

"Well, shit. I guess I been told my own bidness."

CHAPTER 23

They met nightfall at the edge of south Chicago—once four separate neighborhoods that U.S. Steel lashed together with chains forged of its economic might. Crossing Avenue O, they arrived at Park No. 523, which provided a stunning view of Lake Michigan and the paved-over inlet where Costas Cartage stood. The sky was a darkened canvas upon which the steel mill boilers loudly belched burnt orange. The glow was both beautiful and ominous. The Polish, Irish, and colored workers here may have cooked the nation's refined steel, but the quintet from Southville made sure to bring their own.

Amos was the first out the car. True to his conditioning, he surveyed the lay of the land.

"I'm nawt likin' deahs only one route in or out," he said, as he raised a pair of binoculars to his eyes. "And I'm nawt likin' dat deah."

Amos handed Elliot the spyglasses. He positioned him by his shoulders down the sight line.

"Aw naw," Elliot said. "Naw, naw."

George took the binoculars. He scanned the freight building until he saw a set of narrow barred windows. Inside were four women, maybe Chinese, dressed in brown laborer's outfits. The two on their feet then cowered. The two on the metal bunk turned their gaze away. A large white man in pea coat entered, grabbed one of the women, and attempted dragging her out. The woman standing next to her pleaded, but he pushed her out of the way. She valiantly pulled the unfortunate woman's arm, but the bruiser punched her in the gut, sending her to the floor.

He pulled a gun from his jacket and waved it around, shouting. He dragged the poor woman he had chosen from the room by her hair. She screamed and reached for the other women, but they turned their backs, covering their faces in resignation. The brave woman on the receiving end of the punch didn't get up. She could have been dead, she laid so still.

George lowered the binoculars, staring off into the black distance over the waters of Lake Michigan. His hands shook.

"You didn't mention this," George said.

"I knew it was in his wheelhouse," Elliot said, hands on hips, facing Costas Cartage as if he were across the River Styx awaiting Charon. "I didn't know they'd keep them here."

"Staging," Amos said. "Likely dey're movin' 'em someplace else soon."

"We gotta help," Frank said.

"This ain't a rescue, Big Fella," Amos said.

"We set it in motion, they're going to kill them first," George said.

"Boss?" Frank was mortified. Elliot stared off, but at nothing. He calculated his pound of flesh.

"Look here," Elliot said. "Anyone wants to sit it out, I probably won't be alive to hold it against you later."

"Not everything is about you, Elliot," George said. Amos reclaimed the binoculars to scan the perimeter.

"Two ships. One cargo an' a smalla skiff," he said. "I'm countin' one, two, chree...five guys. Just dock hands. Nuthin' too tough."

"Kansas City shuffle," Elliot said.

"Gawda be enuff kindling on that dock for a wickit fiyah" Amos said. "I take da big fella deah, we make up da wreckin' crew. You chree hold da dawk. We make it up da stairs and get 'em out."

"Then what? We set a bunch of kidnapped women loose in the wild?" Ned said.

"Costas is placing a call to Creamer in..." Elliot said, checking his watch. "...seventeen minutes. I'd give him fifteen more to get here. It's a chance."

"A fool's chance," Ned said.

"You can stay here, Ned," George said.

"Shut up, Georgie. You already know what I'm gonna do. For once, goddamnit," Ned said, turning to Elliot. "Please, for once, could you think things through ahead of time?" They locked eyes. Elliot, though he wouldn't acknowledge it, didn't deny it either.

Ned stormed off to the car. The rest followed. Amos unlocked the trunk. Ned grabbed a Remington 11-18 and began loading. He chambered a round before he handed it to Frank.

"Squeeze slow. Aim at what's aiming for you. The spray will take care of the rest."

"Youah comin' wit' me, kid," Amos said. "Careful wit' that thing."

"You ain't gonna carry no gun, Mr. Doyle?"

"Don't need no gun," Amos said. Da Wreckin' Crew division marched over to the footbridge alongside the river locks that led across the Calumet.

"He's green, Amos," Elliot said.

"He's a big boy."

Ned handed Elliot another Remington. He pumped a round into the chamber. The loud *shik-chack* echoed in their ears. He watched until Amos and Frank fell out of sight around the side of the building.

"Let's give it a bit," Elliot said.

"How will we know?"

"We'll know."

"You remember back when all we were risking was a whipping?" George said.

"Elliot, always draggin' us into his messes," Ned said. George chuckled.

"Best times of you jokers' lives," Elliot said.

A flash from the waterfront side of the dock lit up the clear night. It was followed by the loud roar of flames. Elliot led the trio across the bridge. They double-timed toward the large doors at the front of the gigantic gray cinder block and wooden building. He put the first shell of the twelve-gauge into the lock. George kicked open the doors. The dock gate was wide open. Elliot could see Amos and Frank running away from the smaller transport boat, the deck of which was fully engulfed. Smoke rose from the lower hull of the larger cargo ship out its port windows. Wearing brass knuckles, Amos ran down the water side of the dock, his new student Frank Fuquay covering his flank. They ducked into a doorway and ran up a flight of stairs that led to the second level.

Elliot stood on the platform walk. He pumped a shot toward the wooden trussed ceiling. It hit one of the large pendulum lanterns, which exploded, the raining sparks a welcome dramatic effect. George, without hesitation, entered behind him and shot down to a stack of pallets. The two colored dock hands hit the deck. The three whites faced down their intruders.

"Anyone ain't tryin' to get dead best to fade on out the back!" Elliot said.

A white dock hand opened his mouth to say something, but Ned Reilly put a shot right at his feet.

"You Negroes best to get on!" George said. "This is white folks' problem!"

The two colored hands rose slowly, looking to George for confirmation.

"Get on! Next time don't take work from criminals."

They took off running but the white men remained, defiant.

"You know who we work for?" said a shorter, stockier white man, hook in hand. A low rumble out the door behind them got Ned's attention. Two sets of approaching headlights came up the gravel road from Ewing Street.

"Shit," Ned said. George and Elliot turned to see for themselves. The air horn of a cargo ship rang out. One of the other ships was making it in from Great Lakes.

"You assholes picked the wrong man on the wrong night!"

More dock hands emerged. Both boats were now ablaze. George was halfway down the stairs on the right. Ned advanced down the left, covering him from the side as the odds tipped further into the impossible. Elliot was left alone on the walk, dead center. The Sheriff's Department stood paralyzed. The cars were almost to the building. His friends were going to die.

Elliot closed his eyes. He listened to his own breath above the taunts from the now army of dock workers. He took a deep breath, exhaled slowly and, when he opened his eyes, time stood still. That's when he gave George and Ned the plan, communicated with a shotgun blast to the face of the loud-mouth holding the hook. Every other second-string gangster on the warehouse floor either froze or scattered.

"Take cover!"

Elliot walked out the door, firing the shotgun over and over at the first Buick in line, spraying his malice through the air. As the rear cars skidded, the first car's windshield exploded. It careened forward, hopped atop the two shallow stairs, flew off the platform walk, and down onto the warehouse floor. It nearly crushed George and Ned, but the odds were improved as it took out more than a few goons.

Outside, the clicks of the trigger of the impotent shotgun came at the absolute worst time. The other two cars were now upon him. He yanked the 1911 from his coat and fired slow, deliberate shots at discreet targets. The first enemy bullet grazed him across his right shoulder. He held his position. The next bullet he fired caught a well-dressed goon in the throat. Goons fired back. Elliot took one in his left shoulder in nearly the same spot as that fateful night in Bill Drury's garage long ago. He hit the gravel, but continued firing blindly from his back. He heard a man shout in pain. As he got up on his feet to run back into the warehouse, angry voices promised death.

The entire dock was now an inferno. George and Ned took cover behind the overturned luxury car, firing their shotguns at the portion of the horde that was now armed. Elliot discharged a clip and reloaded. The dark, acrid smoke of diesel fire filled the air. The familiar sound of a Thompson machine gun rang out in the smoke. The roof timbers groaned and crackled. More shouting, but from fewer soldiers.

"If we don't get off this dock, we're dead," Ned said. The Thompson blared out another short burst. Elliot shot in the direction of the sound. He looked around until he could see a strain of light through the small window of an access door on the far side. He returned to cover. His shoulder throbbed. He figured he wouldn't bleed out if he could calm himself so he breathed shallow.

"We gotta get around this car," Elliot said. "I took care of a few, but more are coming behind us. They'll have the higher ground."

"Tommy gun is really pissing me off," Ned said. His shotgun was spent so he brandished his revolver.

"There's too much smoke. He can't see us," George said.

"Three points after the next burst," Elliot said.

More machine gun fire rang out. Lead filled the car door, giving away the shooter's position. George rose first, firing dead center. Elliot and Ned covered the angles. They took three shots each in tandem, forming a triangle of death. From behind cover, after ten seconds, George peeked out. A stiff lakefront breeze blew away enough smoke for them to witness the dead. George grabbed the machine gun off the dying shooter, now lying prone. He covered the main door.

"Outside, I counted four. Got one." Elliot held his wound. "They can't all be brave."

Gunfire entered from the outside where he left the Buick toughs.

"You're dead!"

"Make me a hole. I'll find Frank and Amos," Elliot said. "You two, get lost. This thing is tits-up."

More gunfire. George shot the Thompson. One of the proper

gangsters fell hard. Elliot took off for the door. George rose from his perch and sprayed fire at both sides of the doorway above. The two stepped backward, through the smoke, over the dead as they went toward the dock. Nickelson's men ran in. George and Ned escaped out the rear.

As soon as Ned's face met fresh air, the insides of the cargo ship exploded. It rocked the dock. Ned flew forward on his face, collapsing into a heap on the wooden walk. The bruiser in the pea coat ran through the dock gate. George recognized him from the spyglasses. As Pea Coat drew down on them, George raised the Thompson. Another explosion sent Pea Coat into the water. George turned to see Ned struggle to stand. Before he could help him, Pea Coat had pulled himself back up on the dock, but then caught a few in his chest. He had fallen back in the water before George realized he had pulled the trigger. He dropped the Thompson into the water in disgust. Southville County Sheriff George M. Stingley, Jr., Associate Pastor of Greater Grace Pentecostal Church, a man who lived his life right all his days, notched his first kills in an unsanctioned sting operation.

"Ned, are you hit?"

"Naw. Ribs are broken, though."

George felt no guilt whatsoever.

"C'mon."

Ned groaned aloud as George helped him to his feet. He supported his body as they ran as fast as they could, down the dock, across the bridge, back to the car. Ned sat on the grass, propped against the driver's side door while George reloaded his shotgun.

"I'm going back in."

Ned nodded, pulled himself up, and climbed into the driver's seat.

"It was him or us, George."

George looked away.

"You saved my life."

"You saved mine in Sugartown."

"What are we doin' here, Sheriff?" Ned chuckled through his pain.

"Give me ten minutes before you get out of here."

Ned nodded.

Everything turned to shit. George prayed as he ran back to the bridge, asking for better luck for Elliot. As a man of faith, he'd never admit he didn't believe those prayers would be answered.

CHAPTER 24

Elliot crawled up the two narrow flights on all fours. The fire door had yet to trigger, giving him a clear view of the far end of the warehouse where Amos and Frank tried to fight off a throng of Nickelson's men. Amos, wearing his brass knuckles, moved ferociously through the crowd. He grabbed the back of the head of one of the greasy goons and tattooed his forehead. His face exploded. He went down, screaming into his bloody hands. Amos turned to aid Frank as he had been set upon by two; one behind him holding a pipe around Frank's neck, one in front throwing whopping hooks to the body. Before Amos could reach Frank's puncher, two others grabbed him and forced him down to the floor. They beat down upon him with wooden planks. Elliot, from his distance, squared the .45 to get a shot off, but they were far too enmeshed for him to pick a clear target. He grabbed a wood slat of his own and ran in their direction, only to be cut off by machine gun fire. Elliot barrel-rolled to his left, coming down hard on his wounded shoulder. He crashed into a stack of wooden shipping crates that were far too thin to offer true cover. Another burst of machine gun fire splintered the crates spewing glass and packing hay everywhere. He felt wetness under him. Some of it was wine. Some was his blood. Splinters were stuck in his back.

The two younger, faster thugs were too much for Amos. They stomped him on the ground. They used the wooden slats on him when he was down. The goon behind Frank pulled the pipe harder into his throat, cutting off his wind. He watched Amos struggle less and less as he himself began to black out.

Amos' attackers taunted him after each kick.

That was when Frank Fuquay, all the way from Yazoo, Missip, lost his shit.

The mope holding him from behind wore alligator shoes. Frank wore steel toe boots. The oily asshole screamed as he felt three of his five toes shatter. The pain was enough for him to let go of the pipe. Frank head-butted the puncher square in the center of his face. His nose bloomed like a cherry blossom. Frank reached down, picked up the pipe, and went to town, beating his man until he was unconscious. He turned back upon broken foot guy to stomp him at the knee. Delirious, but determined, he stumbled into the crowd over Amos and swung away.

"Get off 'im! Get off, goddamnit!"

He went wild, moving back and forth, the whop and ping of hollow steel meeting flesh, over and over again.

"Kid! Frankie!"

Frank looked down to see Amos, still alive.

"I think you gawd'em all, Big Fella."

Frank looked around to see all four men, either moaning or unconscious. He dropped the pipe in contempt. Amos raised his arm.

"Gimme a hand, willya."

Frank helped Amos to his feet.

"You gonna be alright?" asked Frank. Before he could answer, they both heard a long burst of machine gun fire.

"Keep on, goddamned greaseballs!" they heard Elliot shout. "Y'all ain't hittin' shit!"

Frank looked to Amos.

"We all gawd'ah pahts ta play, kid."

Frank looked back as he followed Amos, hoping that somehow Elliot had a chance.

Elliot took cover behind a desk in a small observation office with large windows. The fire spread to the upper floors. Through the skylights, he could see the roof burning. It would give way soon. On the catwalk across the warehouse were two men, one in a wool coat and pageboy cap. The other was in a powder blue suit and matching fedora. He had a long scar that reached from his mouth to where his ear met his jaw. They peered into the office from the edges, where the walk met the wall.

"You got a really low kill count for all dem bullets, man!" Elliot said, firing twice at the catwalk. "I'm thinkin' ol' Alfonse made a mistake!"

"You keep talkin', nigger!"

"You're Nickelson, right?"

"What's it to ya?"

"I just want to know the name of the man I royally fucked!"

More Tommy gun fire entered the office, ricocheting off a metal filing cabinet.

"You think I don't know you? You're the half-nigger Caprice!"

Nickelson and his man descended from the catwalk down to the warehouse floor. Elliot changed position behind a group of stacked pallets. Pap-pap-pap-pap-pap went the Tommy. Hot lead hit the wood of the desk.

"Try again, mutherfuckers!"

Elliot looked up through the skylight, noticing the glass giving way to the flames. The ceiling beams started cracking.

"See you brought your pallys!" Nickelson fired again. "Figured you make a play?"

"Sorry about your boats, Bill!"

Elliot fired in their direction, but the glass in the skylight gave way and plummeted toward the floor. Elliot rolled out of cover, exposing himself in a clear line of sight. Nickelson's gun perforated the office with bullets. Elliot blindly returned fire, hitting nothing. He jumped through the window of an adjoining office, landing in broken glass. His face was cut. His shoulder was now bleeding steadily. He crawled across the floor, remaining underneath the dividing wall, uncertain what to do next.

"When this is over, maybe I'll take a drive to Southville. Visit that uncle of yours," shouted Nickelson, firing shots into the crude plywood that made up the wall frame. "Or maybe the kike in Springfield!" He fired more shots. "Heard that nigger bitch of his is a fine piece!"

Elliot stepped out the doorway, sized up the gunsel and fired once. Nickelson didn't expect to get a face full of his man's brain matter. He fell backward into an adjacent stack of wooden crates.

"What were you gonna do?"

Elliot ejected the clip and put in his last.

"Who were you gonna pay a visit to?"

He snatched back the hammer. Leaving a trail of blood behind him, he stalked forward in Nickelson's direction. About ten paces in, he found Nickelson's foot sticking out from cover. Elliot put a slug into it. Nickelson's scream was music to his ears.

"What about my folks up in Springfield?"

Nickelson hobbled away toward more crates. Elliot followed.

"I got all night to blow your brains out, Dutchie!"

The ceiling disintegrated from the intense heat of the spreading fire. Its large truss beams plummeted down like the flaming bolts of an angered god. It was also seconds before the arrival of the feds. One way or the other, the whole thing was ending soon. Elliot turned a corner and made it to a large waste area. Nickelson fired upon him, but he only managed to give his position away. Elliot returned fire and hit Nickelson in the right thigh. Nickelson fell down on his ass. Elliot walked over to him and pointed the gun at his forehead.

"You're lucky I need you alive."

He grabbed Nickelson by the collar and dragged him over to a metal waste chute that was bolted in a large window.

"One way or the other, you're dead, Caprice!"

Elliot yanked him to his feet.

"Hope there's nothing sharp down there."

Elliot pushed Nickelson into the mouth of the tube. Down he went, screaming epithets followed by a loud metallic clang that reverberated up the chute. Elliot ran as best he could to the upper main hall where he found George.

"What are you doin' here?"

"Looking for you," George said. "Where are the others?"

Elliot and George jogged to the corridor where he last saw Frank and Amos. The three Chinese captives ran into them. George stopped them from running down the stairs, toward the fiery dock. Amos and Frank ran in.

"We need to get on," Elliot said.

"I came back in through a stairwell that leads away from the fire."

George showed the women his sheriff's badge, smiled, gestured for them to follow him past the main stairs. After a few steps forward, Elliot could hear high pitched screams like that of a child.

"Get on with George, Frank."

"I go where you go."

"This is the job," Elliot said, pointing in Frank's face. "You said you wanted to do this work, so do it!"

"Kid! C'man already!" Amos was standing at the far end where the warehouse met the side stairs. Frank walked backward as he watched Elliot run down the hall. He turned and hauled ass to his own safety.

Elliot found a windowless room at the end of the hall. Inside was a young Chinese girl, maybe five or six. She pulled at the lifeless arm of the woman dragged off by Nickelson's goon, her naked body sprawled atop a dirty mattress on a steel bedframe.

"*Xǐng lái, āyí! Xǐng lái!*"

"Hey, darlin'," Elliot said. He approached slowly, but the girl bolted underneath the bed.

"Shit on a stick."

He got on his knees to reach for her, but she scooted away, kicking his hand. More timbers crashed to the floor. The roof above the room was ablaze. Elliot finally got her by the ankle, yanked her from under the bed and gathered her up in his arms.

He ran out the room. At the point they crossed the threshold, the roof caved in. The blast threw them forward. The fall reminded Elliot that he was already injured. He picked the kid back up in his arms and ran toward George's exit only to be met by a wall of fire. Elliot ran for the only other escape—the same waste chute he dumped Nickelson. He pushed the girl in. She screamed all the way down. He put the hand of his good arm at the top of the mouth of the tube.

"Schadenfreude," he said to himself before jumping in, feet first.

Once he reached the bottom, he noticed Nickelson wasn't inside and hoped Creamer made it in time to catch him. As he climbed out of the dumpster, he could see the girl running toward firefighters. No one noticed as he made his way toward the bridge. He had almost gotten there when he was stopped by an officer of the Chicago Police Department.

"You alright, fella?" said the dick. Elliot tried to keep walking, but the cop put his hand out to stop him.

"That a gunshot wound?"

The cop waved over another. Elliot figured it was all over. He considered pulling the 1911 and giving it a go. After all, his work was done. He had found Alistair Williams. Bill Nickelson was out of Jon Costas' hair. He even got back the family farm. All accounts were settled. He earned his blaze of glory.

"That'll do," John Creamer said.

"Back up, pally," said the second cop.

John Creamer flashed his badge and FBI identification. He was flanked by the agent he brought to the sit-down at the Palmer House. The one dressed like the hotel detective.

"You're FBI. So what?" said the first cop.

"So maybe I ask how you got here so soon. How you're connected to Bill Nickelson."

The second cop just walked off.

"What's your name and unit?" asked Creamer's man.

"Hold on, hold on," said the first cop.

"I'll need an account of all your activities on the scene."

"Hey, you want him?" said the first cop. "G'head."

The cop walked away.

"Check on Nickelson."

Creamer's man dangled while Elliot and John walked toward the bridge.

"You did tell me to expect fireworks."

"That I did," Elliot said.

"You need medical attention."

"I'll see my doctor back in Southville."

"Nonsense, man." Creamer stopped, but Elliot kept walking. "I'll put the siren on and get you over to Northwestern."

Elliot stopped, but didn't turn around.

"Goodbye, John."

"Elliot," Creamer said. He searched for something to say. "We were friends."

Elliot turned around and watched Costas Cartage, Limited burn. FBI agents and Chicago Police Department personnel argued in the light of the fire, as Chicago firefighters controlled the blaze as best they could.

"Looks like you have enough to do."

Elliot walked toward the bridge.

"I'll let you know what comes of it," Creamer said, watching his only colored friend disappear in the darkness.

He made it across the foot bridge, walked over to the car and got in.

"We done?" Amos asked.

"Yeah."

"That looks bad," Ned said, as he eyed Elliot's shoulder.

"We're going to a hospital," George said.

"Home, George," Elliot said. His voice cracked. Tears formed in the corners of his eyes.

"I just want to go home."

CHAPTER 25

It was a balmy December, atypical to the region, but not the most opportune as that meant snow would likely fall in February and March. They'd have to adjust for a late planting season. As they had the money to bring on a few hands, they resolved to make up the difference planting additional crops. Elliot suggested something simple to gestate, like beans. He cited Thoreau's philosophical works, but Buster and Frank were simpler men and didn't want to hear all that high-minded nonsense. To them, planting was work. No one wanted to work, unless they had it far too good to be farmers in the first place.

On the odd Saturday, Uncle Buster had Frank busy yanking up the old fence posts that had been neglected for so long. Elliot didn't help on account of his shoulder. Though Doc's care was considerably better than the back-alley butcher he saw the first time, he lost cartilage in his rotator. It would give him trouble for the rest of his life.

He stepped out on the porch to see how Frank and Buster were faring. Their mutual connection to Mississippi—and perhaps their mutual skin tone—bonded them together in ways Elliot couldn't share. He knew that Frank was good for his uncle and vice versa, so he resolved to accept things as they were, though he wondered if anything was waiting for him in the world beyond living the life of a rogue.

"Y'all need a hand?"

"All you got is one," Frank said. Buster chuckled.

"That's a lot of mouth for someone who hasn't gotten their pay this week!"

"Gonna do me like the man, huh, boss?" Frank said, raising his hands in surrender. Elliot fished in his pocket for a hand-rolled.

"Hey, boss. You expectin' someone?"

Frank gestured toward the access gate. Elliot looked to see a black car with federal plates approaching the house. Elliot knew it couldn't be anyone else. He opened the door and grabbed his coat off the hat rack. His arm was still in a sling, so he draped it over his shoulder as he walked. The car stopped halfway up the access road. Elliot approached as John Creamer got out. He figured he wouldn't exactly be welcome.

"How are you healing?"

"Slow and painful," Elliot said. "How's life at the bureau?"

"I'm not there anymore."

The wind blew, and Elliot could hear crows chatting amongst themselves. He imagined they spoke about him getting screwed. Again. By the same man.

"Oh?"

"I'm headed out to Menard. Our friend Nickelson is stashed there."

"Stashed?"

John Creamer looked away.

"He's gonna turn, isn't he?"

"He is."

Elliot grabbed John by the collar, even before he realized it.

"Let go, Elliot," John said. He grabbed Elliot's wrist. Frank and Buster watched.

"How many bullets do I have to take for you, Creamer?"

"You brought him to me, remember?"

"You screwed me, just like before."

"Not like before," John said. "They're reconvening the committee."

Elliot turned Creamer's collar loose and stepped back three feet.

"Eisenhower will be in office," John said. "He's got no stake. No extrajudicial interference."

"You sold it to him."

"Elliot, these things work a certain way."

"Just be straight." Elliot couldn't look at John Creamer. "I gave you the golden goose."

Creamer nodded.

"You took it to Washington."

"I did."

Something unique happened within John Creamer. Something, prior to this moment, Elliot figured wasn't possible. His old college friend—the well-intentioned white man with the money to be angry for Negroes, whether they were or not—was guilty.

"Fuck me in the face. You're back in with Kefauver."

John Creamer looked away, saying nothing.

"That motherfucker Wiggins?"

John nodded. Elliot screamed. He kicked the gravel on the road. If he had use of his other arm, John Creamer may have gotten the shit kicked out of him, right at the Caprice Family Farm. Creamer held out his hands in the body language of a man pleading with someone who he knows has good reason to be through with his ass.

"Everything we did together to advance the fight against organized crime is back on the table. And this time, I'm out in front."

Elliot moaned aloud.

"All that bullshit before. It's never going to happen again."

"Sure it isn't."

John put his hand on Elliot's good shoulder.

"When the committee reconvenes, it has a completely new agenda. The Chicago Outfit comes second to the New York and

Sicily connection. Accardo's out. Genovese is in. I'll keep you out of it—"

Elliot laughed in John's face.

"Once you come in as my special witness—"

"What?"

John Creamer smiled wide, as if he was granting Elliot a prize.

"Oh, fuck you."

"It's not a hiding to nothing anymore."

"I'm not testifyin' in open session for the world to see, John."

"Closed door testimony, I promise."

"No."

Creamer stared back at Elliot. His gaze turned cold as steel. It was the same look as in his family's rooftop atrium, the night Elliot's career and life was ruined.

"Then I can't help you."

The two stood in front of one another, silent.

"At the dock, you said that we were friends," Elliot said. John Creamer looked through him.

"This is bigger than friendship."

"How's it goin' down there, boss?" Frank said. Elliot waved without looking.

"Got me by the shorties, huh?"

"I'd like to think of it as finishing what we started," Creamer said. "Doing our duty."

Elliot looked back to Buster and Frank. They now sat on the porch, keeping watch.

"I got a different idea of duty."

John Creamer got back in his car. He rolled down the window.

"So I'll be calling you."

"When?"

"It's going to be a while. You know how Kefauver likes to set up the big show. Don't worry about Nickelson. He's got no friends anymore."

"Imagine that."

John Creamer rolled up the window. Elliot watched as he reversed the car out the access gate before he walked back to the house.

"Takin' a break, huh?"

"What's that about?" Frank asked.

"Just some old nonsense."

Elliot looked at the house. Not even John Creamer's orange weenie could ruin his moment.

"Let's do a white picket fence this time."

"That's a lot of work," Buster said.

"That's why we got the big man."

"Speakin' of that," Frank said. Frank returned to pulling fence posts. Elliot sat next to Uncle Buster.

"I was thinkin', when the weather breaks we can paint the house. Fix the gutters."

"Finish that porch, so you don't freeze to death."

"Mm hm."

"You tryin' to sell the place?"

"Naw," Elliot said. "Least not 'til you dead." He laughed.

"Well, you gon be waitin' a while. I'm feelin' like a new man."

"Is that right?"

Buster nodded. Elliot placed his good arm around his uncle's shoulder. His old frame was as warm to him then as when he was a boy.

"That's good, old man. We got ourselves a lot of livin' yet."

"Then don't leave again."

Buster looked Elliot in the eye. His worry was plain.

"I won't. I promise."

"Yeah?"

"Yeah." Elliot looked at the old oak, with the branches that reached to the section of roof outside his bedroom window.

"Everything that matters is right here."

ACKNOWLEDGMENTS

If you're still reading, you're my kind of people.

By now, you likely have some idea of this book's precarious journey from my fantasies to your lap. I imagine that my first acknowledgment should be my mother, Rosalita, who taught me to say "fuck this shit" to all obstacles, which is a rather powerful signature spell, no wand necessary.

Before Lieutenant William Drury could anchor in the plot of this novel, he was a real human being with a family. The tragedy of his death in 1950 affected not only his wife and children but the entire city of Chicago and helped shape the fight against organized crime. I feel he is a true Chicago hero and his life deserves to be known by everyone. My apologies to his descendants for fictionalizing his story. I attempted to show his memory great love and respect. He deserves a statue in Lincoln Park.

Elizabeth Kracht, of Kimberly Cameron and Associates, saw life in this book's pages and worked hard with me to make it possible for it to live on. She stood with me when a difficult work, then tainted by its rocky beginnings, took the slings and arrows. May it be as fulfilling for her as it has been for me.

Eric Campbell, Grand Puba of Down & Out Books, showed no fear in taking us in and displayed his commitment to our mutual success by beating the hell out of my book. In accepting his findings I was able to enhance and expand my original work into what I always hoped it would be. It ain't the same book. I ain't the same writer. We're both better off.

From the night she purchased two copies of the first edition at a reading in Berkeley, Allison Davis has been my patron, confidante, co-conspirator, and champion. She also gets me into a lot of frickin' trouble, of which I should have been in a long time ago.

Michael King has read every word I've ever written, taught me about my style, argued with me when I'd considered changing course, and has given me every bit of a quality education as he does his students at Harvard. I can only hope I've been as good of a friend to him.

JT Lindroos somehow conjured a frame from the movie that's been playing in my head since I created Elliot twenty-seven years ago and made a boss cover out of it. Once I saw it, I began to accept I was in the clear.

And now the friend list of all time: Joe Clifford, Tom Pitts, Simon Wood, Steve W. Lauden, Josh and Erika Stallings, Christa Faust, Gabino Iglesias, Rob W. Hart, the great Gary Phillips, Michael Pool, dearest Pam Stack, Art Taylor, Renee Pickup, Andre Battiste, Richard Yaker, Joshua Bitton, Jen Hitchcock and BOOK SHOW LA, Eric Beetner, Julian Bevan, Paul Bishop, Scott Waldyn, Sarah Chen, David Cranmer, Kate Pilarcik, Larry Gasper, Elaine Ash, James Ziskin, David Ivester, Les Edgerton, Will "The Thrill" Viharo, Anonymous-9, and everyone else word count prohibits me from listing here. All of you made this thing so much fun. That made giving up impossible.

Finally, a special note to Ashley, Maryam, Danny Jr., and John Laymon. When I think of you, I run out of words.

From his beginnings as a young stand-up comedian (*Def Comedy Jam All-Stars vol. 12*), Danny Gardner has enjoyed careers as an actor, director, and screenwriter. He is a recent Pushcart Prize nominee for his creative non-fiction piece *Forever. In an Instant.*, published by *Literary Orphans Journal*. His first short fiction piece, *Labor Day*, appeared in *Beat to a Pulp*, and his flash fiction has been featured in *Out of the Gutter* and on *Noir On The Air*. He is a frequent reader at Noir at the Bar events nationwide. He blogs regularly at 7 Criminal Minds. He is a proud member of the Mystery Writers of America and the International Thriller Writers.

Danny lives in Los Angeles by way of Chicago. *A Negro and an Ofay* is his first novel.

OTHER TITLES FROM DOWN AND OUT BOOKS

See www.DownAndOutBooks.com for complete list

By J.L. Abramo
Catching Water in a Net
Clutching at Straws
Counting to Infinity
Gravesend
Chasing Charlie Chan
Circling the Runway
Brooklyn Justice
Coney Island Avenue (*)

By Trey R. Barker
2,000 Miles to Open Road
Road Gig: A Novella
Exit Blood
Death is Not Forever
No Harder Prison

By Richard Barre
The Innocents
Bearing Secrets
Christmas Stories
The Ghosts of Morning
Blackheart Highway
Burning Moon
Echo Bay
Lost

By Eric Beetner (editor)
Unloaded

By Eric Beetner and
JB Kohl
Over Their Heads

By Eric Beetner and
Frank Zafiro
The Backlist
The Shortlist

By G.J. Brown
Falling

By Rob Brunet
Stinking Rich

By Angel Luis Colón
No Happy Endings

By Tom Crowley
Vipers Tail
Murder in the Slaughterhouse

By Frank De Blase
Pine Box for a Pin-Up
Busted Valentines
and Other Dark Delights
A Cougar's Kiss

By Les Edgerton
The Genuine, Imitation,
Plastic Kidnapping

By Jack Getze
Big Numbers
Big Money
Big Mojo
Big Shoes

By Richard Godwin
Wrong Crowd
Buffalo and Sour Mash
Crystal on Electric Acetate (*)

By Jeffery Hess
Beachhead

(*)—Coming Soon

OTHER TITLES FROM DOWN AND OUT BOOKS

See www.DownAndOutBooks.com for complete list

(*)—Coming Soon

Made in the USA
Middletown, DE
06 June 2017